SHE WHO DREAMS

SHE WHO DREAMS

KIM PRITEKEL

SAPPHIRE BOOKS

SALINAS, CALIFORNIA

This and other Sapphire Books titles can be found at
www.sapphirebooks.com

Kim Pritekel Books

Standalones
1049 Club
After Shadow
Blinded
Connection
Control – with Alex Ross
Damaged
Shadow Box
Swann Song
The Gift
The Plan
Wild – with Alex Ross
Zero Ward
Unmasked Desire

Dance with Me Series
Curtain Call
Encore Performance

The Traveler Series
The Traveler: The Hunted
The Traveler: The Huner

The Wynter Series
Finding Faith
Taking Liberty
Justice Won
Keeping Hope
Showing Mercy
Having Honor

The Destiny Series
She Who Would be King
Daughter of Ankou
Doors
She Who Dreams

Dedication

To the dreamers - never stop.

Prologue

Part I
Sursha, 1383

Blowing out a nervous breath, Roishin ran a hand through her hair, making the short strands stick up in crazy ways. The heels of her boots thudded dully on the stone as she turned around and began to pace in the other direction. The quilts had long ago been removed, as had the candles. What was left in the little cave she and Elsie had used the previous December were a couple large pillows to sit on. Though, at the moment, sitting still was not possible for her.

Two days after the wedding, Roishin had gone home to see her parents and to wish the "happy couple" of Elsie and Garratt her congratulations. It had been awkward at best, tormenting at worst to see her brother wed to her secret love. Not surprisingly, she'd stayed at the king's residence. While there, she had spent some wonderful time unimpeded with the king and queen and precious little Isabeau.

She smiled at the memory of that. Now at six years old, Isabeau was every bit the handful that Roishin had been. She adored that kid and planned to ask Enori if she could bring Fallon, Cateline, and Isabeau to Duras for a visit soon.

While she'd been there, she'd told Elsie that she'd created an open door between Caisleán Thiar and their cave. It went nowhere else but was a safe meeting place if they needed to speak or—in Roishin's mind, at least—if Elsie ever had any reason to get out quickly. She'd placed the door against the wall in the passageway leading from Elsie's bedchamber to the trunk. It would be absolutely impossible to accidentally use or even see unless the person knew it was there.

So, now she waited. She'd received a note left in the cave—which she checked daily—to let her know Elsie needed to talk. She'd created a small fire in the corner with the flick of her fingers on her second visit there, when she'd created the door for them. It was an eternal flame, so Elsie's way would always be lit.

She watched as the flames made her shadow wiggle and dance across the stone wall as she continued to pace.

"Hello."

Stopping instantly, Roishin looked to see Elsie standing there. This had been her life now for so long, but there were times it still took her off guard at the immediacy of travel through the doors. She smiled, feeling a bit shy. They stood not ten feet apart, but it may as well have been the width of Sursha.

Elsie was so beautiful. Roishin looked her over, avoiding the giant ring that gleamed on her left hand. But, she absolutely glowed in a lovely dress that Roishin had never seen before. Her hair was done up in a fancy updo, much like how Roishin's mamaí wore her auburn locks.

"My goodness," she said softly. "You look like a real princess."

The look on Elsie's face was filled with so much uncertainty as she looked down at her hands, which fidgeted together. "Is that a bad thing?" she nearly whispered.

Roishin walked over to her, yet again caught up in that horrible tug-of-war of needing to be near her yet keeping her distance. Over the past months, she'd been retraining her heart to not need her.

"No," she said, using two fingers under Elsie's chin to lift her head. She smiled when their eyes met. "No," she said again. "Absolutely beautiful."

Elsie gave her a small smile. "Some days I feel like I'm in someone else's body and I'm just standing back watching, wondering."

"Wondering what?"

A little shrug, then, "How did I end up here?"

Roishin's smile was wide. "Because of the incredible human being you are." She dropped her hand. "Because the queen saw herself in you."

Elsie's own smile grew. "I think that is one of the most incredible compliments anyone has ever given me."

"You deserve it. After all," Roishin drawled. "I don't compare just *anyone* with Mamaí."

Nodding, Elsie chuckled. "Aye."

Clearing her throat, Roishin grew serious. "Is everything okay? Your message—"

"I wanted you to know first," Elsie said, the glow that Roishin had noticed upon first seeing her now emanating from her like heat. She took a deep, centering breath and then said, "I'm pregnant."

Roishin stared at her, unable to think, unable to speak, unable to breathe. Finally, she took a slow, steady breath. "And...?" She swallowed, unable to say it. She was too afraid of the alternative.

Elsie took Roishin's hands in her own, their first touch since a polite hug just after Winter Solstice. "It's yours," she whispered, looking deeply into Roishin's eyes. "I know it from the absolute bottom of my soul."

Roishin grabbed her and pulled her to her in a tight hug, Elsie clinging to her just as hard. She buried her face in the fragrant blond hair atop Elsie's head, eyes closed. She, too, felt it in her soul—that Elsie spoke true and the baby was hers. The tears pricked the backs of her eyes even as she felt the warm, watery emotion shed upon her neck.

Cradling the back of Elsie's neck, she asked, "What can I do to help?"

"Carry her?"

A bark of laughter burst from Roishin's throat, she was unable to stop it. She pulled back from the hug to see a smile upon Elsie's tear-streaked face. Bringing up her hands, she gently wiped away the tears with her fingers.

"I want you in her life, Roishin," Elsie said, growing serious once more. "I know this is a complicated situation, but I want you there." She placed her hands on Roishin's arms. "I want her to know you, I want her to learn from you and I want her to *be* like you."

Roishin grinned. "You sure about that?' she asked, an eyebrow quirked. "I drove you pretty nuts during most of your teenage years."

"Aye, and look where that got you," Elsie murmured, her tone sending sensations cutting right through Roishin and heading south. Elsie looked away. "My apologies." She took a step back. "But, I do want you in her life," she said. "I feel it's important." She met and held Roishin's gaze. "Especially for them to go to all this trouble, to want this."

Nodding, Roishin ran her hand through her hair again. She was still trying to get her body to behave. It was absolutely not something she could afford to give in to. "I agree." She looked back at her. "When are you telling my parents? And," she added, "Garratt?"

"Well, he's not home at the moment." She sighed, shaking her head. "Fallon is actually really angry with him. He's out on some campaign or other. As for your parents," she continued, giving Roishin a shy smile. "I was wondering if you'd be willing to come with me. I really want you there."

Roishin eyed her, hands clasped behind her back as she rocked on her heels. Finally, she said, "What are you doing right now?"

Elsie looked a little nervous. "Why?"

Walking over to her, Roishin held her arm out. "Milady?"

Elsie, who looked utterly amused, placed her hand at the bend of Roishin's arm. "You are serious about this?"

Roishin said nothing, simply clicked the heels of her boots together and said, "There's no place like home!" Yes, Elsie looked at her like she'd lost her mind, but it was worth it to be able to use the quote from the book she'd so enjoyed.

Within moments, they were in the hallway just outside her parents' closed chamber door. Not entirely sure where they'd arrive exactly, she was grateful to see the fire glowing from the family chambers. It was then that she heard the soft voice of her mother. From the flowing cadence, she knew she was reading.

Roishin smiled, so easily able to picture what they'd find: Cateline sitting on the couch, Fallon's head resting in her lap. The queen would be reading from their chosen tome, her fingers absently running through her wife's hair. She'd seen it a million times growing up and had been herself in the very same spot many times, her mother's beautiful voice so calming as she read.

Taking Elsie's hand in hers, Roishin put a finger to her lips, Elsie nodding in understanding. Together, they quietly crept up to the closed side of the double doors, the fire's glow inside reflecting on the open door. Grinning like the mischievous kid she'd once been, Roishin raised her hand and, with loud, firm knocks, knocked out the rhythmic tune that used to be hers alone.

When she, as the youngest at the time, had become old enough to be self-sufficient in the evenings, or could ask for what she needed, her parents had begun to close their bedchamber door. It was understood that signaled their private time after family time had ended for the night. And, unless it was an emergency, the children used this as their own private time as well. A time to read, knit, whatever made them happy.

Initially, and in retaliation, seven-year-old Roishin had devised the obnoxious knock to make her presence—and her upset at the change in household ways—known. Over time, however, it had just become her signature to differentiate her presence from that of two other siblings, who both had their own ways.

She glanced over at Elsie, who was valiantly trying not to laugh. In her days as a servant in the castle, she'd heard that knock many, many times. Cateline's voice stopped immediately, no doubt initially startled by the noise and then recognizing the knock. Fallon, on the other hand, must have flown over there, because about two-point-five seconds later, she threw herself into the hallway from the room beyond.

The joy in seeing Roishin, who usually showed up unannounced, turned to shock and then clear concern when she saw Elsie with her. "What's wrong?" she immediately asked, a protective arm going to Elsie's shoulders as she looked from one woman to the other. "What happened?"

Cateline joined them, going to Roishin and pulling her to her side. The reaction of both mothers warmed Roishin, and she knew in that moment that, no matter what, Elsie and the baby would be fine. She also knew that she would create an open door from one castle to the other that only the four of them knew about. Even if it was never needed for emergency purposes, she absolutely wanted Fallon and Cateline to have a strong presence and influence on her daughter.

"Everything is okay," Roishin assured them. "Truly." She looked to Elsie, deferring to her to share the news as she wished, as it was she who would be doing the heavy lifting.

Elsie met her gaze and held it for a moment before she looked to the older women. "I think we should go into the family chamber."

The four of them went inside, Fallon closing the door behind them. A full round of exuberant hugs commenced. Roishin's eyes closed as her daidí held her to her. She held on just as tightly. Something strange had begun to happen. Since she'd taken her parents to the waterfall to reunite them with Livia, and now that they were part of this child's coming existence, she was feeling the chasm between them closing.

Somehow, by sharing her world with them as much as she'd been able to, and with their suggestion of this baby, she felt she was beginning to be understood. It meant everything to her, because her *parents* meant everything to her.

Cateline had one arm around Elsie's waist and

one around Roishin's. She looked as though she were in absolute heaven. When she rested her head against her daughter's shoulder, Roishin smiled.

"So," Fallon said, looking from one of the younger two women to the other. "What news?"

Roishin looked over her mother's head to Elsie, giving her a soft smile and nod. She braced herself though, because she knew her mother was going to explode with happiness and excitement, and she might well find herself victim of a wayward hand or arm.

Elsie looked from Cateline, who had lifted her head to Fallon, then nearly gushed, "We did it! Roishin and I are having a baby."

As expected, Cateline squealed, grabbing her daughter-in-law in a bone-crushing hug. But Fallon… Looking utterly shell-shocked and as if she'd been punched in the gut, she literally staggered backward a few steps until the seat of the couch caught her at the backs of her knees and caused her to flop upon it.

Roishin knelt before her, hands resting on her leather-covered knees. She looked into the violet eyes, which were welling with tears. She took one of the larger, deeply tanned hands in her own.

"We made it happen, Daidí," she said softly. "The line will continue." She smiled. "And, you'll be an honest-to-goodness daideó."

Fallon met her gaze, seeming too moved to even be able to speak. Instead, she cupped either side of Roishin's head and held it as she leaned forward and left a kiss to her forehead before resting her own against it.

"I love you," she finally managed.

Roishin smiled, looking at her when Fallon lifted her head away. "I love you, too. I cannot wait to see you and Mamaí with her."

"You know it's a girl?" Fallon asked.

Roishin nodded. "Didn't realize what I knew, but I've known since I was twelve." Using Fallon's strong thighs for leverage, Roishin pushed to her feet before tugging the warrior to hers.

Without a word, Fallon gathered Elsie into her embrace, cuddling the younger woman to her like she was a precious egg that could break and must be protected. Elsie leaned into her, accepting the enveloping hug. Fallon murmured something to her that was for her ears only. Elsie smiled and nodded.

Roishin accepted the nearly painful hug from Cateline, who was still crying over the news. She squeezed her eyes shut as noisy kisses were rained all over her face like she was, indeed, that seven-year-old girl again.

Finally, Fallon took Roishin's hand in her left, Elsie's in her right. The chain continued, Cateline sealing it by taking Roishin and Elsie's other hands. Fallon looked from one woman to the next.

"We must do all we can to ensure this baby's safety," she said softly.

"And Elsie's," Roishin added.

Nodding, Fallon said, "And Elsie." She held Roishin's gaze. "I give you my word, I will protect her with my life." She, again, met every pair of eyes on her. "We are the four guardians for this child." She slowly shook her head. "Never forget that." She brought Roishin's hand to her lips. "We didn't understand that with you, Roishin, and I am so sorry."

Roishin smiled at her. "No need, Daidí," she said. "None of us knew."

Fallon nodded. "But now we do." She looked to Elsie. "And, with your blood, too, we know not exactly what's to come."

"But," Cateline added. "We'll all do it together."

Fallon nodded, sending a look of pure love to her wife. Releasing the hands she held, Fallon opened her arms to bring them in for a group hug. As if by silent understanding, the two smaller women ended up more in the middle, Roishin and Fallon acting as the outer barrier. Their gazes met over Cateline and Elsie's heads, an understanding passing between them.

Whatever it takes, we will protect them.

Part II

Starting, Elsie nearly had a heart attack, only to roll her eyes when she realized the weight on her rounded belly was Roishin's hand. She looked over at her grinning face.

"I knocked, but nobody answered," Roishin said, the twinkle in her eyes belying her claim.

"I see," she drawled. She covered Roishin's hand, their fingers entwining. "It's good to see you."

"I'm sorry I scared you." Roishin lifted her head to rest in her open palm as she lay atop the covers next to Elsie. "I wanted to see how you're doing," she explained. "I can't exactly show up during the day when Garratt is actually in town."

"What has happened between you two?" Elsie asked, her fingers beginning to absently run along the top of Roishin's hand where it lay upon her six-months-pregnant belly.

Roishin shrugged her shoulder. "I honestly don't know. I think part of it is he feels I've abandoned the family." She looked down into Elsie's eyes as she looked up at her. "I also think he's somewhat threatened by all of this." She indicated herself, with her short hair and the blue cloak with the gold stitching that she was now rarely without.

"Why would he be threatened by that?" Elsie asked, finding it sad. She'd always worried that she'd played some part in the chasm that had begun between the siblings, once very close. It seemed to get wider all the time.

"I'm not the typical woman, Elsie," Roishin said simply. "Our mother is very, very strong," she said, "But, at the heart of it, her soul is a wife and mother. Mother to an entire nation," she qualified with a grin. "What he expects a woman to be. I'm not that and never will be." She smirked. "I don't think he knows what to do with that, so he fears it."

"Well, I don't know," Elsie said. "Seems to me you'll be a mother here in a matter of months." She took Roishin's hand and moved it just a bit until it rested along the left side of her belly. "Wait…"

Roishin's eyes and mouth slowly opened as the baby moved, then kicked. She looked at Elsie as though she'd just experienced the most astonishing thing. "Oh my gods!"

Elsie smiled, so happy that Roishin got to feel it. She popped in so unexpectedly and was never able to stay long enough to get to feel it. "What do you think?"

Roishin had tears in her eyes as she looked down at the bulging belly. She slowly shook her head. "I don't even know." She looked deeply into Elsie's eyes. "Thank you," she whispered, emotion making the two words thick.

"For what?" Elsie asked.

"For agreeing to be her mamaí."

Smiling, Elsie reached up and cradled Roishin's cheek. She lifted her head just enough to leave a lingering kiss on her lips "No." she murmured, resting her head back down on the pillow as her eyes began to grow sleepy again. "Thank you."

"I'm sorry," Roishin said, beginning to move away. "You need your rest." She was stopped by Elsie holding firm to her hand.

"Will you stay?" Elsie asked. "At least until I'm sleeping?"

Roishin studied her for a moment but then nodded with a smile. "Can you turn to your side?"

Without question or comment, Elsie did as asked, smiling when she felt Roishin spoon up behind her. She placed her hand on Elsie's hip—a favorite spot for her—before, with a contented sigh, Elsie closed her eyes.

⁂

"Martha, if you don't mind, can we add some carrots to tonight's dinner?"

"Certainly, milady," the older woman said with a chuckle. She placed a hand quickly to the huge belly. "Little one cravin' some, eh?"

Elsie rolled her eyes. "Every single day," she said in a singsong voice, hands on her belly. "Pretty sure I'm going to turn into one."

Martha threw her head back and laughed. "My fourth son loved him some carrots, too. Now?" she said, eyebrows shooting up. "Won't touch 'em."

Elsie laughed, touching her cook on the shoulder with affection. "Thanks, Martha."

"Supper, same time, milady?" Martha asked.

"Aye," the princess said, then raised her hand with two fingers. "For two. Well…" She placed her hand on her belly and laughed. "Three."

The two women shared a laugh as Elsie headed out of the kitchens and back toward the stairs. She headed back up to her bedchamber, where her supper would be delivered. She was having Isla to her rooms for supper and was very much looking forward to it.

Being the official royal dressmaker and

seamstress, Isla was not only responsible for Elsie's wardrobe needs, but Cateline had also wrangled her talents as well. Elsie had been thrilled when Fallon had suggested they use Livia's old rooms to create a wonderful work and living space for Isla, who was not seen as a servant in her role.

Initially, Elsie had felt terrible using the space, knowing just how much Livia had meant to the family, but she finally came to the realization that Livia would probably be pleased. Isla, a woman on her own making it on her own talent and her own steam, was much like the woman who had once inhabited those rooms.

"Good eve, milady," Agnes, Elsie's lady-in-waiting greeted as Elsie entered the room. The shy seventeen-year-old with her pale blue eyes and light red hair looked shyly at her as she was folding the tablecloth she'd spread out over the wood table not twenty minutes before.

"Good eve, Agnes. What are you doing?"

The young woman spared her a glance before returning her focus to her task. "His Highness told me to clean this up, that supper will take place in the dining room downstairs."

Dark blond eyebrows shot up. "Oh, he did, did he?" Fury washed through her. "No. Agnes, supper will be exactly here," she said, pointing at the floor at her feet. "Please do as I instructed you to do."

"Aye, milady," Agnes said with a deep curtsey.

Elsie wanted to be angry at the girl, but she knew better. Garratt had put her in a terrible position: who to listen to? Turning on her heel, she went in search. Stepping out of her bedchamber, her head whipped to the right when she heard Garratt's loud, boisterous laughter coming from his own bedchamber.

A woman on a mission, she marched her eight-months-pregnant self down to his open chamber doors. Inside, she saw Garratt in his military garb—though he'd been home for three days—laughing and talking loudly with two other military men. She didn't know their names but knew their faces.

"And I'm looking down at her," Garratt was saying, partially turned away from the door and anyone entering. He was using his hands to help pantomime his story, seemingly gripping something or *someone* in front of his hips. "There's a lot there!" he exclaimed, the two men bursting into laughter. "I'm not entirely sure where to—"

One of them sobered immediately, clearing his throat as he noticed Elsie standing just twenty feet behind Garratt. The second man looked away, blushing. Garratt stopped his enthusiastic storytelling, hands still where they had been during his tale. He glanced over his shoulder at her before quickly looking away.

Elsie waited, pleased that he was clearly embarrassed. She had little doubt he did as he pleased when out in the field with his men and frankly, didn't much care. But, to bring that into *her* home? Bragging to his men about his exploits in the very chamber she was forced to spend her wedding night? And, in which Garratt was convinced he'd "done his job."

Turning to face her, he pasted a large smile on his tanned face. "Good eve, love," he boomed.

She wanted to quirk an eyebrow. *Love?* Considering in the eight months they'd been married, he'd been home for roughly two months' worth of days, if that. She absolutely despised falsity to benefit others.

"Godwin, Jasper, you remember my beautiful bride," he said, presenting her as if the two men hadn't been at their wedding.

Both men bowed deeply to her deference, the one still refusing to look her in the eye. The other gave her a genuine yet somewhat sheepish smile. "Milady."

Garratt strode over to her to stand behind her. He placed his hands on her bulbous belly. "My son!" he declared.

Elsie took his hands in hers and, as gently as she was capable of in that moment, removed them as she stepped away from him. He met her gaze, a bit of surprise in his blue eyes. "A word," she said quietly, about to head out of the chamber, but he grabbed her hand, stopping her.

"No," he said. "You'll be joining us downstairs as we dine—"

"I will not," she said, glaring at him. She pulled her hand free. She was absolutely not in the mood for him. "I'm tired and will be dining—"

"With us downstairs," he repeated, his own voice lowering.

She continued out of the bedchamber. If he chose to follow, they could talk. If not, she'd made her intention clear. He did follow, the slamming of the doors startling her. In the hall, she turned to him.

"Don't ever make me look bad in front of my men again," he warned.

"Then, perhaps you should have done as I suggested and followed me away from them to talk," she said, arms folded protectively over her belly. "Or, better yet, let me know when you plan to have company and I can leave you to your chatter, stories, and laughter undisturbed."

He slowly crossed his arms over his chest, chin raised a bit as he looked down at her. "Are you telling me what to do in *my* own castle, Elsie?"

"Garratt," she said, her exhaustion returning. "I honestly don't care what you do, my issue is when you try and tell *me* and *my* people what to do." She glared up at him. "Don't ever tell Agnes to change the instructions I've already given her."

He looked away, jaw muscles bulging. She couldn't quite tell if he was angry at that or embarrassed at being confronted with it. Finally, he looked at her again. "You will join us for supper downstairs."

"I will not," she said again, doing her level best to keep her calm. "I am eight months pregnant, Garratt. I am exhausted, and it's extremely hard on my back and my legs to trudge up and down the stairs." She held his gaze, wanting those words to sink in. "I already went down earlier to ensure supper instructions were imparted to Martha, which, honestly, *you* could have done, considering you're actually here."

He snorted. "Why on earth would I do that? That's not my job."

All she could do was stare at him, disgusted. What would Fallon say? She so badly wanted to voice that but instead said, "And, entertaining your men is not mine." With that, she headed to her chambers and closed the door.

❧❧❧❧

"You may retire for the night, Agnes," Elsie said, giving the young woman an affectionate smile. "Thank you for all you do."

The young woman gave her a sweet smile and a curtsey before heading to her quarters just off Elsie's. She closed the door behind her, leaving Elsie and Isla alone. They sat in the chairs before the fire, working on the knitting project Isla was helping Elsie with. She'd never been the best knitter but wanted to learn how.

"Good gods, you're all tangled." Isla grinned, setting her own project into her lap as she reached over to help.

Elsie relinquished control of her material and needles as she watched closely. "It is absolutely astounding to me," she murmured. "You just seem to have this innate gift for anything cloth." She met Isla's gaze, so close to her own in the dressmaker's current position. "Amazes me."

Isla smiled, returning her focus back to the knot Elsie managed to create. "My mam taught me," she said softly. "And, her father taught her." She sat back up straight in her chair. "Can you do it now?" She grinned. "You're all unknotted."

Elsie chucked. "No promises." The two women worked in companionable silence once again. Finally, Elsie asked, "Did you ever have children, Isla?" The fact that the dressmaker currently had none with her had given Elsie pause to ask such a thing of a woman of twenty-six who had been married at one time.

"I was pregnant three times," Isla said quietly, never taking her eyes off her task. "As an old wash woman who lived in my village once said to me, 'The good Lord didn't see fit to leave any of His blessings with the Devil.'"

Elsie reached a hand over and took hold of one of Isla's. The seamstress met her gaze and held it for a moment. Communication of sorrow and understanding passed between them before Elsie squeezed the warm fingers she held within her own.

"I promise you," she said. "You'll never be hurt

like that again, Isla." She gave the fingers another squeeze. "Ever."

Isla's smile was soft, her brown eyes so filled with life and gratitude. That was one thing Elsie was learning from the woman she was truly beginning to see as one of her closest friends. No matter what life threw at her, somehow she managed to smile through it.

During the most difficult day of Elsie's marriage thus far—the day after her wedding, and wedding night—it had been Isla who had held her and assured her that it would all be okay. No, she didn't know the full extent of Elsie's grief that morning, but she certainly understood the grief of having to be in an unwanted marriage and certainly of having to share her body for the first time with the unwanted husband.

Yes, Elsie thought. She, too, was feeling gratitude.

Part III

Being a woman of taller stature, it was easier for Roishin to portray the role of a male than it was for Enori or some of the other women. A person could don a "mask," as it were, but to add or subtract height without practical means was not a possibility. She looked good, she knew that. And, she'd gotten damn good at holding her intention for as long as needed.

Currently, her intention was a man in his forties, dark hair slicked back from a handsome, angular face. Beneath the mask, she was all eyes, looking for her target, while the intention was calm, poised, and just knew he absolutely belonged there. His black tuxedo fit him just so, shoes shined to a polish.

Chatter filled the space, as did the notes played by the pianist in the corner seated at the keyboard of the baby grand. She held a tumbler filled with something, though she hadn't taken a drink. It was far more of a prop than intoxicant.

"There she is," Livia said inside her head. "Talking to the woman with the fur coat on over to the right."

Roishin looked in that direction and sure enough spotted the target. She looked at the fur coat with distaste. No clue why anyone thought that was a fashion statement in 1983. She tossed that thought aside when she caught just the barest bit of an emerald sequined dress. She took a step back and was able to fully see her.

Yes, indeed. That was her. "Is Isaac finished yet?" she murmured.

"He is not. Keep her inside."

Taking a deep breath, she put herself into the mode of her role and, with a hand tucked into the pocket of her trousers, strolled on over to the lovely blonde. Hair straight and long and pulled up on one side, shoulders revealed in her cocktail dress, and the heavy makeup of the era completed the package. She was lovely and, as Roishin neared, hazel eyes glanced her way.

Roishin raised her glass in salute to the young woman who was looking her over. It had taken time, but she'd finally gotten to the point where she could separate herself enough from her intention to react as she or he would and not internalize it.

The woman with the fur coat glanced up at Roishin's face, giving her a heavily lipstick-coated smile before she wandered on. Now, it was just Roishin and her target. She grinned, using that which she'd practiced in the mirror for days before this mission.

"Great party," Roishin said, the voice of her intention deep and smooth.

The blonde, whom Roishin knew was named Suzanne, cocked her head slightly to the side. "You know I'm here with someone," she said, teasing in her voice.

Steve's—Roishin's intention—eyebrows shot up. "Now, you wound me." She put the hand that wasn't carrying the drink to her heart. "I come over here just to be friendly and you assume I'm up to no good."

The woman dropped her gaze to the floor then back up to her eyes. "It's good to see you, Steve." She reached out and ran a long, painted fingernail along the lapel of the tuxedo jacket. "I hadn't expected you back from Chicago so soon."

"Eh," Roishin hedged. "Couldn't miss Richard's big five-oh, now, could I?"

"I suppose not," she admitted, sparing her a glance. "You being the good little brother and all."

"All right, Romeo," Livia said. "You have three minutes to get her to the second floor."

Roishin took the woman by the hand and lightly tugged. "Come on," she said. "Let's get caught up." She grinned at the woman who eyed her skeptically. "Oh, come on." She gave Suzanne the smile she knew from her research that the blonde loved from Steve. "What do you think I'll do?"

"That's what I'm worried about," she muttered, allowing herself to be pulled through the crowd.

Roishin set her drink down on a small table they passed before heading for the stairs, leading her target by the hand behind her. She felt her heart begin to race as she knew they were on the countdown. She had to play it cool and not let on that something was wrong, nor make Suzanne believe she was trying to get her upstairs for anything else other than to talk.

Suzanne and Steve had a patchy past, but also one much like a boomerang, which was why Roishin had chosen his likeness as her intention. Truth was, Steve Wilkes was in fact in Chicago with his new wife at that very moment. The stairs in the impressive house led to bedrooms, bathrooms, and a lounging area where a few were sitting and chatting.

Roishin led her down the hall and to one of the bedrooms that was empty. She smiled at the woman before stopping just outside of it, indicating she should go first. When she did, Roishin glanced both ways to make sure "Steve" hadn't been seen. It was a challenge to not only hold your intention but also keep certain people disinterested enough in you that they basically ignored you, as she'd had to do for a large portion of those gathered.

Once the bedroom door was closed, Roishin was stunned to find her arms filled with a lovely blonde kissing her. She fully returned the kisses, even as her senses were acutely attuned to what was happening beyond that bedroom. She knew it would happen very soon.

Right on cue, Livia said, "And, ten, nine…"

Roishin moved them away from the door, which she'd been pushed up against, and deeper into the room. They ended up on the bed, she on top of the smaller woman. She had to force herself not to panic when Suzanne's hands began to grab at her fly. The mirage only went so far and was truly skin deep. Beyond that, a rude awakening for them both.

"…three, two…"

Roishin broke from the kiss and covered Suzanne's entire body with her own. A second later, a massive blast rocked the night, and the building. The windows of the bedroom exploded inward, showering glass down upon them. Suzanne was crushed against Roishin's chest and screaming. Distant police sirens rent the air, shrill in the sudden, deafening silence after the cacophony ended.

"Get out!" Livia called.

Lifting herself from Suzanne, she looked down at the terrified woman. "Be right back," Roishin said. "I'll go see what happened."

Knowing her target was safe, she hopped up from

the bed and with long strides ate up the space between the bed and the door. She yanked it open to see the lights were dark, no doubt electricity knocked out in the blast. Standing out in the hallway, she looked to the right—the direction they'd come from—and then to the left. At the end of the hallway was a window.

"Steve?" Suzanne called from the room behind her. "What happened?"

Yes, it was time to go. Roishin took off at a dead run toward the window, shedding her intention as she went. Cloak fanning out like a cape behind her, she threw her hand out, bowling ball style. She saw the window shimmer and threw herself into it…

…and landed squarely on her right shoulder in the Crystal Palace. She groaned, rolling to her back. Isaac stepped out, looking down at her. His grin caught by the luminescent red, he held a hand down to her. Taking it, she allowed herself to be pulled to her feet.

"Ow," she whined, rotating her right shoulder and rolling her neck.

He slapped her on her other shoulder. "Great job, Roishin."

She nodded as they headed out of the Crystal Palace. "You, too. Was he, uh…Was he…"

He nodded. "Yeah. He was sitting in the car at the time." He smiled, teeth stark white against the mahogany of his skin. "You get used to it," he assured. He squeezed her shoulder, wincing when she hissed. "Sorry. See you next time."

He pointed his fingers at her like two six-shooters as he backed away from her, then turned and whistled a happy tune as he headed off down a path in the spokes-like design of the garden surrounding the energy hub. She chuckled, shaking her head as she headed down her own path.

All he needed, she thought, was to be carrying a lunch pail that he lightly swung as he strolled home from "work." She headed home herself, ready for the day to end. This had been an intense mission, and she needed to clear her head. It had been the most research-intensive mission she'd been on to date.

Though she'd been there for less than an hour, it had been many hours of planning. Weeks, really. She was so glad to get home. Letting herself into the cottage, she immediately trotted upstairs. Enori hadn't been downstairs, but she felt her, though not in the house proper. That meant she was taking a shower.

Heading into her own bedroom, she tugged her cloak ties loose, the heavy garment sliding off her shoulders. She hung it up on the hook jutting from her door before she tossed herself to her bed, careful to avoid her jammed shoulder. She raised her arm, moving it this way and that, trying to loosen the joint.

Roishin!

Pausing, she lifted her head. No Enori. She slowly began to move her arm again.

Roishin! Please!

Sitting up, she threw her legs off the bed and hurried to her bedroom door. Listening, she heard nothing. Immediately, she jumped across the hall and through the bathroom door. Enori glanced over her shoulder at her where she stood beneath the spray.

Her panic hadn't even let her think that one through. Swallowing, Roishin looked away. "Sorry," she murmured.

The utter perfection of the woman's body was already emblazoned on her brain from when she'd been seventeen and had seen her in the Underground's waterfall. She definitely didn't need round two.

"Everything all right?" Enori asked. To Roishin's horror, she walked over to her, not even bothering to grab her towel. "Roishin?"

Swallowing again, Roishin looked back to her, desperately trying to avoid looking below her neck. Short blond hair was smoothed back from her perfect face, the expression a mixture of concern and amusement.

"Um," Roishin managed, looking into her eyes. "I heard someone calling my name. It sounded like someone was in trouble, and I worried it was you."

Shaking her head, Enori brought her hand up. Confused, Roishin began to recoil but Enori's thumb ran along her bottom up. When she held it up, there was a smudge of Suzanne's red lipstick on the pad.

"Oh, jeez," Roishin muttered, wiping at her mouth with her own fingers.

"Went well, I take it?" Enori grinned.

Sheepishly, Roishin nodded. "Got the job done. She's safe and he's not."

"Well done," Enori said. She smiled up at her, seeming quite pleased.

"Thanks." Roishin suddenly felt really stupid now that her panic had evaporated with the steamy air around her. "I'm really sorry I burst in on your shower, Enori. I honestly thought you were in trouble."

Enori's smile was sweet. "Do not apologize," she said softly. That sweet smile turned decidedly wicked. "We are two women. What could possibly go wrong?"

Nearly choking on her own spit on that one, she watched as Enori turned away and walked back to the waterfall. Roishin's gaze was pinned to the backside of an absolute goddess. She honestly had no idea if

Enori was even human, sometimes. It just didn't seem possible for one woman to be given so many physical gifts.

She forced herself to turn and leave, giving her mentor and friend the privacy she deserved. She headed back across the hall to her bedroom, her mind continuing on its thought path. She'd never seen Enori act in any real sexual way with anyone. She was affectionate, certainly, and could flirt the feathers off a bird, even when Roishin didn't think that was her intention.

A naturally sensuous woman, but there didn't seem to be any ties to anyone, male or female. She just kind of…was. Roishin had been living in the cottage with her now for over a year and cared very much about Enori. She'd made what could have been a difficult situation, what with leaving all she knew, not near as bad. She'd been patient with Roishin, caring, and gave the best hugs ever.

She felt they were close—as close as anyone could get to Enori, she supposed. She was the ultimate onion, and so often Roishin felt she'd just barely peeled away the surface layers. She suspected those still waters ran very, *very* deep.

Roishin's thoughts were shattered when this time she heard an all-out scream of agony. Eyes wide, she grabbed her cloak and twirled it around her shoulders as she jetted through the door that was against her wall…

…and into the cave. She continued…

…stepping out into the passageway that led to the trunk from Elsie's bedchamber. She was about to turn to the closed wooden door that was hidden by a tapestry on the other side when she heard it again. This time, however, it was very real and coming from Elsie's bedchamber.

"Push, milady!"

There was absolutely nowhere Roishin could go. She couldn't open that door and waltz on in there for many reasons. So, she had no choice but to stand there in the pitch darkness. Another agony-filled cry from Elsie, her voice giving out by the end. Hands resting on the cool wood of the door, Roishin rested her forehead there, too, and listened.

"One more, Elsie!" another voice called out. "One more push!"

It sounded like Elsie put everything she had into that push as her cry echoed throughout Roishin's very soul. A moment later, the unmistakable cry of a baby. Roishin's eyes closed as the tears slipped past her lashes and slid down her cheeks. Every cry from the baby brought another tear from her.

"'Tis a girl, milady!" exclaimed the first woman's voice.

Pushing away from the wall, Roishin had to get in there. She quickly created another door to get out of the passageway and then, in a distant hall, focused her intention and became an average young woman, a servant girl in a plain dress with long, dark hair pulled up.

She hurried back toward the princess's bedchamber, careful not to be seen. Anyone she may run into in the hall would know she didn't belong there. But, in the post-birth chaos of the bedchamber, she hoped her identity would go unnoticed.

Once she reached the bedchamber, she eased inside and stood by, looking as though she were waiting for instruction. The bed had been stripped of its normal bedding, a special quilt placed atop it to catch blood and other birthing juices, to be burned after. Two midwives were there, one cleaning the crying baby of all the white goop that covered her flailing little body. Another was examining Elsie, who lay back on the bed looking utterly exhausted.

She was naked, a thin sheen of sweat covering her body and her long hair splayed out across the pillow like a sweaty, golden wave. Her legs were raised and spread still, the midwife who was examining her using a rag to wipe off the blood from the insides of her thighs and privates.

"Girl!"

Starting, Roishin looked to see the woman with the swaddled babe was waving her over. Roishin hurried over to her, stunned when the baby—*their* baby—was handed to her.

"Take her over to the princess."

Roishin bowed and cradled the newborn in her arms. She looked into her tiny face and for just a moment, those deep green eyes looked up at her. Roishin couldn't look away, a true connection between mother and daughter.

I love you with all my heart.

Reaching the bed, Roishin had to remember the intention she was in as she gently lowered the bundle to a waiting Elsie. Though exhausted, sapphire eyes looked up at Roishin with confusion in them.

"Congratulations, milady," Roishin said softly, easing the baby into Elsie's arms. "Perhaps you should name her Mariota, milady?" she murmured into her ear.

Elsie gasped and looked at her again, studying Roishin's face. Tears welled in her eyes, even as they were desperately, seemingly, trying to look through the mask. Roishin gave her a lopsided grin. Elsie gasped, eyes widening. Roishin nodded.

"Come, girl," one of the midwives said. "Let the babe feed."

"I'd like for her to stay," Elsie said.

Though looking a bit confused, the two women began to gather the bloody towels and dressings as well as the large bowl of water that had been used to clean the baby.

"I'll be back shortly, milady," the older of the two midwives said. "Get all this disposed of, then I'll help get you cleaned up, too."

Elsie nodded. "Thank you."

Once they were left alone and the doors closed, Roishin helped to stack the pillows behind Elsie so she could sit up a bit. She climbed up on the bed next to her, her intention fading.

Elsie stared at her, eyes wide and lips open. Roishin grinned at her before she leaned down and placed a soft kiss on those lips. Shaking herself out of it, Elsie turned her attention back to the baby. It took a moment, but they finally got her to suckle.

Roishin watched, absolutely in awe. She rested her chin on Elsie's naked shoulder. "She's so beautiful," she whispered.

Elsie nodded, not taking her eyes off the suckling babe. "She is. I already love her so much."

"So do I." Roishin reached across Elsie's body and lightly touched the soft skin of a chubby cheek, tiny little hands, and a sausage-like arm. "She's perfect."

Elsie nodded. "How did you know?"

"I heard you." Roishin smiled when Elsie looked over her shoulder at her. "I know, it sounds crazy. But

I did."

"I'm so glad." She left a small kiss on Roishin's lips. "I love you."

"I love you, too."

Chapter One

I promise with all my heart," Fallon murmured, glancing up from her granddaughter to Enori, who gently took the swaddled newborn from her after the king unwound her hands from the dangling bits of ribbon that were wrapped around the sleeping baby's body.

Roishin watched as next, and finally, it was Cateline's turn. She was asked to exact the same promise as Roishin, Elsie, and Fallon had: to love, protect, and encircle two-week-old Mariota with all she had and all she was.

"I promise," Cateline said, leaning down and leaving a kiss on the baby's forehead. She unwound her hands from the ribbon.

Enori walked over to Roishin. "Take her, please," she said. Once Roishin did, Enori wrapped her own hands in the flowing ribbons. "I, Enori," she began softly, "will love this child, daughter of Roishin and Elsie, granddaughter of Fallon, Cateline, and Ankou. She will have my protection, my honesty, and my counsel for all time." She looked across the baby's sleeping body and met Roishin's gaze for a moment before carefully removing the ribbon wrapped around the bundle. "So it be."

"So it be," they all said in unison.

Roishin cradled Mariota against her chest, bouncing and swaying gently where she stood to keep the little one sleeping. She listened as Enori began to speak again as she wrapped the ribbon, the same shade of blue as the cloaks they both wore.

"In this very building," she began, indicating the structure around them. "I performed the ceremony to bond Fallon and Cateline together as one many years ago."

She smiled at the couple, Fallon's arm immediately going around Cateline's shoulders as the smaller woman leaned into her. The two shared a soft look and kiss before returning their attention to the priestess.

"Fallon," she continued. "Youngest child of the great King Carthac of Sursha, turned warrior, turned king." She smiled, beautiful and genuine. "A true hero, and one of the greatest to rule." Her cerulean gaze turned to Cateline. "The beautiful daughter of a French nobleman, turned beloved Queen Cateline."

Cateline smiled at her, resting her head against Fallon's shoulder.

Enori turned to Elsie. "A young girl from Scotland, orphaned far too soon. Brought into the great nation of Sursha for a second chance." Again, that beautiful smile. "Now, mother of one of the greatest queens Sursha will ever know." She raised her chin slightly, almost as if in pride for such a wonderful accomplishment. "And," she added. "To be a beloved and hailed queen in her own right." Enori tilted her head, slightly studying the other woman. "You will break the rules and break boundaries, Elsie," she said, her voice so soft, as if those words were only for the princess. "Your time is coming."

Roishin looked from Enori to Elsie, who looked riveted by what was being said. She knew Enori would only speak the truth, so she wondered what it all meant. She held Elsie's gaze when she looked at her. The two shared a smile now, connected in a way they weren't with anyone else on earth. All due to the precious bundle in Roishin's arms.

"And you." Enori's tone toward Roishin made them all laugh.

Roishin gave her a sheepish look. "Uh-oh."

Enori's teasing, quirked eyebrow fell and that same, beautiful smile spread across her lips. "From the humblest beginnings of all," she said, a touch of wonder in her voice. "A newborn babe found in the woods, only to be the greatest gift of love from Ankou to your mothers." That eyebrow quirked again. "From young, curious, *mouthy* girl to a woman of bearing, profound dedication, and love." Her smile was soft, meant only for Roishin. "A girl I once called protégée and mentee. Now, a woman I call friend." She smirked. "And, still mouthy."

Roishin burst into laughter, shaking her head in amusement. "Whatever."

Enori grinned for a moment before growing serious once more as she turned to those gathered. "We are all bonded now." She looked at each one in turn. "Ankou blood flows through your soul, Fallon, Cateline, and Roishin." She looked to Elsie. "You, the blood of your daughter's namesake, the great Mariota, a powerful Druid priestess. You two," she said, indicating Elsie and Roishin. "Have created a very powerful being. Make no mistake."

"Will she be a target?" Roishin asked.

"Always."

That one word, spoken easily and without hesitation, made Roishin hold her daughter even tighter. She looked down into her sleeping face, unable to keep the smile from hers. She was so beautiful, and she'd never felt such an almost painful love and sense of protectiveness as she did with Mariota.

She wished with everything in her that she could be with her every single day, live in the same house with her. She wanted to see her every waking moment, but it just wasn't possible, for all the same reasons it wasn't possible for she and Elsie to be together. Also, though Garratt was relatively disinterested in her, so convinced he'd have his son, Mariota still needed to be seen as his.

Mariota looked absolutely nothing like him, and eerily like her "aunt." And, though no one would even consider for a second that Roishin would be the other contributing parent, they didn't need whispers of perhaps an unknown family member that was. So, distance would be kept, except in the quietest of night hours, or in their cave, where Elsie brought Mariota to spend time with her.

Once she was old enough to no longer need to feed at her mother's breast, Roishin would take her into Duras with her for visits. She felt it was incredibly important for the girl to learn as early as possible who—and what—she was.

❧❧❧❧

Up in the family chambers, a private dinner had been consumed and many laughs had. To Roishin's surprise and delight, Enori had joined them. She looked to her parents, who were talking with Elsie, who had just finished breastfeeding, about something amusing. All three were gesticulating dramatically and laughing. Roishin smiled at that as she sat by herself, Mariota resting against her shoulder as she burped her.

She couldn't remember seeing her parents look

so happy. The only thing missing for them, she knew, were their other two children. Garratt was gods only knew where on some campaign, and Laigen was at her home in Spain. But what charmed her the most was Enori. She was sitting on the couch, Isabeau curled up in her lap as she spoke to her.

As she watched, she saw that the six-year-old was very engaged in whatever Enori was telling her. She giggled or spoke or nodded vigorously. Then, they began to sing quietly. Roishin recognized the song, a silly little song sung to children, replete with hand gestures that made the song interactive.

It brought to mind how Enori had been with Roishin so long ago. Now that she'd gotten to know Enori as an adult, it was easy for Roishin to forget that she'd been there all along. So patient, so kind.

Now, watching her with her baby sister, Roishin was absolutely enthralled. Why did she have no children of her own? She was wonderful with them. The smile she bestowed upon Isabeau was so filled with happiness and a joy that Roishin had rarely seen. Enori had a calming presence about her, and that was always calming to others. Isabeau in her lap, now talking excitedly about something, Enori herself seemed to be the one at peace.

Roishin gasped playfully when she heard a little burp in her ear. Pulling her daughter from her shoulder, she braced the back of a wobbly head as she held the infant. "I think you burped. I do!" she exclaimed softly. She left gentle but noisy kisses on chubby little cheeks and a warm neck. "Good girl," she cooed. She smiled at her daughter, who focused on her. "Someday," she said softly. "Someday I'll teach you all you need to know."

"Like what?"

Roishin was surprised to see Isabeau suddenly standing next to her chair. She glanced to the couch and saw Enori still sitting there, Cateline now beside her. The two women were talking. Turning back to Isabeau, Roishin smiled.

"All kinds of stuff," she said with a grin.

"I love my sister," Isabeau said.

"Well, sweetheart, Mariota is your cousin—"

"She's my sister," Isabeau insisted, her deep blue eyes boring into Roishin's.

Roishin could tell this wasn't the confusion of a six-year-old girl trying to understand complicated family relationships. She truly believed this. "Did someone tell you that, Isabeau?" she asked gently, not wanting her to think she was in trouble or any such thing.

Isabeau shook her head. She took one of Mariota's tiny hands in her own, holding it like it was the most precious egg on the planet. "She just is." She met Roishin's gaze. "I feel it."

Roishin wasn't sure how to feel in that moment. She'd certainly be asking Enori about this later, once they got home. But for now, she cradled Mariota in one arm while using the other to hug Isabeau to her. She kissed the side of her head. "I love you, Isabeau."

Isabeau beamed at her, as though she'd just been told the most amazing thing in all the world. Roishin had to hold the baby tighter as she suddenly had a six-year-old grabbing her neck in a tight hug.

❧❧❧❧

"Thank you," Roishin whispered, easing the baby down into her cradle. She'd been fed, changed, and swaddled. Roishin had helped where she could, clearly not on the feeding part.

Elsie stood aside, holding back the curtains of the beautiful cradle for their daughter. Once she was safe and sound inside, the curtains could be released to give the baby a warm, dark space to sleep in her mother's bedchamber. For now, Roishin and Elsie stood side by side, looking down at the wonder of what they'd created.

"Some days," Elsie said softly. "I cannot believe she's real."

Roishin nodded, moving to stand behind her. She wrapped her arms around her and rested her chin upon Elsie's shoulder. Her hands were covered where they rested at Elsie's belly. They just stood in silence watching Mariota sleep for a long time, nothing said, nothing needing to be said.

It had been a wonderful day for Roishin, to be able to spend the *entire* thing with those she was closest to in all the world. She and Enori and the rest of them were all so busy with their tasks and missions, it was easy for her to lose touch with where she came from. Her world in Duras and all that entailed was so vastly different from Sursha. She'd gotten a really good reminder that day that she needed to do all she could to bring those two worlds closer together, somehow.

Finally, the curtains were closed and the two moved away from the cradle to sit before the fire. Roishin looked over at the woman sitting in the matching chair to her own. She smiled, enjoying the lovely profile she was presented with.

Sometimes, it amazed her that she'd been given the privilege of loving this incredibly special woman. It was a love she knew she'd always carry, no matter what.

She'd gotten to touch her, and she'd gotten to see all that she was. And now, they'd been given the ultimate gift.

Reaching across the short distance between their chairs, she took Elsie's hand in her own. When the lovely princess looked over at her, Roishin smiled. "Thank you for being so incredible, Elsie. For all you've done for Mariota. For being the perfect mamaí for her."

Elsie's smile was so beautiful, lit up her entire face. "And," she said softly, fingers wrapping around those that held them. "I thank you for giving me a gift I never could have even imagined, Roishin." She looked deeply into Roishin's eyes. "A gift of *us* that can never be taken away." She squeezed Roishin's fingers. "One thing that, no matter what, can express the depth of love we have for each other."

Roishin brought their joined hands to her lips and left a lingering kiss on Elsie's fingers. "Always." They shared a long look before the spell was broken. "So," she said conversationally. "And, I want you to be honest with me, Elsie. How are things?"

Elsic shrugged, looking to the fire. "I'm learning to create a life for myself," she said. "Garratt is rarely here, and to be honest," she added, glancing back to Roishin. "I'm fine with that. I don't think he wants this any more than I do."

Roishin was about to get really angry, but Elsie's sweet smile stopped her. She forced herself to calm and listened to what she said next.

"Roishin, his heart is in the military. I think it always was. Even when he's here, he's still dressed and ready for battle, has his men here all the time. I think it's comforting to him."

Roishin considered her words for a moment, and as much as she wanted to smack the living crap out of him, it made sense. Nodding, she asked, "How does he treat you? Be honest."

"We're not really friends," Elsie admitted. "I don't know much more about him today than I did a year ago. And, this may sound awful, Roishin, but I'm really fine with that. I think he tried to convince himself, and perhaps your parents, this was what he wanted." She indicated herself and then the cradle twenty feet from them. "But, ultimately, I don't think it would have mattered who the woman was." She shook her head. "I don't think he has it to give."

For a moment, Roishin wanted to cry, then she wanted to march on over to her parents' residence and scream: *Why? Why did you condemn her to this?* She stared into the fire, her jaw working as she berated herself. She should have never left. She should have—

"Hey."

Roishin didn't even realize she was clenching her fist until she felt soft fingers on her hand. Relaxing as much as she could, she looked over to see concerned eyes on her. Without a word, Elsie got to her feet and pulled Roishin to her.

"Come on," she said, leading her toward the bed. "You are going to lay down with me."

Roishin dutifully followed. She helped the other woman undress down to her chemise, a job her lady-in-waiting would normally do, but she'd been given the day off. As Roishin removed her boots, Elsie unpinned her hair and brushed out the long, golden strands.

The two eventually got settled, understanding that Roishin couldn't stay for all sorts of reasons, one largely being that Agnes would be in first thing in the morning and it just wouldn't do for her to be found there. But for now, Roishin accepted Elsie into her arms to snuggle up against her.

Something she'd noticed since the conception of Mariota was that things between them were much easier, more relaxed, somehow. It was almost as if the expectation had been released, and now they were free to love each other on a deeper level, a larger level, than waiting for that kiss or that arousing moment.

Holding her now, it was just pure contentment. She wanted nothing more from her but to be with her, enjoy the closeness and trust that had happened over years, long before that first kiss.

"I've made a new friend," Elsie said at length, seeming to continue their conversation from earlier. "She's definitely made things so much easier, nicer."

"Who?" Roishin asked, resting her cheek against the head that rested on her shoulder.

"She's a dressmaker," Elsie explained, her hand curving around Roishin's side so her fingers were lightly tucked beneath her body. "A widow. Her name is Isla and has been a true gift. One thing Cateline said to me, and now I understand why, was to have a friend. Have someone to trust and keep away the loneliness."

For just a moment, a very short, very selfish moment, Roishin felt a stab of jealousy. She forced it away, as it had no place here. After all, she'd essentially made the decision for both she and Elsie. Granted, not entirely sure how much choice *she'd* had in leaving, but still…

"Tell me about her," she said, running her fingers through soft hair.

"She's just a really nice person," Elsie said, seemingly unaware of the conflict inside Roishin. "She's had some horrible things happen to her, yet somehow she remains a good soul. Very talented dressmaker, too. Even the queen utilizes her skill."

Roishin smiled at that. "I'm so glad, Elsie." She kissed her head. "I so badly want you to be happy and not stuck in an empty life."

"No," Elsie said, her voice growing soft as she seemed to be getting tired. "I won't let that happen. Early on I decided that Garratt would have little to do with my fulfillment, Roishin." She cuddled in a bit more as her body began to relax with her sleepiness. "With or without him, or even completely on my own, I'm finding my way."

Roishin smiled at that. One of the things she'd loved most about Elsie from the very beginning was her strength. She was a survivor, no matter how sweet and beautiful she looked on the outside, both of which she truly was. On the inside was a will of iron. She had so many of the wonderful traits that Roishin loved most about her own mother.

She waited until she knew that Elsie was deeply asleep then gently moved out from beneath her. She replaced her body with a pillow, which Elsie immediately wrapped herself around, making Roishin smile.

"I love you," she whispered against her head before leaving a soft kiss there and slowly climbing out of bed.

Walking to the cradle, she checked on Mariota, leaving a kiss on her tiny head before she took one final look around. Everything looked good. A small move of the logs in the fireplace renewed the flames to ensure warmth for both her girls. It was time for her to go home.

Such a bittersweet thing, she thought. Most times she was ready to go, no matter how much she knew she'd miss her family. Mariota had changed so much. Blowing out a tired breath, she walked to the door that would take her to the secret passageway that would lead the way home.

Chapter Two

The woman—young, perhaps twenties? Her dark brown hair was long enough to drape over past the front of her shoulders. Her eyes were nearly as dark as her hair. Skin tone a little darker, the color of a person with a suntan, perhaps. Not Caucasian.

It had been a close-up image of her face that was slowly pulling back to show more of her. She had a young boy sitting in her lap. His dark brown hair, short and shaggy, almost looked as though it had been cut with a knife's blade. His eyes, the same color as the woman who held him, looked shy, almost afraid. Hers looked haunted.

Motherand son? Sister and brother? Aunt and nephew?

The images vanished, leaving pure darkness. As if typed on a computer, letters then words began to appear:
Rio de Janeiro—2002—favelas
Bruna Barbosa—age 23
Carlos Barbosa—age 5

Green eyes blinked open, the dimness of her bedroom all around her. She didn't see any of that, however. She moved her lips as she silently repeated what had appeared before her mere moments before she'd snapped to wakefulness. She sat up, still going over it, whatever "it" was. Running a hand through her hair, she finally decided to get up.

She did her morning business then trotted

downstairs in her pajamas, making her way to the kitchen and through the open door that led to essentially a small stone room. It acted as a root cellar, fridge, and storage. There, she gathered a fine selection of fruits from the veritable army of baskets that lined the shelves into the empty wooden box left there for just this purpose.

Returning to the kitchen, she set her bounty down on the counter and grabbed a knife. She was still going over what she'd seen and read, no clue what it all meant, as she peeled, sliced, diced, and cubed.

"Good morrow," Enori said, padding into the room.

Roishin sent her a smile over her shoulder. "Good morrow."

Enori raised an eyebrow as she went to the percolator to start getting it ready. "Sleep well, did you?"

Roishin chuckled. "Ironically, no."

"Uh-oh."

"Do you know who Bruna or Carlos Barbosa is?" she asked, knife still in hand as she turned to rest her lower back against the counter. She watched as the other woman got the little machine ready for Roishin's coffee.

Enori sent her a quick gaze. "Context, please?"

"Well," Roishin said, bringing back to her mind's eye what she'd dreamed. "This morning, just before I woke up, I saw this woman and a little boy. Got a really good look at them, then suddenly all this information. I assume it's about them, but I have no idea."

Enori paused in what she was doing. Slowly, she turned and met Roishin's confused expression. "Congratulations," she said softly. "You have been given your first target."

⁂

From the Crystal Palace, Roishin headed to the Conference Room, which was nothing like what one would normally think. There was no long table lined with chairs inside a secure room with a door. This was a pitch-black room with a huge rectangle of shimmering air the size of a movie theater screen.

She was watching intently as image after image appeared on the "screen," committing to memory everything she was seeing. The information came fast and it was a lot to absorb, but she was determined. Finally, the show came to an end, leaving her in darkness other than the very dim light of the shimmering space.

"Go back three minutes," she said, and the screen immediately glowing back to life. Everything she'd seen in those last three minutes zoomed backward until stopping suddenly. The images moved forward once more at regular speed. Once it finished up, again the screen began to shimmer.

"Anything else, kid?"

"Nope. Thanks, Frank," she called out to the man known as "The Projectionist" to some. She turned away from the screen and sent a wave into the darkness before heading back toward the Crystal Palace exit doors.

Frank Weatherby had been born in the late eighteen hundreds, the era of the silent movie hitting the world hard during his childhood. He'd been obsessed with them, then even more so when the talkies came out. He'd gotten a job as a projectionist in one of the cinema houses in his hometown of Akron, Ohio at the age of twelve. He did that job for the rest of his life, until he died in the seventies.

She once asked him why he'd chosen to spend eternity essentially being a human movie projector and not either have a life in Duras or follow his wife, Ethel, into Yewa, the land of the dead, no living anywhere in sight. His response had made her laugh.

"Ethel yelled at me for sixty-six years straight," he said. "I needed some peace!"

Now, she had a whole lot on her plate and a whole lot on her mind. She needed to decide how many people needed to be on this mission with her—just a partner or a larger team. As she headed home, she considered. She definitely knew she wanted Livia with her. She considered Enori. Her immediate thought was that she absolutely wanted her there, too.

But, would it be better to do this first mission on her own? Prove herself to Enori? She'd never been the team lead before, and whereas she was excited, she was also nervous as all get-out. She knew Enori believed in her, but…

The house smelled of coffee when she got home. She couldn't help but smile at that. Enori didn't drink it, so unless they had some coffee-drinking company she didn't know about, it had been made for her. What she also noticed as she walked further into the house was a basket sitting at the center of the kitchen table. A covered basket.

Getting closer, she saw there was also a clay jar. Roishin stood there, absolutely stunned. She could now smell the fresh bread beneath the basket covering, and she could see Millie's honey butter spooned inside the jar. She knew Enori wasn't in the house, which Roishin was a little disappointed by, but she was deeply touched by the trouble Enori had gone to.

Hurrying upstairs, she shed her cloak and grabbed a notebook and pen she kept for missions from her bedroom, then trotted back down the stairs. Leaving paper and pen on the table, she readied herself a cup of coffee in her mug, left out on the counter for her, then buttered herself a piece of Millie's amazing bread.

As she munched, she got to a clean sheet of paper and began to jot down everything she'd learned that was necessary to impart to whomever she chose to take with her. This would also help her decide how many. She wrote, she scribbled out, she wrote again. She ate one piece of bread, not even noticing another buttered piece had appeared on her plate. She worked out strategy, sipping from her coffee until she finished the liquid inside. No clue how many minutes or hours later, she reached for her mug only to find it was full of fragrant, steaming brew.

Night fell and the glow of a warm, popping fire spread across the downstairs. Realization hit, and Roishin looked around. The bread basket had been cleared, as had the clay butter jar. Her coffee mug sat on the table, half-filled with coffee, whose steam wafted up from the warm brew. A book sat on Enori's loveseat, closed and left for the night. It hadn't been there before—that she knew.

She was alone downstairs, though she could feel Enori's presence in the house. She was tired. Her eyes hurt, her back hurt, and her brain hurt. She stood from the bench seating of the kitchen table and raised her arms above her head. Stretching as high as she could, a little squeak escaped as she stretched her back, too.

Looking down at her notebook, she saw that she'd

filled nearly half of it with preparation notes. Sighing, she clipped her pen to the page she was on and slapped the notebook closed. She dumped out the rest of her coffee before washing the cup and letting it drain overnight. A flick of her wrist doused the flames in the fireplace as she grabbed her notebook off the table on her way to the stairs.

Enori's door was closed, so Roishin went into her own. She tossed the notebook to the top of her dresser. A quick shower made all the difference, allowing the soreness to ease out of her muscles. She quickly dried off and dressed in her pajamas before heading back across the hall to her bedroom.

Looking out the window, she saw the peaceful village beyond. Stone cottages much like the one she currently lived in dotted the area. She saw smoke coming from one of the chimneys, firelight flickering through the windows of the residence unseen. She smiled at that.

What were they doing in there? Was it a family? A couple? A single person? Were they laughing? Talking? Fighting? Making love? What was that like in Duras? Was it different than the other world? A place with laws and rules provided by science. Was it more potent in Duras?

Everything was so much brighter, seemed so much more intense here, she thought. The food, the coffee, colors, everything. So, what about touch? Kissing? Orgasms? She smirked as she looked away from the window, absolutely no idea why that had popped into her mind. Crazy thoughts.

She finger-combed her hair back from her face as she walked to the bed, turned down the covers, and climbed in. As tired as she was, her mind was still swirling with information, ideas, worries, thoughts, and anxiety. She got herself settled on the side of the bed she slept on. Even back home, sleeping in that big ol' bed in Caisleán Thiar, she'd slept on only one side.

Lying on her back, she tucked her hands behind her head and stared up at the ceiling. Intending to either continue her mental strategy or try to sleep, she realized she felt lonely. It was a strange feeling, something she hadn't felt in a long time. Certainly not while in Duras; she was too busy.

Her attention was grabbed by a soft knock on the closed door. "Come in," she called out.

A moment later, Enori peeked her head in. "Did I wake you?"

Roishin smiled and shook her head. "No. Everything okay?"

The door was pushed open more and Enori stepped inside the room. Walking to the bed, she lowered herself to sit on the side. Sitting there, her gown white against the paleness of her skin and color of her hair, Roishin thought she looked absolutely ethereal in the moonlight filtering in through the very window she'd just been looking out of. For a moment, Roishin's breath caught.

Forcing herself to look away, she cleared her throat softly then looked to her friend for explanation of why she was there.

"How are you feeling about everything?" Enori asked, seeming unaware of Roishin's momentary and confusing issue.

"Nervous," Roishin said easily. "What happens if I fail, Enori?"

Enori stretched her body out on the other side of the bed atop the covers. She held her head up on her hand as her other arm ran down the length of her side, hand resting on her own hip. She studied Roishin for a moment before she asked.

"Why do you think you would fail?"

Roishin looked at her like she was from another planet. "Because I've never done this before."

"No?" Enori challenged. "So, it was not you with me, or with Trudy, or John, or…"

Roishin grinned shyly, looking away. "Yes, of course it was. But it wasn't *my* mission."

"So," Enori hedged, her fingernail lightly running along the top of Roishin's hand, which lay atop her own stomach. "You had nothing to do with the planning, then?"

Roisin ignored the little shiver that coursed through her system. "Well, yeah. I mean, I had to create my own role, figure out how it played into the mission." She shrugged a shoulder. "That kind of thing."

"Hmm," Enori murmured, sounding bored even as her eyes twinkled. "Sounds to me like you have done this before, then." Her hand fell harmlessly to the bed. "But," she added. "That is just my opinion."

Roishin smirked. "You make it sound so easy."

Enori shook her head. "What we do is not easy, Roishin," she said. "Which is why only a select number of us do it. But," she added, her smile beautiful. "If Ankou did not believe in you, you would not have received your target in your dreams."

"Is that how it always works?" Roishin asked, turning to her right side and mirroring Enori's position.

The priestess nodded. She studied Roishin for a long moment, almost making Roishin nervous as it was like she was looking into her very soul. Finally, she spoke. "Roishin, you are brilliant. You understand all this more than you think you do."

Roishin believed Enori believed what she was saying, but she was so worried she'd disappoint. She wanted to beg her to go with her but worried that would make her seem weak. She so badly wanted to please Enori.

Looking away from those beautiful eyes, turned a light gray in the dimness, Roishin looked down at her hand, which rested on the blanket that covered her body. "I want to help them," she finally said. "So badly."

"Of course you do," Enori said kindly. "It is who you are, Roishin." She covered Roishin's hand with her own. "Who you have always been."

"Do you think I can do this?" Roishin asked, sounding like a little girl.

"No," Enori said, a little smirk curling her lips. "I *know* you can."

❧❧❧❧

The next morning, Roishin awoke feeling refreshed. Her body felt good, her mind clear, and a complete plan in mind. She shoved her covers off her and got to her feet. Gratitude filled her as her stress was gone, almost as though her brain had had the most incredible massage overnight that she was completely unaware of.

She quickly made her bed, hopped across the hall to do her morning business, then trotted down the stairs, skipping the final two to land on the main floor. She grinned over at Enori, who was curled up on the love seat enjoying the book she'd left there the night before. Walking over to the couch, Roishin plopped down and rested her elbows on her spread knees.

Her gaze boring into Enori's, she said, "Okay, I think I've fully got this. I'd really like it if you'd be on my team. Will you?"

Enori studied her for a moment, head slightly tilted to the side. Finally, she smiled. Such a lovely, soft smile. "Of course. All you had to do was ask."

Roishin looked at her shyly through her bangs, which had gotten a little long. "Yeah, well…"

Grinning, Enori nodded. She reached over and mussed the bangs. "Shaggy dog."

Roishin grinned and nodded. She ran her hand through her hair to push it back from her face. "A haircut is on the agenda before we go."

"When does that happen?" Enori asked, her voice growing serious as she fell into work mode.

"Three days from today. So, that being said, my plan is to gather you and Livia here for a meeting this afternoon—if you're okay with us doing it here?"

"Why would you ask? You live here, too, Roishin."

Roishin rubbed the back of her neck, feeling shy. "Yeah, but it's your house." She looked away for a moment and shrugged. "It's come up before, but you told me when I moved in that it was while I was training, so I wouldn't have to worry about anything." She looked down at her bare feet. "Training is over. Right?"

"Hey. Roishin, look at me."

Roishin did, meeting Enori's gaze.

"You have choices," she said softly. "If you want to move out and start living on your own, you can."

It was the second time that had been brought up and offered. And, it was the second time Roishin felt nauseous at the thought. Clearing her throat, she said, "Would you rather I go?" She raised her hand to forestall a response before she added, "I know it's my choice. I understand that. But would you rather have your house back?" She gave her a sheepish grin.

Enori smirked. "I never lost my house to begin with."

Chapter Three

The air was hot and sticky as they made their way to their destination. Sitting in the back seat of the dusty black SUV they'd gotten their hands on, she was doing her level best to not be nervous. Over the years, decades, and centuries, she'd been on some dangerous missions, but this one was particularly so.

For one, it was taking place in one of the most dangerous places on earth, and for two, there was a very young leader at the wheel, literally and figuratively. She glanced to the driver, who to all looked like a Brazilian man in his early forties. He was the son of the sixty-something Brazilian woman sitting in the back seat looking at his reflection in the rearview mirror.

For just a moment, his dark brown eyes met hers in that mirror, but she could see the nervous green of the woman beneath. The gaze returned to the darkness of the wee hours of the morning beyond, spotlighted by the headlights.

They were in the outskirts of Rio de Janeiro in a particularly poverty-stricken place. The so-called favelados lived in favelas, which were basically shacks made from anything that could be borrowed or stolen. It was a shantytown filled with the poorest of the poor. It was also a place to hide or be hidden.

"She and the boy are sleeping," Livia said, her energy in the car with them once more after returning from surveilling the location.

"Is she alone?" Roishin asked.

"No. I fear we'll have to take action," Livia said.

Nodding, Enori met Roishin's gaze again quickly before Roishin refocused on the road. They reached the crooked tree they'd all decided was the best place to stop and continue on foot. Beforehand, Enori had mixed up concoctions of what they'd need for both the woman and the boy, and for any trouble they may encounter.

The SUV slowed to a stop, the gravel beneath its tires crunching. The engine was cut, followed by the headlights. "Frank," Roishin said softly. "Go ahead and project."

Frank, "The Projectionist," was a walking, talking search engine of memories and current, previous, or future maps of any given area. He was currently sending them all a mental projection of the terrain in their exact location. It was pitch black for their eyes, but he was showing them through the camera in their minds where they were, almost like internal night-vision goggles.

The process was incredibly draining on the energy and disorienting, so it wasn't often used. But, at times it was necessary. It was shocking what lay before them. Humanity piled atop humanity, dirty, some wearing mere rags if fully clothed at all. The smell was horrendous, the stench of the rotten core of greed. The Haves simply—and literally—shitting on the Have Nots.

Enori had to push that out of her mind and focus on the two souls they were there for and the incredible wrong that tonight would be set right. Livia guided them to what amounted to a lean-to made of cardboard, a partially rotten sheet of plywood and a tarp that smelled of moldy rainwater.

Inside, mother and son were huddled together, lying on their sides. They were filthy and dangerously thin. The man who snored softly a foot away lay on his back. A handgun was on the ground covered loosely by his left hand. No doubt, he could grab and fire within a second of wakefulness.

She glanced to Roishin, who was already looking at her. In that one look, an entire conversation passed between them. Enori nodded, understanding her role. She reached inside her pocket and retrieved the tiny glass vial, which she kept herself as it was a more dangerous substance that could not be overused or the result would be death. She handed Roishin the pouch that she'd also retrieved. Back at home, she'd shown her how and where to administer it, in case they ended up in the situation they were in now.

It was a mixture much like that she'd created for Fergus all those years ago, except this one was far more potent, meant to work in a single dose, not over time. They went to their assigned parties and would have to act in concert with each other and very quickly. It would be far too easy for the situation to get out of their control if they took too much time.

The fact that Ankou had given this to Roishin as her first mission told Enori just how much he believed in her. She had shown incredible ingenuity and intelligence and maturity over the past year. Though Enori had kept her praise largely muted in volume, she'd been constantly impressed with her.

She absolutely was the daughter of Ankou.

Enori focused on the two sleeping forms. She pulled the tiny cork free from the glass vial and poured a bit on the pads of both index fingers. She recorked the vial and, careful not to get any of the liquid on any other skin of the two and with lightning quick reflexes, she smeared the liquid beneath their nostrils, knowing the second it was inhaled, they'd immediately fall into a calm, almost hypnotic state. Too much and their entire system would shut down.

Two sets of dark brown eyes opened, both mother and son awakened but calm. It would be easy to control them for now. They only had a small window before the effects wore off, but by then, they'd be out of danger.

A glance over to the man showed Roishin doing exactly as she'd been taught in their demonstration work together the night before. She used the curled knuckle of her forefinger to perfect effect and punched into the hollow of his throat. He instantly opened his mouth as he gasped for air at the incredible pain that just exploded in his throat, and the contents of the pouch were poured in.

They didn't wait around to see what happened next with him. No need. In minutes, he'd be dead. They just had to hope there was nobody else around or watching. Together, they got the boy and his mother to their feet. Neither made a sound, simply followed dutifully. Enori's head was beginning to ache badly. She knew they needed to get out of there and stop the mental projection before it became incapacitating. No doubt it was hitting Roishin at least as hard.

"You get her, I'm going to carry the boy," Roishin whispered into her ear.

Nodding, Enori grabbed the woman's hand and tugged her along behind as Roishin slung the five-year-old potato-sack style over her shoulder. They made nary a sound as they traversed their way back to the street where their SUV was parked. She could see it now and was relieved.

Especially relieved, in fact, as Bruna Barbosa's fingers were beginning to squeeze Enori's. She was starting to come out of it. They had mere moments before she or her son Carlos were fully out from under the effects and would become extremely frightened or emotional. Hearing her name hissed in the darkness, Enori turned around just in time to see keys tossed to her.

Catching them with her free hand, she quickly unlocked the back passenger door and pulled it open. She shoved Bruna inside before climbing in and accepting a woozy Carlos nearly on her lap. She had left the keys in the door for Roishin to grab once she secured their door.

Enori was working to secure the two in seat belts as Roishin threw herself behind the wheel and got the SUV started. Headlights kept off, they shot off into the darkness until they were far enough away they could slow down and rejoin humanity on the road without suspicion. As if on cue, Bruna began to look around frantically.

"My son!" she screeched. "Where's my son?"

Responding to the young woman's Portuguese tongue, Enori wrapped a motherly arm around her shoulders. "He's right here, meu bem," she said softly. "He'll never be taken away from you again," she added, knowing that had been how they'd gotten hold of her in the first place.

Bruna looked into her eyes, her own widening. "Who are you?" she asked, a bit calmer.

Enori had chosen the intention she had for this very moment. She carried a motherly figure with a large bosom, which Carlos currently rested his head against, and soulful, kind eyes. "Pascoal is deeply worried," she said. She knew the mention of the woman's father would help put her at ease.

Immediately, Bruna burst into tears. It seemed to Enori that she felt she was finally truly free or simply overwhelmed with everything happening. "Papai?" she whispered, hope in her tone.

Enori nodded, urging the young woman to rest her head against her shoulder. She glanced into the rearview mirror to see that Roishin was looking into it also, though not at Enori, but past her. She looked very worried.

"What is it?" Enori asked in Gaelic, knowing they wouldn't be understood by the other two.

"We're being followed," Roishin responded in the same language.

"Are you sure?" Enori asked, not looking, as she didn't want to alert Bruna that anything was wrong.

No need, as a moment later, a shot rang out and the back of the SUV was hit. Bruna cried out in fear, little Carlos burying his face into the large bosom of Enori's intention. She had to keep her focus or he'd fall flat on his face in her lap. She wrapped her arms around the bodies on either side of her and forced Bruna to duck as she held the boy in place.

The tires screeched in protest as Roishin began to drive erratically, trying to lose their pursuers. Another shot took out the passenger side mirror. Enori gasped softly in surprise, doing all she could to stay calm. Bruna was terrified enough for all of them. Roishin gunned the engine, whipping the wheel to the right.

The maneuver didn't lose the car speeding behind them. Another shot rang out, and this time the back window of the SUV's cargo area cracked into a million little spiderwebs from the small bullet hole. Glancing up, as she, too, had ducked her head, Enori saw a large cinder block building looming up ahead.

"Roishin!"

Roishin said nothing, simply gave the SUV even more gas. From the look on her face in the rearview mirror, Enori could see incredible focus and control. It may have been her intention's face, but it was *her* eyes.

They were close enough for the double spotlight of the headlights to hit the wall when Roishin waved her right hand across like she'd just thrown a Frisbee. The wall of the building shimmered, and then…

…they plowed through the sand, which washed up over the hood of the SUV like a tidal wave. A squabble of seagulls exploded into the air, screaming down at the encroaching vehicle in the morning sun that shone down on them all. The SUV came to a stop and, other than the birds and waves of the ocean beyond the beach, it was dead silent.

"Everyone all right?" asked Pedro, Roishin's intention. His voice sounded as stunned as no doubt the woman behind it was.

Lifting her head fully, Enori met Roishin's gaze. The priestess was absolutely stunned, and she was sure that was written all over her face. She had become quite good at keeping her emotions and thoughts close to the vest over her very long lifetime, but what had just happened, she had never seen before.

For a moment, Roishin looked downright scared, which made Enori wonder what had escaped into her expression. Both were distracted when Bruna began to exclaim excitedly.

"I grew up here!" She looked to Enori, wonder in her eyes. "I grew up here! Papai lives here!" She threw herself at Enori, who hugged her back. "Thank you," she cried into the hug. "You are an angel."

Enori gave her a squeeze before she released her. "Let's get you home, okay?" Bruna was still crying, valiantly trying to wipe her eyes, but nodded. "You know how to get to your papai's house from here?"

"Oh, si!" Bruna exclaimed.

Enori met Roishin's gaze quickly in the rearview mirror before Roishin opened the driver's side door and then pulled open the back door. Carlos looked at the man who stood there.

Roishin grinned at him and pulled out a coin from her pocket. She showed it to the boy, making sure he was watching. Then, with a gasp from the little guy, the coin vanished. A moment later she pulled it out from his ear. He giggled with delight, especially when she gave him the coin.

Stepping aside, she allowed him to climb out of the back seat, followed by Enori. Bruna let herself out on her side. The foursome gathered on the driver's side, Bruna immediately hugging both "mother and son" before taking her own son into her arms.

Roishin held out the keys to the SUV. "You drive?" she asked. At the young woman's nod, Roishin smiled, dangling the keys down to her. "You take Carlos to your papai's house," she said. "Mamãe and I will follow after you're safe," she said, indicating the heavyset woman who stood next to her.

Bruna took the keys, looking at them as if they held the answers to all the hardest questions in the world. Finally, looking to Enori, who smiled at her and nodded in encouragement, she turned to the open driver's door and loaded Carlos inside, indicating he needed to get settled and buckled in. No car seat for him, but Enori knew it wasn't far.

She felt Roishin take her hand and lightly tug on it. The second Bruna's back was turned as she climbed into the driver's seat, Roishin stepped backward into the door she'd opened, Enori following…

…and stepped into the Crystal Palace. They both just stood there for a long moment. Enori glanced at Roishin, easily able to feel that she was completely shell-shocked even without the random luminescent strands of energy washing across her face.

She took her in a hug, cradling the back of her head as it rested on her shoulder. She held her tighter when she felt Roishin's body shaking with her silent tears. No doubt she was completely overwhelmed by the entire experience, and Enori held her as she let it out.

"You did so good," she murmured into her ear. "I am so proud of you." She smiled when she felt Roishin wrap her arms around her and pull her tightly against her.

After several moments, the tears calmed but the hug remained. It had been a harrowing situation and it could have gone so terribly wrong. She understood Roishin's need for that human connection, perhaps even a bit of grounding. If she were honest with herself, she needed it, too. But then, she'd noticed far too often lately that she found herself needing that grounding.

Finally, her hand cupping the back of Roishin's neck, Enori pulled out of the hug just enough to look up into Roishin's face. She smiled, her hand sliding around from the back of her neck to the side of her jaw. Roishin's hands rested upon Enori's wait.

"Are you all right?" she asked softly.

Roishin nodded. "Sorry." She gave her a sheepish look, just barely seen in a passing red wave. Her hands fell from Enori's body. "Ready?"

❧ ❧ ❧ ❧

Enori gasped, head popping up as she looked around. She was in her bedroom in her bed. It was late, she could feel it. That last push of night before bleeding into the early hours of morning. She heard it again. She looked to her left, the direction of Roishin's bedroom. Whimpering and quiet murmurs, though it was impossible to understand what was being said.

When they'd arrived home, Roisin had been quiet and very withdrawn. Enori had let her be, not pushing her to talk. Even still, she'd kept an eye on her. They'd eaten dinner, though Roishin had barely touched hers before heading upstairs to shower and go to bed early. It had been strange, curled up on her loveseat by the fire reading, all alone.

How many years, *centuries* had she lived alone? Spent quiet nights curled up reading, alone? But now, it had become part of her new normal for Roishin to be there, too. On her couch, doing whatever her little heart desired, from reading to writing to playing chess or card games by herself. Eventually, it had felt entirely too lonely, so she'd headed up to bed to read.

Pushing the covers back, Enori climbed out of bed and walked over to a small cabinet she kept in the corner of her bedroom. She knelt down in front of it and pulled open the door. Inside were all her pouches of special mixes for this, that, and the other. She found the one she was looking for and closed the cabinet door as she pushed to her feet.

She headed out of her bedroom and to the closed door of Roishin's. Listening for a moment, she heard more whimpering and bedclothes ruffling. She pushed open the door and, sure enough, Roishin seemed to be in the middle of a nasty dream. Her face was contorted into pain as another whimper escaped her lips, her chest heaving with her nocturnal anxiety.

Walking over to the bed, Enori sat on the side. "Roishin," she said softly, not wanting to scare her awake but allow her voice to slowly seep into her subconscious. "Wake up."

Roishin whimpered one more time, though it was a bit quieter, less forceful. Her brows knit as if something was getting her attention. Enori reached out and lightly ran her fingers through dark strands.

"Wake up." Her fingers smoothed their way out of her hair and to her face. She caressed the soft skin with her fingertips, following the lines of a strong cheekbone down to the proud jaw.

As Roishin's body began to still and calm, her breathing becoming more even yet not the deep breaths of sleep, her eyes slowly opened. They blinked a few times before coming into focus as she looked up at Enori, who smiled at her.

"Hi," Roishin murmured.

Enori's smile widened. "Hello, yourself." She scooted farther onto the bed until she was on her side, somewhat leaning over Roishin. "Are you all right?" She continued to caress the soft skin, backs of her fingers brushing over Roishin's cheek.

Eyes closing as Roishin leaned into the touches, she nodded. "Bad dream."

"What was it about?" Enori whispered, moving a bit closer until she was able to cradle Roishin's head against her breasts. She smiled as Roishin cuddled into her, partially turning to her side so she could wrap an arm across Enori's waist.

"I didn't save them," she murmured into the embrace. "They were shot."

"But," Enori whispered, resting her cheek against Roishin's head. "They were not." She left a kiss there. "Because of you, a young mother and her son, kidnapped more than a year ago by a wealthy father's rivals, are returned home."

"But, what if—"

"Shh." She pulled back enough to look down into Roishin's face. "No 'what if,' Roishin." She brushed long bangs out of her eyes. "No need." She reached behind herself and grabbed the little leather pouch she'd pulled from her cabinet. "I want you to take some of this."

She pushed the little drawstring open wide enough to dip her fingertip and thumb in to grab a very small amount. Drawing them out, she held the granules between them.

"Open." Roishin did as asked and Enori dropped the powder onto her tongue. "This will help you rest tonight," Enori explained. "No more thinking, no more dreaming, no more wondering 'what if.'" She smiled. Leaning down, she left a kiss on Roishin's forehead. "Lay on your back."

Roishin once again did as she was asked to do and Enori moved off the bed. She tucked her in, making sure she was comfortable. She cupped Roisin's face even as green eyes were already growing heavy.

"We'll talk tomorrow," she whispered.

Chapter Four

The entire car?" He stared at her, clearly stunned.

Enori nodded. "Yes."

She crossed one leg over the other where she sat on the beautiful window seat in Ankou's quarters. The stained glass window behind her was massive, looking more like it belonged in a cathedral somewhere rather than in the living space of the God of the Underworld. The entire space looked like a private library.

With dark wood trim, coffered ceilings, and shelves filled with leather-bound tomes in every language filling every wall, it was an incredibly calming space. The furnishings that were scattered, and the padded seat in the window, were upholstered in a deep maroon.

It was an exquisite room, and Enori loved spending time there. For now, Ankou, in his ever-present simple monochromatic outfit in shades of brown, stood in front of the massive fireplace, staring into the flames.

Much like his daughter, he used small gestures of hand or fingers to change the size of the fire randomly. It reminded Enori of someone who might absently bounce a small ball or worry something in their hand. It was a gesture of deep thought or concentration, and Roishin had begun to do it more and more.

Enori waited patiently for his response or

directive. She'd known he'd be quite surprised by what his little girl had been up to. When he'd initially told her of his plans to create such a being with Cateline and Fallon, Enori had admittedly been dubious at best. Primarily, Fallon and Cateline did not live in Duras, nor had the surrogate. The energy in both realms was so vastly different, she wasn't entirely sure it would take, honestly.

"When Roishin was taken from here," he said at length, garnering Enori's attention from her musings. He spared her a glance over his shoulder, a small smile on his lips. "The first one," he clarified, "I'd been devastated." He looked back into the flames.

"I know you were," she said softly, remembering all too well. She'd been part of a group of leading voices who had talked him down from sending his personal troops of the Order to attack Ireland and bring her back.

"She was meant to rule by my side," he said softly, a fact Enori knew, but it was clear he was working out a point, so she just let him talk. He let out a sad sigh. "My daughter. Well," he amended. "My *first* daughter." Finally, he turned to look at her. "But, strangely, I think it worked out as it should. As we've seen with Ava, my plan never would have worked."

"Born here," Enori said, "Roishin would never have been able to live in the other world for a long amount of time, just like Ava wasn't."

He nodded with a very heavy sigh. "Roishin was so sick all the time," he said softly, almost more to himself. "She suffered greatly." After a long moment, he cleared his throat, seeming to force himself back to the here and now. "It was worth trying," he said, snapping himself out of his morose musings. "With Ava. How is she, by the way?"

"She's been returned here and is doing well." Enori's smile was easy. "Roishin got to her just in time."

He nodded, looking pleased. "I want you to pair her and Roishin up," he said. "With Ava's immersion hypnosis and her half dozen years living in the other world, I believe she can be a resident expert on the era."

Enori nodded. "I agree, and it will be done."

He smiled at her, the smile of a loving father. "I know it will," he said softly. His entire demeanor changed as he walked over to an elegant chaise lounge. His gaze never left her as he got comfortable. "How are things?" he asked casually. "Cohabitation, and the like?"

Enori smirked, amused by his word choice. "Well, I must admit I thought you were trying to punish me when you suggested she stay with me during her training." She grinned as a rare and loud bark of laughter left his lips.

"And, did I?" he asked, the smile still on his lips once the laughter died down.

Enori looked away from him, instead watching her fingers as they lightly pulled her flowing white gown free of a slight fold at her knee. "I have very much enjoyed having her in my home," she finally said. She suddenly felt very defensive of her feelings and had no real idea why. It wasn't something she wished to talk about, but if he insisted, obviously talk about it she would.

"Her training is complete," he continued, eyeing her. "The main phase of it, anyway. Obviously, there's more to come. But," he said, both feet planted on the floor and forearms resting upon his thighs. "She could move out at any given time. Decide where she would like to go here in Duras."

Enori met his gaze but said nothing.

He stared her down for a long moment before slapping his thighs with large, meaty hands and pushing to his feet. "I am very proud of you, my darling," he said. "I want to reward you."

She looked at him, confused. "Reward me?" She shook her head. "There is no reason, Ankou. I love my work. You know this."

He nodded. "I do." He walked over to her and held his hand out. She took it and, amused, was led around the spacious library in a waltz. "I remember I once asked you," he said into their impromptu dance, something he'd often done with her throughout the many, many years she'd effectively been his right hand. "Why do you work so hard?" He smiled. "Do you remember your response?"

She smiled, nodding. "I said, 'Because if I do not, I am afraid you will strike me with lightning where I stand.'"

He burst into laughter again. She was surprised; twice in one meeting! Something clearly had him very happy. "I had forgotten about that initial response." He lifted the hand he held delicately on his own to allow Enori a spin before they continued their dance without music. "The response I was referring to was, 'Because it is who I am.'"

Enori nodded, feeling that to her very soul. "And it still is."

"I agree." He spun her again, smiling at the little smile that touched her lips at his antics. "But part of that has been because you had no family. The Order has been your family and what you had."

Though at times it made her sad if she really

stopped and let herself think of that, but it was the truth. "Yes."

"Now," he added. "Your family has expanded, hmm?" He quirked a bushy eyebrow in question.

Again, she said nothing but was beginning to feel a bit nervous. Truth was, she wasn't entirely sure why. But, she continued to give him her full attention.

"I want you to organize a wonderful visit for this expanded family, Enori." One more spin and a small dip, and Enori was back on her feet. He smiled at her and left a light kiss on her fingers before releasing her hand. "Thank you for the dance."

She allowed herself to be taken in a quick embrace by him, by the being who had been the only father figure she'd ever had. The only true "family" she'd ever had. Well, except… Not allowing her mind to go there, she focused on the present.

"Are you giving Roishin the time off to spend with them, then?" she asked.

He nodded. "I am." He looked to the fireplace and, with a small gesture, the flame vanished, letting her know their meeting was concluded.

"It will be done, Ankou." She gave him a smile and small bow before heading to the door, though stopped at the sound of her name. She turned to look at him. "Yes?"

"I want you to join them," he said softly, then stepped through a door and was gone.

❧ ❧ ❧ ❧

Arriving back home, Enori wasn't entirely surprised to find Roishin still asleep. Her powder mixture had ensured a truly good, deep sleep. A tremendous amount had been put on her shoulders and very, very quickly. No matter how mature Roishin may be, she was still a nineteen-year-old young woman who was still learning.

That was a fact that Enori had to remind herself of. Though the two women didn't look all that far apart in age anymore—by physical appearance, just four or five years, perhaps—but in chronological age, Enori had centuries of experience and understanding on her side. As she quietly entered Roishin's bedroom, she thought about herself at the younger woman's actual age.

She'd been with the Order but five years at that point. She had her earthbound skills, given to her by the ancestral Ankou blood that ran through her veins. But, honestly, they were little more than the simple parlor tricks of seeing a bit into one's future, or feeling the energy or motives of a singular person.

They were raw and inconsistent. They'd been just helpful enough to keep an orphan of the streets alive. It had been Ankou's personal tutelage and patience that had honed her into the tool she'd become, Ankou's emissary on Earth. Now, as she looked down at the sleeping form beneath the covers, she smiled.

Roishin lay on her side, her back to the door. She honestly wasn't sure what made her do it, but Enori shrugged out of her cloak and climbed onto the bed beneath the blankets. She hesitated for just a moment before scooting a bit closer to the woman who was breathing the deep, even breaths of truly peaceful sleep.

She felt Roishin's warmth against her front as she spooned up behind her, her thighs tucked up under Roishin's bent legs. She wrapped an arm over Roishin's waist, smiling when, in her sleep, the other woman placed her arm over Enori's. She closed her eyes and inhaled the scent of dark hair and skin just a shade darker than her own.

As she got settled, she allowed herself to admit, if just for a moment, that she needed this. She wasn't ready to delve into the reasons why, but she would admit that much. Her life, her very reason for being, had become Ankou's agenda and his mission. She didn't resent that. In fact, she felt absolutely privileged and honored that he trusted her and believed in her when she had desperately needed someone to.

She'd continue that commitment, loyalty, and dedication for the rest of her being. But, that commitment, loyalty, and dedication had come with a steep price—the cost of her own individuality. It was about the bigger picture, the larger meaning, and needs of everything, not one single woman.

Much of it was a true belief in the mission and what they were doing, but—and it was hard to admit this to herself—some of it was self-imposed denial of herself for fear that she'd get too distracted and she'd lose Ankou's belief in her. The first fourteen years of her life was nonstop loss, and she couldn't take it if she lost Ankou, too—the loss of Brielle had almost killed her. His trust in her, his need for her services of the Order...it was all she had.

She held Roisin tighter to her. So, why? Why had Ankou put this young woman in her house? In her life? Under her care? Almost a hundred years ago now, had he not seen the devastation she'd gone through? Another powerful young woman had been placed in her path, Ankou's orders to teach her, to mentor her.

A young, beautiful Scottish high priestess of the Order of the Druids.

She felt unseen eyes on her, but she proceeded. Enori entered the small village, tucked into the trees. It wasn't an ordinary Scottish village as she'd seen before. This was more like a cluster of homes built literally into the trees, nearly vanishing into nature. On the ground, she felt incredibly vulnerable and was very open to attack.

She wondered what on earth Ankou had been thinking but continued with his orders. The Romans had destroyed much of the Order hundreds of years before, but this last, stubborn group refused to bend a knee to the predominant religion of the country and the Western world—Christianity.

Just up ahead, she saw a young man who was carrying a large bundle of sticks. He glanced at her, steps slowing as she advanced on him.

Reaching up, Enori brushed her hood back. "Good morrow," she greeted. "I am here to speak to—"

"I was shown you'd come."

Enori turned away from the young man to see a woman climbing down a rope ladder from one of the tree houses. Her own cloak was dark brown, the dress she wore beneath not very visible within the billowing material of the cloak.

Reaching the forest floor, she walked over to Enori, her own hood pushed back to reveal golden blond hair and sapphire blue eyes. Enori could only stare at her.

"I was not told your name," the woman continued, looking into Enori's eyes. "But," she added with an affirming nod of her own words. "I was shown."

"I am Enori."

"And I am Mariota," the woman said softly. "I am who you seek."

Angry at herself, Enori brought up a hand and swiped at the tear that managed to escape. She hadn't allowed herself to think about that in a very long time. And, as she lay there now holding Roishin, she felt shame pass through her.

She could no longer remember what Mariota's hair smelled like. Could no longer remember what her skin felt like, tasted like. Could no longer remember the softness of her mouth, nor the sounds she made in passion. She did, however, remember her strength. She remembered her iron will and the love she had for her infant daughter, Camma.

She remembered the last gift she'd been able to give Mariota once the attack began.

"No!" Enori raged. "I will not leave you."

"You must!" Mariota stepped up to her, the fires already burning all around them. She placed her hand on Enori's face. "You must," she murmured against her lips, "save her." Looking into Enori's eyes, the pleading was there as much as the fear. "You know where to take her."

Tears in her eyes, Enori nodded, cradling the wrapped bundle to her chest beneath her cloak. She knew there was no other way, and as she looked deeply into Mariota's eyes, she saw all the love she felt reflected back at her.

Mariota took her in one final, lingering kiss. "I love you," she whispered against Enori's lips, then ran away from her and into the fight to help protect her people, the last of the Druids in that part of Scotland.

Enori watched her go, then with her own steel courage, ran with the baby to her horse. She mounted the steed, then with a kick of her heel and loud cry, galloped into the darkness. A baby of Druid blood could not enter her world, nor was there a door anywhere close to just get them to another part of the country, so she rode hard through the night until she reached the small stone cottage, the place Mariota had told her many times to take the baby should anything happen.

Without a word, she'd handed the swaddled Camma to the older woman who had answered her frantic knock. With welling teras in blue eyes much like Mariota's, the older woman had taken the child, then slowly closed the door.

Two days later, Enori had returned to find the charred bodies of the leaders of the Order, still tied to the crosses used to burn them alive. Another wooden cross had been planted in the middle of the carnage. A message left behind, a warning for anyone who dare not follow the One God.

The few survivors of Mariota's sect had gone deep underground, so deep they disappeared into the pages of history.

Enori readjusted her head on the pillow as she considered all that had happened so long ago. She wondered what Mariota would think of her namesake. She couldn't help but smile, knowing in her heart that she'd be deeply pleased, and even more deeply pleased that she'd been born of the love of two women—one of whom was her very own blood.

Chapter Five

L et's see what we've got here!" Isla sang, eyes open wide to match those of the baby looking up at her. She made a silly face as she gently rested the measuring rod across the tiny body, her mother holding her tiny hands in order to keep her little arms outstretched. "You are getting so big!" She gasped big and loud, garnering another giggle.

Elsie watched, charmed. She loved it when Isla spent time with Mariota. She was so gentle with her, and she had the most wonderful silly side that came out when around the baby. Mariota was always left in giggles that had both women laughing soon after. This time, however, was so the dressmaker could get current measurements to make the baby some new outfits.

"She is growing like a little weed," Isla said, moving to her ever-present parchment to record her findings.

"She is," Elsie agreed, leaning down and leaving noisy kisses on her baby's neck, which continued the giggles. "Do you need me to pick her up like last time.?"

"Aye," Isla said with a grin, holding up her ell measure. Once the babe was held up so her little feet were resting on the bed, the dressmaker was able to measure her length. When she was finished, she bent down so she was on eye level with the little one. "Do you know what?" she asked a very serious-looking Mariota. "I think I love you," she whispered loudly and dramatically. The baby giggled at the silly voice she used. Grinning, Isla stood erect again, meeting Elsie's amused gaze. "I'm pretty sure the entire castle has fallen for that little one, milady."

Elsie smiled. "I tell you, Isla, I'm grateful for her every day." She brought the baby up to rest against her shoulder, one hand cupping the back of her head. "She amazes me every single day."

"She's so beautiful, milady," Isla said, the gentlest of smiles on her face, if a bit wistful.

Elsie looked at the other woman, whom she'd genuinely come to like and trust. "Isla?"

"Aye?" The dressmaker glanced over at her as she made a few notes upon her parchment before rolling it up.

"When we're alone, I'd like you to call me by my name, Elsie." At Isla's wide-eyed look of surprise, the princess smiled. "Truly."

The most beautiful smile spread across Isla's face. She nodded. "Aye. Elsie."

Elsie watched as Isla gathered up her things, but she had the distinct feeling that the other woman wasn't keen to leave just yet. She kept sending small, surreptitious looks over to the chair where Elsie had carried Mariota and sat down. It was time to feed her. As Elsie glanced toward the other woman, she realized that she, too, wasn't ready quite yet to be alone.

"Isla?" she said.

"Aye, milady?" Isla said, nearly springing to attention. "I mean, Elsie." She gave the princess a sheepish grin.

"Could you hold her for a moment?" Elsie asked, holding up the baby.

"Of course!" Setting her parchment and measuring rod down, the dressmaker hurried over to

Elsie and took the infant in her arms.

Amused, Elsie worked on the very clever flap design Isla had created for her to nurse. She unbuttoned the little buttons that allowed a flap of fabric to be released so the baby had access. Isla glanced over at her, saw her exposed breast, and—to Elsie's surprise—blushed and quickly looked away, focusing her attention on Mariota.

"Um," she muttered. "Are you ready for her, milady?"

Elsie quirked an eyebrow at the other woman as she lowered the infant back into Elsie's arms. She couldn't help but smile at the most adorable sheepish look she got.

"Sorry," Isla murmured with a little smile, holding the baby's body safely as Elsie got her placed to nurse. "Elsie"

The princess smiled at her. "I'll forgive you." She looked down at her breasts, ensuring Mariota was comfortably suckling, which she was. She spared a glance back up to the other woman, who still leaned over her a bit. "This time."

Yet again, Isla blushed. She tugged her bottom lip beneath her teeth for a moment as she stood erect. Rubbing the back of her neck, she released the full bottom lip before sending a shy glance Elsie's way. "Aye," she said quietly.

In that moment, Elsie thought she was just about the most adorable woman she'd ever seen. She didn't know whether to laugh or hug her. She did neither, instead asking, "Would you like to join me for dinner?" She smiled, a little sheepish herself. "That is, if you're not busy, Isla."

Quickly, the dressmaker shook her head. "No,

mi…Elsie."

Elsie quirked an eyebrow. "No, you're not busy, or no to dinner?"

"Well," the dressmaker said, looking as though she wished she could fall through the floor. "I'm not entirely sure how to answer that."

Confused, Elsie cocked her head slightly. "Why?"

Isla nodded toward her rolled parchment and measuring rod that still lay on the bed. "I can't very well tell my princess that I'm not busy when I just took measurements of her baby to make a new set of outfits for her." She grinned. "Yet, I'd very much like to join her for dinner."

Elsie burst into laughter, startling her daughter. "Oh, sorry, my love," she murmured, rubbing the baby's arm and shoulder until she began to suckle again. Assured the baby was fine, she looked back up at the other woman, still amused at the predicament she outlined. "I grant you an evening free of making baby clothes," she said, unable to hide the mirth from her tone.

Isla looked away, but not before Elsie saw her grin. Clearing her throat, she looked back to the princess. "Aye, Elsie," she said. "I will join you for dinner. Thank you for the invitation. For now, is there anything you need?" She indicated the baby in her arms. "Anything I can do before I take my leave until then?"

Touched, Elsie shook her head. "No," she said softly, reaching out a hand. Isla took it and, for just a brief moment, it felt good to touch the warmth of another human who counted their age in years instead of months. "Thank you. See you later, then."

Isla gave her hand a squeeze then released it. Walking over to the bed, she gathered her belongings and, with a glance and smile to mother and daughter, Isla left the bedchamber, closing the door softly behind her only to return a moment later,

"Forgive me," Isla said, holding up a missive. "He saw me leaving so asked me to bring you this." She walked back over to Elsie, handing her the note, folded and waxed with Prince Garratt's personal seal. With a little bow, she hurried from the room once more.

An internal groan at the ready, she set it aside. She'd have to wait until Mariota was finished so she could walk to her personal desk and grab the small dagger she used to open such correspondence. She looked at it, noting it was smudged with gods only knew what. He was out in the field, so it could be anything from dirt to manure to blood.

Looking back to her daughter, she smiled. Nothing could put a smile upon her lips like Mariota did. No matter Elsie's mood, worries, thoughts, and fears, always her daughter could conjure instant joy. She had come to understand that, in her marriage, she was truly alone. The strange thing was, she liked it that way. She was becoming stronger by the day, becoming the scrappy little girl from Scotland that begged, stole, and worked her fingers to the bone to keep herself and her mother alive while her father was constantly away.

The doors Roishin had set up for easy passage between the two castles were wonderful. Several times a week, depending on the happenings at the king's residence, Cateline or Fallon—sometimes together— came to see her and the baby once everything had calmed for the night and they wouldn't be missed.

But day to day, it was just her running the entirety of Caisleán Thiar, and she loved it. She relished it, and she was doing a good job. The baptism of Mariota into the Order of the Ankou had given her a renewed wind to prove Garratt wrong. It wasn't that he wanted her to fail, she didn't believe, but he did want to be proven right that she needed him.

She did not.

It confused her so much how he could have two incredible women who raised him, one who very much lived as and was known as a woman. Yet somehow he wished for a wife to be weak and needing of his guidance. It baffled her. But, at the end of the day, it mattered not. He was rarely there, and when he was, it was easy to keep her distance as he wanted little to do with Mariota.

Everyone was supposed to believe she was his daughter, but secretly, Elsie absolutely loved that he wanted nothing to do with her. As she stroked the soft blond hair that was sprinkled across her daughter's head, noting the little hand that rested against Elsie's swollen breast, she knew this child would forever be loved by her parents.

No matter what happened between her and Roishin personally, this child was made from absolute love, as it should be. Even if she had been Garratt's daughter, no matter how much Elsie would love her as she would love any children they might have, she would have been made of obligation to create heirs in general and specifically to inflate Garratt's ego with a son.

That thought disgusted her. No longer wanting to think about him, she allowed her baby to finish her dinner then got her burped, changed, and put down for the night. She had been offered a servant to do all those things for her, including a wet nurse, but she'd refused. She was Mariota's mother and would act as such until her dying day.

With a resigned sigh, she carried the letter to her desk and eased the blade of the dagger under the wax seal and unfolded the protective outer parchment to find the folded note inside. Opening it, she read his hurried hand.

Dearest Wife—

I shall be back in Sursha within the fortnight, which should give you plenty of notice that I would like to try for our second child—a son. Your body should be well enough by then for such matters.

Your loving husband—
Garratt

She read it two more times. She felt even more disgusted with each read. What on earth? Who takes the time away from a battle of some sort to write his wife a note that basically says, "When I get home, I expect to fuck. Be ready"?

All she could do was sit there and stare at the few lines. She was surprised to hear a knock on her bedchamber door. At her acknowledgment, the servants to serve her dinner entered, Isla helping them.

She quirked an eyebrow when she caught the other woman's gaze. She got a *What?* look before Isla was gone again. Shaking her head, she began to organize the dishes on the table to make places for them both when Isla reappeared by herself, carrying the last couple items.

Meeting Elsie's gaze, Isla set the plates down. "What?"

"I invited you *to* dinner, not to *serve* dinner."

"Aye. Well..." Isla gave her a little grin. "I knew Erin had hurt her arm in a nasty argument with the butter churning paddle, so, figured I'd help."

Elsie slapped her hand across her mouth to keep in the loud laughter that nearly burst forth. She knew it would wake Mariota. Isla grinned at her, adorable dimples winking as she placed the last two plates on the table.

They continued readying the table in silence, a little giggle escaping from time to time as Elsie got yet another mental image of the diminutive kitchen worker trying to handle The Beast, as she'd heard Millie refer to that very paddle. Finally, they were seated and began to eat.

"I appreciate you helping, Isla," Elsie finally said. "Truly. That was kind of you."

Isla nodded, a bite of dinner in her mouth. After she took a drink from her wine to swallow the food down, she added, "I also wanted to ease my guilt for not working on the new clothing right now."

Again, Elsie found herself amused. "You are full of piss and vinegar today, my friend." She chuckled quietly, glancing at the grinning woman across from her. "So. That letter today."

Isla nodded, her mouth full, letting her know she was listening and knew of which she spoke. Elsie wasn't even sure why she'd brought it up, in all honesty. It wasn't really Isla's business, per se, but she needed to talk about it, and she certainly didn't feel it was something she could talk to Cateline about.

"It was from Garratt," she said. For some reason, she felt ashamed to say that. She wasn't entirely sure why. Perhaps it was shame of that sort of demand on her that she had no real right to deny once he returned.

Isla was looking at her, the little twinkle so often in her eyes that Elsie loved gone. She seemed to sense the seriousness of Elsie's mood. She simply continued to eat, glancing at her from time to time to assure her attention.

"He's coming home in a fortnight, he said. And," she began, but stopped. She looked down at her hand, which rested around her cup.

Suddenly, another hand came into her line of vision. It gently took the cup out of Elsie's loose hold and covered the fingers with its own. Elsie looked up to see an incredibly understanding gaze. Elsie held that gaze for a long moment, so grateful for what she saw there, but also realizing how beautiful the warm, brown color was.

She quickly pushed that thought out of her mind as she took a deep breath, her fingers still held by Isla's. "Well, he wants his son."

"As you know," Isla said at length. "I've not had children of my own, but I helped a midwife in the village a few times with local women giving birth. It is the most traumatizing thing a body can go through, so much damage done to a woman's body. It doesn't matter if it's made for birthing or not."

Elsie nodded, certainly understanding that one. It had been three months and she still found herself sore in her most private place at times.

"And then," Isla said. "You have these selfish men who have no idea what it even means to go through something like that, because it's not 'appropriate' for them to be in there. Why ever not?" she asked, anger in those very eyes Elsie had just been admiring. "They put the blasted thing in you, why can't they watch what happens when it comes out?"

Again, Elsie found herself trying unsuccessfully to hide a smile. She nodded. "Aye."

"And then," Isla continued. "To come back after only a few months and expect you to be ready to go again?" Her eyes were wide with her rhetorical question.

"I remember back in Scotland," Elsie began, realizing that they were still holding hands and also realizing that she rather liked it. It felt good to connect with someone on such a simple yet intimate physical level. "There was a woman who lived near us. Iona was her name. She lived with a man—I never even knew his name, honestly. But that poor thing would pop one out and it seemed within two days, she was expecting another." She shook her head, looking into a past that seemed like a lifetime ago. "Most miserable looking lass I ever did see."

"No doubt. A girl like that," Isla added. "Used up before her time."

Elsie met Isla's gaze again. "I don't want that for me, Isla. I could see Garratt insisting we try until he got his damn son, no matter how many girls are ignored by him in the meantime."

Isla smirked. "Well, he's not often home long. You can claim you have your bleed."

Elsie gave her a devilish grin. "Aye, and that may work once or twice."

"Once or twice is one or two times less you have to deal with him."

Elsie took her hand from Isla's and took her cup. "To one or two times less."

The devil having jumped from Elsie's grin to Isla's, she raised her own cup. "To one or two times less."

With a clink of their glasses, the two giggled as

they sipped.

⁂

She wasn't sure how late it was, but Elsie's eyes slowly opened when she heard the softest, sweetest humming. Not much more than a silhouette in the flames of the fireplace, she saw Roishin holding Mariota. She was slowly dancing with her, humming a mindless tune.

The baby was tucked safely in her arms, and Elsie could see she was staring up at Roishin, the flames reflecting in the very eyes she'd inherited from her second mother. She noticed that Roishin had changed her diaper, and it was all bundled on the floor next to the cradle, ready to be removed from the bedchamber.

As she watched her, she was so charmed, so deeply touched. And, as she watched her, she knew that was what she wanted. She wanted what Cateline and Fallon had. She wanted to love and be loved. She wanted to touch and be touched. She wanted her daughter to have *two* parents, even if only in the bedchamber or their quiet moments as a family.

In her deepest heart, she wanted, after the humming stopped and the little dance stilled, for the baby to be put back to bed to sleep. She wanted the nighttime dancer to crawl back in bed with Elsie, where she'd started from in the first place. Perhaps she'd hurried from the bed to take care of the baby's cries before they woke Elsie. Or, Elsie would have hurried before they woke the woman asleep beside her.

Yes, she thought. That's what she wanted. And she knew Roishin would never be able to give her that dream.

Chapter Six

Elsie listened carefully, even though she was quite uncomfortable sitting on the throne in the throne room, the heavy crown atop her head. She looked from the older man who stood at the bottom of the dais stairs, his face red with his insistence his dead son's land now become his.

Meanwhile, the widow of said dead son held a page, claiming it was signed by her husband and stated his wishes for her to keep their holdings to raise their five children upon. As she listened, Elsie couldn't help but think that this could have been Isla's story. It could very easily have been her pleading her case to keep her home after her husband's drowning.

A surreptitious glance to the lead adviser for the prince showed he was already looking at her, subtly shaking his head. She was surprised by his silent advice, his expression clear: give it to the man and get on with it. She turned back to the pair.

She studied the woman, clearly a hard worker. Her hands looked strong, her dress simple, and hair a bit messy in its updo. She looked as though she'd been in a rush to get herself together that morning to appear before the Court.

A look to the man, who also looked hardworking. His face was leather from years spent out in the sun on his farm. But, his clothing was neat, if not a bit worn. Pushing to her feet, a hush broke over the throne room. One of the castle guards began to step forward, and she raised a hand to him to stop his progress.

Taking the stairs carefully, a bit unsteady with the heavy crown, Elsie looked from one to the other before her gaze settled on the woman. She stopped a stair away. "How old are your children?" she asked softly.

"Me oldest is fifteen, milady, me youngest just six months," the woman said, barely above a whisper. She looked so frightened in that moment, and Elsie realized that she was, in fact, trembling.

Stepping down one more step, she stood just in front of the woman, who looked to be perhaps ten years older than herself.

"My daughter is just a little bit younger," she said, unable to keep the smile off her face.

The village woman spared a glance at her, the two sharing a smile that only another mother could understand. For just a split second, they were just two women, both doing their best to raise a tiny human who was totally dependent upon them.

"Does your oldest help you?" Elsie asked. She realized that the huge chamber had gone so completely silent, a mouse twitching its nose would be heard.

"Aye, milady." A small smile of pride graced the woman's tanned face. "He's strong like his father." Emotion hitched the last word.

Before Elsie stood Isla, Elsie's own mother, and so many other women she'd known who had been left in a similar situation, all with different circumstances. "What is your name?"

"Jane," the woman whispered, head falling. Elsie could tell she was barely keeping it together.

"May I see the note, Jane?" The woman handed her the piece of parchment and Elsie looked it over. It was no note at all, but a Bill of Sale from William Brown to Jane Brown, dated five months prior. Looking to the woman again, she asked, "When did your husband die?"

"Just three weeks ago, milady."

Nodding, Elsie held the parchment in one hand and took one of the villager's hands in her other. "Can you read, Jane?"

The woman looked absolutely crestfallen as she shook her head. Elsie could see it written all over her face. She was terrified that the piece of paper said something different than she claimed it did. No doubt, she'd simply repeated what her husband had told her it was. Squeezing Jane's hand, Elsie looked back to her adviser.

"Fetch me a quill," she said to him. While she waited for her request to be fulfilled, she turned back to the grieving mother. "Jane," she explained. "Your husband was thinking of you and your children long before he died." She held up the page. "This isn't a note. He effectively sold the family property to you before his death to ensure that you'd be safe."

The woman broke down, Elsie catching her before she could fall as her legs collapsed beneath her in her profound relief. As she held the crying villager, Elsie glared over at the old man.

"Do *you* read?" she asked, knowing many in Sursha were educated in the basics. It was one thing that set the country and her customs apart from many in the Western world.

He clenched his jaw stubbornly then nodded. "Aye."

"Then you knew this woman had rights," Elsie said, her voice deadly calm as she held Jane to her. "You tried to manipulate your own daughter-in-law out of what was rightfully hers, what *your* own son made clear he wanted for her and his children."

He looked away, at least having the dignity to look somewhat ashamed.

The quill was delivered, and Elsie released Jane. She asked the castle guard who had brought it to her to turn around. Using his back, she scribbled something on the back of the parchment before handing both quill and small bottle of ink back to him with a smile of gratitude.

"This property," she declared loud enough for all to hear, "shall belong to Jane Brown and her five children for a minimum of fifty years." She looked to the older man, both knowing damn well he'd not live another fifty years. "And, for putting this grieving woman through this," she added to him. "From your own farm, about which you stood here regaling us how well it produces, you shall give Jane Brown and her children one pound of food per person for every single day since William Brown has died."

His mouth fell open and his eyes widened. "But—"

"Which," Elsie continued, voice booming over his protestations. "From my calculations of three weeks' worth of days and six people, is one hundred and twenty-six pounds of food. This shall be fruit, vegetables, and grain." Turning back to Jane, who looked utterly shell-shocked, Elsie handed her the Bill of Sale with Elsie's notations written upon the back of her ruling. "Keep this safe," she advised. "I assure you, I'll make sure your family is watched to ensure your safety." She eyed the older farmer with those words.

With one more hug to the grateful villager, who now was crying tears of joy, Elsie headed back up the stairs to her throne. She could not keep the little smile off her lips. Yes, she thought. Now she understood her job.

❧ ❧ ❧ ❧

There was yet another hour of complaints and decisions after Jane and her father-in-law, but Elsie was still riding high on her wave of righting what was about to be a horrible wrong had the farmer and her own adviser had their way. This had put some thoughts into her head, some of which she planned to speak to Cateline about.

That thought made her smile even wider as she headed up the stairs. The queen was here for a visit to spend some time with Elsie and Mariota, as well as work out details for some new dresses with Isla. The amusing thing was, though Queen Cateline had traveled the old-fashioned way—overland in a carriage—Elsie knew her king would be joining them nightly during the duration of Cateline's visit.

Reaching the double doors to her bedchamber, she smiled anew when she heard giggling on the other side. Pushing open the door, she saw Cateline standing there in her chemise, Isla measuring her with her ell measure and telling a story.

"And, I'm looking at this woman like, 'Madam, I truly have no idea what exactly you think I'm doing, but I assure you, you cannot use this measuring rod on your husband.'"

Cateline erupted into more laughter, a downright cackle, as she stood with arms held out from her body. "What did she do?" the queen asked, putting her arms down as requested as Isla began to measure the length from the nape of her neck and working her way down to the floor.

"She took this right out of my hands!" Isla crowed, lightly tapping Cateline on the shoulder with the measuring implement.

Cateline dissolved into more laughter, making Elsie smile as she watched the two. She spied her daughter lying at the center of her bed, a virtual little pillow fort surrounded her so there was no danger of her falling in any sort of way.

Mariota was beginning to try to rock herself this way or that. Other mothers in the castle told Elsie that it would be no time at all before she'd figure it out and get herself turned over. Once the two women spotted her, Cateline's laughter stopped and she walked over to the princess.

Without a word, she took her into a tight hug, which was happily returned. "I am so proud of you," she finally murmured.

Elsie basked in her maternal love and approval. "You heard?" she asked.

Cateline nodded, leaving a kiss to the side of Elsie's head before pulling out of the embrace, though she still held her by the shoulders. "Isla told me when she came in for measurements." She smiled, so much affection packed into that one look. She lightly cupped Elsie's cheek. "Believe me, I know how hard it is to do what's right when faced with a horde of advisers and male power that seems insurmountable."

She hugged her again, though this time seemed more of a hug of camaraderie from a battle-tested princess-turned-queen than from Elsie's decision. Utterly relieved, blue eyes fell closed as she sank into the embrace. She knew what she'd done was right but was so worried that it wasn't right for the region, as for all intents and purposes, Garratt ruled that portion of the island. Well, his *name* did, anyway.

With Garratt as heir apparent, everything Elsie did, every decision she made, was in Garratt's name and reflected upon him. It was a tremendous amount of pressure, as she knew the two hardly saw eye to eye on what was right and what was the status quo.

Cateline pulled out of the second hug and held Elsie's hands. "What you did today was act like a queen, ma cherie." She smiled.

Moved, she nodded, tucking her lips in for a moment to hold back her emotion. "Thank you," she finally managed." Looking past the queen, she saw Isla watching, the softest smile upon her lips.

⚶ ⚶ ⚶

"Here's my thought on that, Mamaí," Elsie said, glancing over at the queen, who rocked a sleeping Mariota. "Aye," she continued. "We have a law where women can own property after the death of a husband or father. But," she added passionately. "That's only if a man doesn't dispute the claim." Shaking her head, she glanced at the other woman who occupied the matching chair in front of the fire. "Doesn't that undo all the good that law, progressive in its day, affords?"

"Agreed. I know Fallon had spoken with her father for years about that, but Carthac was of another time, another generation." She kissed the sleeping baby's head in her arms before looking back to her daughter-in-law, who was treated far more like a daughter.

"Well, she is king now," Elsie argued, surprised at just how deeply she'd been touched by the events of earlier that day. She kept thinking about that poor woman and how vastly different her day would have ended had Garratt been sitting on that throne—or likely any other man, for that matter.

Cateline gave her a smile, a twinkle in her beautiful gray-blue eyes. "I think you should petition the king, Elsie."

"Petition the king to do what?"

Elsie turned her head at the voice, and her smile was instant. She popped up from her chair and hurried over to Fallon, who was closing the door of the secret passageway where the door had been placed to connect the two castles. It was just a little ways down from the one that would take Elsie to the cave where she and Roishin so often met to spend time together with Mariota.

Elsie was taken in strong arms, literally pulled off her feet in the tight hug. After the bone-crushing squeeze, Fallon left a kiss on Elsie's cheek and gave her a loving smile before releasing her. She walked on, Cateline meeting her halfway across the expanse. Baby still in her arms, Fallon wrapped them both up in her embrace.

It was the most extraordinary thing, Elsie thought. Though it was her daughter Cateline held, it wasn't at all hard to see a glimpse back in time when that baby had been Roishin, unknowingly created from the deep love and passion they had for each other. It was still there, the joy of reuniting after only two days apart during Cateline's travels.

An entire dialogue passed between them in a look, sentences of love punctuated by a kiss. The moment was over, and Fallon took Mariota in her arms. Everything about her softened to the point of nearly turning her into mush. Fallon, all woman for sure but tall, powerfully built, and a commanding presence, was completely and totally wrapped around the tiny finger of her three-and-a-half-month-old granddaughter.

The couple and baby cuddled on the couch, Fallon cradling the baby as she looked to Elsie. "So, my dear girl," she said with a wide grin. "I am *so* proud of you!"

Elsie nearly melted at the words. "My goodness," she managed. "How on earth did it get all the way across the island so quickly?"

Fallon's grin widened. "Well, I was down by the harbor earlier today," she explained. "Someone who heard from someone who heard from someone who knows Jane Brown told me."

Elsie smiled, unable to help herself. "Aye, well it was only one person—"

"Whose life is forever changed," Cateline finished. She turned to Fallon, resting her hand on her thigh. "Before you came, we were discussing the current laws allowing women to own or inherit property."

Fallon's entire countenance darkened as she looked down at the baby who had promptly fallen asleep in her arms. "Aye," she muttered. "As long as it's not a claim disputed."

Elsie sat forward in her chair, which she'd turned to face the couch. "Then, let's change this," she said. "Looking into that woman's eyes today..." She shook her head. "I saw my own mam all over again. I saw Isla, also a widow."

Cateline looked to Fallon. "Millie."

Fallon nodded in agreement before returning her gaze to Elsie. "This has been a long-standing law, Elsie," she said, the tone of her voice making it clear that it would be a fight.

A little glimmer entered Elsie's eyes. "So were women not wearing trousers," she countered.

Cateline gave her a huge grin of approval. Fallon quirked an ebony brow, which made Elsie's grin grow. "Is this something you really believe in, Elsie?"

"With all my heart."

Fallon nodded. "Then we need to get the advisers here," she said, indicating the castle around them, "with my advisers. Us," she added, indicating the three adults in the room, "and hash out a plan. It'll have to come in stages," she warned. "We cannot afford a country-wide revolt over something that will be perceived as quite radical to some."

Elsie's gaze fell, feeling a bit deflated. "I don't have any advisers," she said softly. "Only those of Garratt. And today, Robert, the main one, was trying to get me to side with the man and drop it."

Fallon's eyebrows fell as he glanced to his wife then back to Elsie. "Garratt would have backed this woman today. Why on earth would he keep such an adviser?"

Elsie said nothing, simply bit her bottom lip. She loved Fallon and Cateline dearly, and she wasn't about to alienate herself from them by telling an ugly truth about their only son. She was a bit surprised, however, that Fallon looked utterly stunned while Cateline held something else in her eyes. Cateline met Elsie's gaze and held it for a moment before looking back to her spouse.

"I think it's late, my love," she said softly. "With this little one, 'tis a very early morning for our Elsie."

Looking troubled, Fallon nodded. Clearly there would be a discussion in the future sometime between the couple, but tonight was not the night. She pushed to her feet, hugging the baby tightly and leaving a kiss on her head.

"Good night, Mariota," she murmured against the soft skin. "I love you." She handed the baby to her wife, giving her a solid kiss good night before she walked over to Elsie, who accepted a tight hug.

"We'll talk soon about this," Fallon murmured into the hug. "I promise."

Elsie nodded, relieved. "Thank you so much."

Fallon smiled down at her. "Absolutely." She raised her eyebrows as she studied the shorter woman with her unusual and beautiful violet eyes. "Just as Enori said." She lightly tapped Elsie's upper chest with a finger. "Someday," she said. "You will help to shape the greatest queen Sursha will ever know."

Chapter Seven

Roishin wandered to the next bedroom, the fourth she'd come across in the beach house that was nearly twice as large as Enori's. With the four bedrooms upstairs, larger kitchen, and much larger living space, she was confused. Also, two of the bedrooms had balconies that overlooked the beautiful white sand beach below.

She hadn't seen another living soul when they stepped out of the door from their house to this one. She could hear the soothing sound of the ocean waves outside and even the squawks and cries of seabirds. She walked out of the fourth bedroom, furnished like the rest of the house. She saw Enori leaning against a wall in the upstairs hallway, seeming to give Roishin space to look around.

"So," she drawled, hands on hips as she took one last look around the bedroom, nothing near as large as the family bedrooms back home in Sursha but larger than theirs at Enori's house. "Is this where I'm going next?" she asked, confused. She'd been given no explanation, simply Enori's quiet, *I want to show you something.*

Enori's expression was amused as she stood with arms crossed over her chest. "For a bit."

Roishin cocked her head and raised her eyebrows. "Care to elaborate?"

Enori pushed off the wall and gave Roishin a quick side glance before she turned and headed back down the stairs, her flowing white gown fluttering behind her. The movement mesmerized Roishin as she followed. It was like watching water cascading over Enori's body, pure movement and grace with every step.

She forced her eyes off it and paid attention to where she was going in the unfamiliar house rather than chance walking right into a wall…or Enori. She was led downstairs to the main floor and right out the door. There was a wraparound porch, several rocking chairs set out with little tables for drinks or plates of food.

They bypassed all that and headed down the three stairs that took them to the path that led to the beach. Beyond was ocean as far as the eye could see, bluer than the bluest skies. Lazy, fat, white cotton-like clouds floated around overhead.

"My god," she whispered, hands on hips. "This is paradise."

"Do you really think so?" Enori asked.

To Roishin's surprise, she heard actual uncertainty in her voice. "Aye, absolutely." Roishin took it all in again, from the house to the beach to the ocean and its calm waves to the shore. Nodding to emphasize her words, she looked back to Enori. "What is this place?"

Enori shrugged a shoulder, sparing a shy glance up at Roishin before she looked down at her fingers, which fidgeted together a bit.

"The past half dozen years have been trying for you and your parents," she said softly. She looked up into her eyes again. "I know you want your parents to experience this." She indicated the space around them. "This," she said, nodding toward the house and the beach. "Is private. Essentially, it does not exist to anyone but those who will stay here."

"Wait," Roishin said slowly. "Are you saying what I think you're saying?"

Enori gave her a little smile, a bit of the Enori she knew coming back. "Depends on what you think I am saying."

Roishin grinned. "Fine. Are you saying this is for my parents to come visit?"

Enori cocked her head slightly to the side, eyeing her. "Yes. I am saying that this house is big enough for a visit where everyone can stay and be comfortable."

Her excitement completely taking over, she grabbed Enori into a tight embrace, literally picking the shorter woman off her feet and swinging her around in a circle. Enori held on for dear life with her arms tight around Roishin's neck. When Roishin stopped, she eased Enori back to her feet on the warm sand, grinning at her.

"Sorry," she muttered, unable to stop smiling and, for reasons she didn't want to think about, unable to unclasp her hands from Enori's lower back.

Enori's own arms remained where they were, the fingers of her right hand lightly playing in short, dark strands at the nape of Roishin's neck. "So," she said. "You think they would like it? Isabeau, too."

Roishin's eyes fell closed and her forehead rested against Enori's for a moment as pure joy at the thought of it all washed over her. She felt soft fingertips run down her face and briefly along her jaw.

"You all deserve it," Enori said.

Roishin lifted her head, looking down into the beautiful face, the beautiful eyes. The beautiful lips. She forced her gaze off those and back to Enori's eyes. "So, you're not kicking me out, then?"

Enori eyed her. "Not yet," she murmured, lightly

trailing a fingernail up under Roishin's chin before stepping away from her. Roishin was both parts relieved and sad. "I wanted a place where Fallon can truly be herself," Enori explained. "Come."

Roishin followed as Enori walked down the beach a bit. It was then that she saw the familiar shimmer. They stepped through…

…and onto what amounted to a little island. There was plenty of shade from palm trees but also wide-open sand and beautiful ocean. Enori turned to Roishin.

"Here," she explained. "They can truly be themselves. This is a completely isolated space. Even those back at the house or the other beach cannot see them," she said, indicating where they'd just come from.

"Wow," Roishin breathed, taking it all in. "Daidí has never had that."

"Exactly. Here, they can swim naked, walk around topless, make love on the beach…"

The image that popped into Roishin's mind nearly took her breath away, and it had nothing to do with her parents. She literally had to turn away, rubbing the back of her neck to try to catch her breath.

What the hell is wrong with you? She couldn't face the woman who strolled along the beach just off to her left. Blowing out a breath, Roishin forced herself—and her mind—to be a good girl.

"And," she said, somehow managing to keep her voice sounding mostly normal. "Since it's Duras, no time will pass in their world. Right?" A question she already knew the answer to, but she needed to force her mind to focus on this.

Enori met her gaze, the warm breeze lightly brushing her hair off her forehead. She nodded. "They could leave in the middle of the night there and return to finish the night's sleep after a few days here."

"You did all this," Roishin said softly. "Didn't you?"

"At Ankou's request," Enori acknowledged.

A bit surprised to hear that, but as she looked across the several feet of sand at Enori and into her eyes, she saw something there, not entirely sure what it was as Enori looked away. Roishin strolled over to her but kept her distance, sensing Enori needed that. Truth was, she did, too.

"Are you going to join us?" she asked.

A small smile tipped Enori's lips as she looked down as her bare foot toed the sand. "Ankou wants me to."

"To supervise?" Roishin teased. Her smile grew when she saw that Enori's did as well.

Finally, the smaller woman met her gaze. "I think he thinks I need a bit of a break, too."

"Well," Roishin muttered. "It *has* been, like, five hundred years or something." She smiled at the beautiful burst of laughter that escaped Enori's lips.

"You make me sound so old." Enori chuckled, coming down from her amusement.

"Oh, come now," Roishin teased. "You're not *all* that older than me. What, like, five years?"

Enori quirked a brow and raised her chin a bit. "That's five *hundred* and five years."

Roishin's turn to laugh. "Jeez," she muttered, turning away from her and heading toward the door. "You're old."

Roishin was nearly on pins and needles as she chewed on her thumbnail out in the hall. She could hear the gasps and oohs and aahs as her parents took the tour. The house had already been absolutely stunning, but she'd made sure everything they liked was there for them. What she really looked forward to was being able to do for them what Enori had done initially for her, and that was to introduce them to a whole bunch of new types of food they'd never be able to try otherwise.

She was rocking on her heels by the time the two found their way out of the bedroom. Fallon pointed a finger at her, an eyebrow raised like when Roishin had been a kid and was in for it. Crossing her arms over her chest, Roishin grinned. She was taken into a seriously painful hug.

"I can't believe you did this for us," Fallon whispered into the hug, which was returned.

"Well," Roishin admitted, next accosted by her mother. "Enori deserves most of the credit." After she was finally released, she said, "Come on. There's more."

Like a little kid, she went bounding down the stairs and outside. The two had already seen the inside of the entire house and where they and Isabeau would be sleeping as well as Enori and Roishin's rooms, so now it was time for the wonders of the outdoors. Enori was already out on the beach with Isabeau, who had instantly been enthralled with the ocean.

Sursha might have been an island, but there was no safe place for an excited six-year-old to play in the water. Now, she was doing just that. She was giggling as she ran around barefoot, her leather shoes placed back on the sand far enough away from the water to not get ruined. Roishin stood, transfixed as she watched the two play.

"Ready?" Enori asked, grabbing the vigorously nodding girl and swinging her around as Isabeau squealed in delight.

Roishin felt eyes on her and turned to see Cateline watching her carefully. "What?" she asked. Her mother said nothing, simply smiled.

Ahead of time, Enori and Roishin had decided to wait to show Fallon and Cateline their special little island when one or the other of them had Isabeau inside the house. They wanted that to be just for them, unless they opted to bring the little girl in with them. But, if Isabeau saw where the door was, chances were good she'd jet through either by herself or interrupt their private time together.

Later that night, the five of them sat around the kitchen table, a bounty of fresh fruit before them. Roishin was thoroughly amused, as no doubt the looks on their faces were exactly what Enori had put up with from her in the early days.

"Come on," she said, holding up a cube of pineapple. "It is *so* good."

Isabeau eyed it suspiciously. "Then you eat it."

Roishin popped it into her mouth with a flourish. Large deep blue eyes watched intently, a tiny pink tongue slipping out and licking over her bottom lip. She looked from Roishin to Enori, who was casually working her way through a slice of cantaloupe, then back to Roishin.

Amused, Roishin nudged the bowl of the yellow cubes closer to the girl. Finally, Isabeau snatched one. She looked at it, then with a quick glance to both women, took a little nibble with small, white teeth.

Cateline, for her part, was all about the fruit. She was trying a little bit of everything and even handfed a more reluctant Fallon a bit of kiwi. It was fun to watch the three of them, Roishin thought. She had never seen her parents look so...*free*. There was a light behind their eyes that wasn't there the day before, back in Sursha.

Her parents had a good life back home, but the weight of the entire kingdom rested upon their shoulders, and she knew how much they both loved their people. But, here in Duras, they could literally forget everything, understanding that they'd return to exactly what they'd left, essentially when they'd left it.

Glancing over to Enori, who sat to her right, Roishin felt an immense sense of gratitude toward her. Though she was still quiet and somewhat reserved, she, too, seemed to be a bit lighter, perhaps a little less weight on her slight shoulders. And, as the other woman popped a cherry into her mouth, she met Roishin's gaze.

"You and your cherries," Roishin teased quietly.

Enori gave her a little grin.

❧ ❧ ❧ ❧

"Okay," Roishin said, looking to Cateline and Fallon, who were standing on the beach watching. "Tell me if you can see me." Roishin turned to the door and stepped through. On the little island, she waved madly, kicked, and shouted. A moment later, she stepped back to the regular beach. "Anything?"

Fallon slowly shook her head, looking at Roishin like she'd lost her mind. "Uh, no."

Grinning, Roishin turned back to the door, waving her parents to follow. She stepped back so they could fully enter. Eyes were wide and mouths were open. She really wished Enori could see this, but she was currently helping little Isabeau bathe. They'd simply created a temporary door from here to their existing bathing cave. It was the perfect opportunity to show her parents the island.

"What is this place?" Cateline asked, turning in a slow circle to take it all in.

"This is all for you two," Roishin explained. "As you saw, nobody can see in here, totally isolated if you want it to be. Isabeau has no idea where it is, though," she added with a grin. "Obviously, you're more than welcome to bring her here. But..." She shrugged, a bit shy. "This was actually Enori's doing. But, I agree with her." She turned to Fallon. "You can be totally free here, Daidí. You're safe."

Cateline wrapped her arms around Fallon's, leaning her head against her shoulder. She looked at Roishin with absolute adoration in her eyes. "My sweet girl," she whispered. Auburn eyebrows raised to emphasize her next point. "Both of you."

Roishin walked over to them and gave each a kiss to the cheek. "You guys can swim here, rest, read, frolic in the sand, whatever." She shrugged again. "Just enjoy it, and each other."

⁂

Later that night, Roishin sat out on the beach by herself. The moon was full overhead and the sound of the waves was so calming and peaceful. A light breeze brushed up against her skin, her bare feet buried in the warm sand. She heard someone walk up to her and glanced up, surprised to see Fallon looking down at her.

She was dressed in the simple, comfortable

clothing they'd left for all three of them in their bedroom. No need for weapons, armor, or fraud here. Fallon was dressed similarly to Roishin. The white, lightweight cotton pants flowed around her legs as she walked and the simple tunic shirt showed the outline of her breasts, visible for the first time in both their lives.

"Mind if I join you?" she asked, nodding to the sand next to Roishin, which the younger woman patted in invitation.

Fallon sat down, stretching long legs out before her and crossing her bare feet at the ankles. She rested back on her hands. They were quiet for a long moment, contented and comfortable silence. Finally, Roishin spoke.

"I think you have the whitest feet I've ever seen."

Fallon chuckled, wiggling her nearly glowing toes. "Hey, you wear boots every day of your life and you see how *you* look." She playfully nudged Roishin's shoulder with her own. "You know," she finally said. "I've been all over Europe and to faraway lands that I can't even remember the names of now. I've seen the best and worst of humanity along the way."

Roishin glanced over at her, noting her profile and the beauty of it. Her long, ebony strands blew lightly away from an absolutely stunning face as the warrior stared out to sea.

"But, I've never seen anything like this." She met Roishin's gaze, the softest, most serene smile upon her lips. "I remember hearing about Albios as a small child." She shrugged a shoulder. "Basically, Heaven." Her smile grew. "Guess this is it." She held Roishin's gaze. "Is all of Duras like this?"

Roishin shook her head. "No. Enori selected this special for you guys. Wanted you to have nothing to worry about, nothing to fear or distract you from just *being*." She pulled her legs up and sat cross-legged. "Duras has many faces, Daidí, and I've only seen a small part of it. I mostly just live here, honestly." She smiled. "I'm so busy all the time with my missions, I haven't gotten to really just breathe."

Fallon nodded. "I very much understand that." She studied Roishin for so long the younger woman was becoming a bit uncomfortable. "I've seen so much change in you, Roishin. So much growth, maturity." She smiled. "You're my second to the youngest, and I'm pretty sure you're older than all of us put together."

Roishin chuckled, thinking of her teasing of Enori a few days before. "Yes, well," she muttered, amusement in her voice. "Living with Enori is a real hardship."

Fallon snorted.

Chapter Eight

Roishin waited until she got an invitation to enter. She glanced over her shoulder to make sure Isabeau hadn't awoken from the soft knocking. Pushing the door open, she closed it behind her and crept over to the bed, all ninja style. Enori, who was still in bed, chuckled silently. Roishin stuck her tongue out of the corner of her mouth in feigned concentration as she "threw herself" onto Enori's bed in slow motion.

Replete with dramatic facial expressions, Roishin "landed" with an, "Oomph."

Enori brought her covers up to cover her mouth, but the squinting of her eyes and shaking of her body made it quite clear she was amused, if not bemused. Roishin, who lay across her legs, rolled from her side to her belly. She grinned up at her as she climbed up the bed to lay next to her.

She turned her head to look at the woman staring back at her. "Hi."

Enori studied her like she'd landed from Mars. "What is wrong with you?" she asked.

Roishin grinned. "Wherever to start *that* conversation."

Lowering the blanket to reveal the lower half of her face, Enori shook her head. "I am going to send you back to Sursha with your parents."

"Aww, baby," Roishin purred, turning to her side. "You'd be so bored without me." She chuckled at the quirked eyebrow that received. "Or not." She looked at Enori and noticed her hair was actually sticking up a bit on the left side. She gasped. "Well, my Moses," she murmured, reaching up to gently ease down the strands. "You *are* human." She looked into Enori's gaze and grinned again. "Sorry. Woke up in a super good mood."

"That is quite clear." Enori turned to her side, the two women facing each other with about a foot of space between them. "So, why are you in here harassing me?"

Roishin could see the teasing in her eyes so decided not to feel bad. "Well," she said, getting to the point of her morning visit. "My parents decided to utilize their little private oasis today, so Isabeau is mine, all mine!" She shrugged. "That is, unless you want to join us. And, she can be yours, all yours, too."

This time, laughter escaped Enori's lisps, again her covers coming up to cover her mouth. Roishin was utterly charmed and damn it, she wanted to reach out and…and, what? Just touch her somehow. When the blankets were lowered again, Enori very obviously trying to hide her smile that was about to pop out again, Roishin rested her hand on her waist.

Enori didn't respond, per se, but she didn't move her hand away, nor did she smack her. "What do you have in mind?" she asked instead.

"Maybe swim in the ocean? Take her exploring somewhere, show her something she can't see in Sursha?"

"You know," Enori said, her tone becoming more serious. "The moment you brought her back, you did that by giving her a little piece of your soul." She looked deeply into Roishin's eyes. "That is why you two have such a bond. She literally feels you."

Roishin considered the softly spoken words and

thought of her time with the little girl. "When I was back in Sursha, the day of the baptism for Mariota."

Enori nodded in acknowledgment. "Yes."

"I was holding the baby, and she came up to me, Isabeau. She told me Mariota was her sister. I tried to correct her that they're cousins, but she insisted." She smiled and took on a determined expression. "'My sister.'"

Enori smiled and nodded where her head still lay on the pillow. "Like Isabeau, Mariota has part of your soul, too. Isabeau recognizes that. She may have no understanding of what she feels, but that is what she is feeling." She reached her hand out and used her fingertips to lightly trace along Roishin's browbone and down along her cheek. "They feel *you.*"

Roishin nearly sighed at the touches, so soft, so gentle. She forced herself to focus. "So, does that mean Isabeau has Ankou now, too?" At Enori's nod, Roishin murmured, "Wow." She studied the other woman's face, so close to her own, for a long moment. *You are so beautiful.* She had to fight herself to not say the words out loud. Instead, she said, "So, would you like to join Isabeau and me in our adventure today, or would you rather some time to yourself?" She smiled and lightly squeezed Enori's waist for emphasis. "No wrong answer."

Enori smiled. "No," she whispered. "I want to be with you."

⁂

Roishin broke the surface, spitting out water as she used her hands to brush her hair back from her face. She saw Enori in water that was just above her waist in depth. She was teaching Isabeau how to float on her back. Isabeau was beginning to panic a bit as her legs began to fall.

"No, no," Enori said softly, moving her hands under the girl's back and legs to help steady her. "Relax."

Roishin treaded water where she was, not wanting to interrupt. She watched the two together. Isabeau seemed to take to Enori just as much as she had to Roishin. And, Roishin could see it in her eyes, Enori was deeply protective of the girl, had a genuine affection for her. She was so amazing with the children, she thought, including Roishin's own child.

As if feeling she were being watched, Enori glanced up, her gaze meeting Roishin's for a moment before it fell back to Isabeau. Roishin decided she needed to cool off, in every way. She needed to stop this constant need to be around Enori, to look at her and touch her. It just had to…stop.

She felt like she was heading into dangerous territory. Enori had been nothing but good to her, patient with her. She'd been a mentor and a friend. She'd taken Roishin into her home, where she'd lived for more than a year at this point. What the hell was Roishin thinking? Doing? She growled at herself as she shot through the water, kicking with powerful thighs.

She needed to get her head back in the game. Yes, Enori was gorgeous, yes, she was unbelievably sexy, and yes, damn it, Roishin knew she was attracted to her. But honestly, who wasn't? She doubted there was anyone, man or woman, who wasn't affected by her. But that didn't give Roishin the right to become so focused on her.

As she broke the surface several yards away from the other two, she forced herself to not look at them.

No, not look at *her*. Roishin couldn't have Elsie, she knew that. It was a painful fact but a fact all the same, and she was coming to terms with that. She smoothed her hair back from her face again.

Maybe that was it—part of the price they had to pay for who they were, what they were given the privilege to know and understand. Maybe it was a road best taken alone. Or a road only taken alone. After all, Enori didn't seem to have anyone, either. Hadn't seemed to in all the years she'd known her. Certainly not in their time living together.

Yes, she thought. They were friends, close friends. She didn't want to lose that. Enori was incredibly important to her in so many ways. She needed to stay focused. They had a mission to accomplish, and it was broken up into endless tiny pieces of that singular mission—to make the world humanity inhabited a better place. Seemed like a bit of a contradiction in terms at times, but it was her job, it was her identity.

Blowing out a breath, she decided to return to Enori and Isabeau. This was their day to spend together, not Roishin to run off by herself like a wounded animal and wax philosophical.

❧❧❧❧

"A little bit more," Roishin whispered, waiting until Enori pulled the covers back enough to clear Isabeau's feet. "Thanks." She gently rested the sleeping girl onto her bed, Enori pulling the covers up over her once she was settled. They stood side by side next to her bed, watching as she slept on. Roishin smiled. "She's absolutely tuckered."

"She is," Enori agreed in a whisper. Finally, she

lightly tugged on Roishin's shirt.

The two left the bedroom, softly closing the door behind them. Heading downstairs, they immediately went to the kitchen to clean up dinner. Isabeau had literally fallen asleep at the table. Enori was rinsing dishes to be washed by hand as Roishin cleared the table, bringing more over to Enori, then used a rinsed rag to wipe down the table.

"Today was a wonderful day," Enori said.

Roishin smiled as she used her hand to capture crumbs wiped into it with the rag as she went along. "It was. You're an amazing swimmer." She glanced over at the other woman who smiled into her task.

"I've been swimming since I was a child." She met Roishin's gaze. "A little fish."

Roishin met her smile with one of her own. "I wish Sursha were a little more conducive for that."

"You do pretty well."

Roishin eyed her with a quirked brow. "It's called four and a half years in the Underground at the waterfall."

Enori's grin was downright devilish. "Ah yes. Of course."

"You're so good with her," Roishin said, wonder in her voice. "You would make an amazing mother."

Enori didn't say anything for a moment. In fact, the silence was so long Roishin worried she'd said something wrong. Finally the priestess spoke. "I love children. They have so much curiosity, so much wonder about everything. They have a clean slate before them, as it were." She briefly met Roishin's gaze. "I cannot stand to see a child hurt, alone, or lost."

Roishin stopped wiping. "Like you were?"

Enori nodded but said nothing. She rinsed the

dish she'd just washed in the bucket of clean water and set it on the towel she had laid out for such a purpose. From all the way over by the table, Roishin could feel the sadness coming off her in waves. And, in the brief moment Enori met her eyes, she saw a deep, profound loneliness that she'd not seen before.

At the same time, she'd never seen Enori so completely open to her. In that moment, it seemed she was fully vulnerable. Dropping the rag on the table, she walked over to her. Without a word, she gently turned Enori so she was facing her and took her in an embrace. Enori allowed it, and in fact leaned into it.

Roishin cupped the back of a blond head, urging it to rest against her shoulder. They were still in the clothing they swam in that day, the material smelling of seawater and fresh air. She could smell it in Enori's hair and on her skin. She felt warm breath against her neck, though she did her level best to ignore it.

All she wanted to do was to show Enori that she wasn't alone and she'd never be alone again if she'd allow Roishin to be there for her. No, she couldn't take away the fear and trauma of that young girl from so many years ago, but she could—and would—be there for the woman now.

After several long moments, Enori lifted her head. Her eyes were still downcast as she stood there, her hands resting on Roishin's shoulders. The air between them was thick with expectation. She had no idea how it happened, but suddenly Roishin's hand was on Enori's jaw, urging her to lift her face.

When she did, Roishin lowered hers. Her lips were so soft, so unbelievably and incredibly soft. The kiss lingered for a moment before Roishin moved away, just a breath before her lips returned. A second kiss, lingering a bit longer than the first, but just as soft. Enori's breath was shaky, and Roishin wasn't sure why. Upset? Fear? Anger at her for doing such a thing?

There was no time to find out as the voices of her parents drifted in from outside, getting closer to the door. Enori stepped back from her and, without even looking at her, turned away.

⁂

Roishin had spent a little time with her parents, who looked remarkably relaxed. They seemed like teenagers in love for the first time, and it was beautiful to watch. After they checked on Isabeau, they'd said their goodnights and so had Enori. Roishin, however, couldn't sleep.

So incredibly bothered by what had happened, by what she'd done, she left the house and went out into the warm night to sit on the beach by herself. She hurt, mostly because she knew in her heart she'd taken advantage of an incredibly vulnerable moment for Enori. She hadn't meant to, but she'd done it, and now she hated herself for it.

No matter what happened, she'd stay in Duras and continue her work, but she couldn't even wrap her mind around doing that without Enori, without seeing her every day, feeling her calm presence. No doubt she'd ask Roishin to leave. Or, even if she was just too kind to do that, she should do it on her own.

Her legs pulled up so her thighs were against her chest and her arms were wrapped around her shins, Roishin looked up into the night sky. It was perfectly black, save for where a star winked down, or where the moon was, seeming to hover over the ocean. Her gaze was taken from the night sky when she heard the screen door crack softly against the doorframe back at the house.

Footfalls made their way over the wood porch then the stairs and finally, the crunch of bare feet over sand. She didn't turn her head, just rested her chin on her knees and waited. She knew who it was even before she lowered herself to sit down beside her. She could feel her. They sat in silence for a moment before Enori spoke.

"Really beautiful out here."

Roishin nodded. "It is. Tempting to get a place like this." She snorted. "Smaller, of course. Just me."

"Are you planning to move?" Enori asked softly.

Roishin shrugged a shoulder, feeling downright sorry for herself. "I figure you probably want me to." Still unable to look at her, she said, "I'm so sorry, Enori. I'm so sorry I did that."

"Why are you apologizing?"

Finally, Roishin looked over at her, replacing her chin with her cheek. "You were upset and my job was to comfort you. Not kiss you."

"And," Enori said softly, mirroring Roishin's position. "Who said that was not a comforting gesture?"

Roishin didn't respond, because if she did, she would have said, *We both know I didn't mean it as comfort.* Instead she said, "Do you..." Words eluded her, not entirely sure what question she wanted to ask first. "Do you love, Enori? *Have* you loved someone?"

Enori nodded. "It was a very long time ago, but yes."

"But you don't now?" Roishin pushed, not asking about specifics but wanting to know if it was even anything Enori wanted.

"Love," Enori said with a sigh as she lifted her head and looked out over the inky blackness that was the ocean, save for the silver-tipped ripples from the moonlight. "It is not something I ever thought I would have any need for again." She shrugged. "I have kept my love for Ankou, my work." Another shrug, looking back over at Roishin. "Those I mentor."

Roishin nodded, no doubt a long line of those over the centuries. "I understand." She sighed, feeling so utterly alone, even as Enori sat not more than six inches away from her. "Is that the price we pay, Enori? Live forever, but alone?" She snorted derisively. "Watch those we may dare to love die?"

"You still love Elsie?" Enori asked. Her voice always had a softness to it, the tone, but this was a quiet that was unusual for her. A quiet of uncertainty.

"I'll always love her, Enori." Roishin looked at her. "She's the mother of my child, my first love. But, as you told me that day before I came to Duras, it's not possible. Our worlds are literally too different. I can't do that to her. Just pop in now and then, get what I need, and go." She shook her head. "It's not right." What she said next hurt like hell to say, but she knew she had to, though she wasn't sure who she was saying it for, Enori or herself. "She needs to be able to find happiness with a woman who can be there for her all the time, not when it's convenient in between missions."

Enori met her gaze and held it for a long time. The smallest smile graced her lips. "You really do love her," she said softly.

Roishin nodded. "I do. Enough to let her go."

Enori brought a hand up and used her finger to gently wipe at the tear that slowly trailed down Roishin's cheek. She gently rubbed the wetness she'd gathered between her thumb and forefinger before she cupped Roishin's face.

Roishin's eyes fell closed at the softness that pressed against her lips. She returned the kiss, another tear sliding down her cheek. Enori left one final kiss on her lips before she gathered her in her arms, holding her there on the beach under the stars.

Chapter Nine

Amused, Enori took another sip of her wine. She sat by herself listening as Roishin and Livia regaled Fallon, Cateline, and Livia's husband with tales of some of their misadventures while on missions. Enori watched the king and queen closely. There was so much going on inside the couple, she could tell, both as individuals and as parents.

For much of this journey with Roishin, Enori felt they were deeply hurt and had no way of understanding why Enori and Ankou had taken their daughter from them. Yes, they understood she had gifts of a profound nature, but no way to comprehend why she had to leave.

But today, she saw it in their eyes. They understood now. And, with understanding can come acceptance and true support. Of course they'd worry about their daughter, but Fallon was a lifelong warrior and understood that battles must be fought, and with that insight, she also knew some wars were forever ongoing.

As she watched Roishin on her feet, pantomiming and gesturing along with an extremely amusing version of her story, Enori saw the pride in her eyes to finally know who she was and why she was, and to be able to impart that to her family. Enori could almost feel the weight lifted from her shoulders.

After their seaside talk the night before, Enori had also come to more understanding of her own about Roishin and the very personal toll everything had taken on her. Just when she'd begun to start the journey of understanding herself as a person, a female and one that was attracted to other females, she'd been snatched from it all.

Enori didn't feel guilty about bringing her back to Ankou and Duras because although Roishin hadn't been born in Duras, her soul had been. Ava Gentry was evidence that the soul knew its way home. As powerful as Roishin was proving to be, it would have been a matter of time before she either stumbled across a door or accidentally created one and would have gone to where things innately made sense.

Even still, Enori didn't sit back and rest on her laurels for that. Roishin had paid a heavy price, just as she'd mentioned the night before. Hearing her thoughts on everything and seeing her pain had affected Enori deeply. Everything, for so long, had been about the greater good, the bigger picture—both of which she still believed in.

But, somehow, that young woman had wiggled her way into a deeper level of existence for Enori, the human side. Once begun, it was easy to stay on the wheel of disciplined aloofness and duty. It was not, however, so easy to put that aside and feel.

And yet, here she was, watching and listening, smiling from time to time at Roishin's antics. As she listened to Isabeau and Livia's son Mattia giggling as only children could as they played together, she felt it.

She felt something she'd never felt before, and that was what it was like to be part of something that was as simple as it was complex: family. These people weren't together because they were planning a mission. There was nothing else involved here but that they loved each other and wanted to spend time together. That was it.

No more, no less.

Even during her time with Mariota in Scotland, they'd had to steal away to be together. Make love under the stars miles from the small Druid compound. Stolen kisses and stolen *I love yous*, for fear Mariota would be found out. Resting her eyes on Roishin, Enori gained an even stronger respect for her heart and her integrity.

The unbelievable strength it took for her to say the words she'd said the night before when asked if she loved Elsie: *I do. Enough to let her go.* Why hadn't Enori been that strong? When they'd begun to hear of suspicions, why hadn't they decided to let it go? Would Mariota have lived to raise her daughter? Certainly she wouldn't have been utterly destroyed, from her earthbound body to her very soul.

The moment Enori had seen Elsie, she'd seen Mariota in her and it had nearly taken her breath away. And now, the baby, Mariota's own great-great-granddaughter. She smiled at that thought, bringing her wine goblet to her lips to sip from the sweet drink inside. The wine warmed her on its way through her system like an internal caress.

How fitting, she thought. The long-lost great-great-granddaughter of the first woman she loved would also be the daughter of the woman… Well, that would have to be dealt with at another time. The story was coming to an end, and Enori felt eyes on her.

⁂

Cateline was quiet as she and Enori strolled. Enori had been surprised when the queen had requested a bit of time with her before she and Fallon returned to Sursha, but she certainly had acquiesced. The day was beautiful, the water lapping gently at the shore before receding back into the bottomless ocean, only to play it out all over again moments later.

Enori had always thought the woman walking beside her was incredibly beautiful. The slight breeze blew long auburn curls back from an absolutely lovely face. Striking gray-blue eyes, so filled with warmth and kindness for anyone they set upon. She had a similar temperament to Elsie, she thought.

Enori could see why Roishin had been drawn to Elsie, considering it was said one was drawn to those who remind them of the parent that has the most profound effect on them, for good or for ill. They strolled in silence for a bit, Enori waiting for the queen to speak her piece.

"I wanted to have a little time with you, Enori," Cateline finally said. "I wanted to personally thank you for what you've done for Fallon and me." She smiled. "And Isabeau." She looked over at her companion. "You're all she's talked about since we've been here." She chuckled. "She already talks about Roishin nonstop, but now you've been added into the mix."

Enori wasn't entirely sure what to say to that or how to feel. But, that same somewhat confusing sense of belonging she'd felt earlier returned. "I hope good things," she finally managed.

"Oui!" Cateline hooked her arm with Enori's, bringing their strolling steps closer together. More silence followed, though it was comfortable, companionable. "You gave Fallon something she has never had, Enori," she finally said. This time, her voice was soft, filled with absolute love and gratitude. She glanced over at Enori. "The chance to just be herself. No preconceived notions, no constricting boxes or roles. Just Fallon."

"Of course." She held the queen's gaze. "I am so pleased."

"You know," Cateline said conversationally. "For a long time, I wanted to hate you. As much as I wanted to understand why you had come back into our lives, seeming to disrupt them by taking Roishin, there was this strange part of me that understood. I don't know how, but it was there. And now, being here and seeing Roishin, I realize you gave *her* that freedom to be herself, also."

"I think she would have found her way back home, Cateline," Enori said.

Cateline nodded. "I agree. She always knew, deep down, that she didn't belong in our world. And," she blew out with a heavy sigh. "I think somehow Fallon and I knew that, too." She grew quiet again before saying, "Will we be able to come back here, Enori? See her? See you and Livia?"

Enori stopped their progress and turned to face the other woman. "Cateline," she said softly, taking the queen's hands in her own. "You and Fallon carry Duras in your soul, in your blood. This," she said, indicating the world around them, "is where you came from. Yes, your lives and your responsibilities for this life are in the other world, in Sursha. But," she added softly, "Duras is your true home." She smiled. "It always will be, and you will always be welcome here."

Cateline took Enori into a warm embrace, that of a mother. "Please," the queen whispered into the hug. "Take care of Roishin."

All Enori could do was nod.

⁂

The apple came off the tree with a satisfying snap. Enori examined the large, succulent red piece of fruit before it was set into the wooden basket that sat at her feet. She reached up to a higher branch to snag another one that had caught her eye.

"I have never known anyone who loves her fruit like you do."

Enori glanced over to see Ankou leaning against a nearby tree in the orchard, amusement in his brown eyes. She looked away from him and back to her task, stretching as far as she could to reach the elusive apple. He stepped over to her and plucked it for her, holding it out to her.

She eyed him, grabbing it before placing it in her basket. She was leery about his sudden presence.

"Perhaps you should have brought Roishin with you," he suggested. "She has those few extra inches." He smiled. "Could help."

"I left her to spend time with her family before they go back to Sursha," she explained.

He nodded, pulling off another apple from a different part of the tree. He held the fruit in his hand, looking it over before he rubbed its ruby skin upon his shirt to shine it. "How did it go?"

Enori nodded, noncommittal. She picked a few apples, which joined the others. "It went very well," she said. "It was nice to see Roishin happy with her parents and Isabeau."

"She will need to be trained, you know," he added.

Enori smirked, sparing him a glance. "I figured." She picked two more apples. "When?"

He shrugged, taking a bite of the apple he held, the crunch loud in the still evening. He eyed her as he chewed, making her shrug in question. "Why do you not live in the middle of an orchard somewhere rather than that rather dreary stone village?"

She turned back to her task. "You know why, Ankou," she said quietly.

He nodded, taking another bite. "Perhaps it's time to move on, hmm?"

She said nothing in response. One thing about Ankou—she was grateful he never pushed a point. He made it, then left it be. Usually.

"I want Roishin to move on to the next part of our business," he said, which she assumed was his main reason for showing up.

She looked at him. "You want her to be part of that side?"

"Do you not agree?" His bushy eyebrow raised as he took another bite.

She chewed on her bottom lip for a moment as she considered. She knew he was right. Roishin needed to be part of all of it, needed to know the entire system. The happy rescues were wonderful, but that wasn't all of it. Finally, she let out a sigh.

"No," she said. "I agree." She reached up for another apple but was stopped by a hand to her arm. She looked over at Ankou, who was studying her very seriously.

"I need to know if you have any reservations about this, Enori." He held her gaze. "It could be catastrophic if she is not ready."

She held that gaze, hers cool and steady. "I have none."

He nodded, seeming satisfied by her confidence in Roishin. He looked up at the tree, then, with a little wave of his hand before he vanished, the biggest, reddest apples slowly began to tumble from their moorings, hovering at eye level for her. With an irritated sigh, she plucked them from the air and dropped them into her basket.

"I hate it when it does that," she muttered. "Picking them is half the point."

⁂

Eyes closed, Enori raised her head back to the warm water that fell over her naked skin. She pushed her hair away from her face, the water pelting it down. It felt wonderful, so soothing and relaxing. She did, however, gasp slightly as it rained over hardened and sensitive nipples. No stranger to sex, Enori had done what she'd needed to do over the years, but it wasn't something she focused on in her personal life at all anymore.

She admitted that more than once she'd had a little fun at Roishin's deeply blushing expense, but that was just part of a day's work, she told herself. Overall, her mind was something she was far more keen on keeping actively in practice than her body. She was very aware of how she physically affected people and certainly used it to her advantage when she needed to.

However, she found the unwanted attention just that—unwanted. Even so, she ran her hands down the soft, slick skin of her upper chest and down to her breasts. Again, a gasp escaped her lips when her palms came into contact with her nipples. She'd forgotten how incredibly sensitive they could be. She'd forgotten the feelings that they could stir deep in her belly, the ache they could cause between her legs.

Playing a necessary role and true arousal—and

need—were two entirely different things. Kissing a man as you waited for him to take his last breath and kissing a woman who was stealing yours were also two entirely different things. She'd been a million different places and played a million different roles, but the one she was most terrified to take on was that of Enori.

Her true self, her true wants and needs, were carefully packed away behind thick walls of ice and stone, carefully constructed over centuries. Now, as the warm water trailed over her body like a lover's caress, she felt the blocks melting and crumbling, and she'd never felt more naked.

Time heals all wounds, it was said. Well, she'd used those wounds as the moat around those impenetrable walls, and she'd used time as the battlements to harden her resolve. And now, as it all crumbled around her, she feared she'd have to send up her flag of surrender.

Then what? What was there to hide behind? Enori was a very honest person, part of her core belief system. However, when it came to herself, that wasn't always easy. She didn't lie to herself, per se, she simply didn't allow in the things that would require her to. But, there was a very real situation in her own home that she could not avoid, one that she could not hide from nor turn her back on.

And, she realized, that very real situation had just arrived back home. Her eyes opened as she felt Roishin enter the house. Her stomach flipped, making her take a moment to gather her wits and her breath. She just stood there for a moment until finally, she reached for the soap to continue her shower.

Dressed for bed and her hair still damp from her shower. Enori was in her bedroom when she heard Roishin make her way up the stairs. She was dumping the clothing she'd worn that day into her laundry basket when there was a knock at her open bedroom door. She glanced over to see Roishin standing there.

"How did the rest of your visit go?" she asked, walking over to her dresser to grab her comb. She began to comb the blond strands back away from her face as Roishin leaned against the doorframe with a shoulder.

"It went really well," she said, crossing her arms over her chest. She held a serene smile upon her lips as she watched Enori work at her task. "I did overhear Daidí mentioning sunburned nipples, and I'm pretty sure I'm scarred for life on that one."

Enori chuckled as she walked over to the bed and climbed on. She brought her legs up to sit cross-legged as she continued with her hair. "Imagine how *she* must feel."

Roishin smirked, pushing off the doorframe and entering the room. She plopped down on her back across Enori's bed. She stared up at the ceiling. She seemed content, and that made Enori happy.

"Did you have fun?" she asked softly.

Roishin turned her head to look at her. "I did. Did you?" she asked, eyebrows raised expectantly.

Enori smiled, nodding. Roishin reached out and playfully tugged on Enori's toes, which just barely peeked out from the sleeping gown she was wearing.

"Why'd you leave?"

"I wanted you to have some time alone with your parents and sister," Enori said simply and honestly.

"They were sorry to see you go." Roishin grinned. "Isabeau kept asking if you were coming back."

Enori finished her combing and set the tool on her thigh as she ran her fingers through the damp strands. "I went and got some apples," she said. "The big, red, sweet ones you like."

"Oh," Roishin nearly purred. "Those are so yummy."

Enori took the hand that lay on the bed next to her foot. "You look tired."

Roishin nodded, curling her fingers around Enori's. "I am. That was a lot of fun, but a lot of chasing a six-year-old."

Enori smiled. "I'm sure all of us will sleep very well tonight." She quirked an eyebrow. "Sunburned nipples and all."

Chapter Ten

The expanse was massive and seemingly endless. As far as a person could walk was as far as the boundaries went. There were no walls, no floor and no ceiling, just endless darkness, like the night sky. But, as they walked, one area at a time lit up, startling Roishin. Enori smiled, glancing over at her. She remembered her first time there.

What was revealed were stacks, rows, racks, shelves, and aisles of clothing, shoes, accessories, wigs, jewelry, and even makeup. Women's, men's, children's, whatever, was ready to peruse. There was also eyewear, small electronics, and small appliances of every stripe, small enough to be carried.

Eyes huge, Roishin finally looked to Enori.

"What is this place?"

"It is called the Warehouse," Enori explained. "It's run by The Scientist."

Roishin looked at her. "The laptop guy that Trudy and I had to get the computer for."

Enori smiled. "Bingo. All that is taken on recovery missions, he replicates." She indicated all that was around them. "All this."

"Wow," Roishin whispered. "Is all this authentic to period?"

Enori shook her head as she led the way to a specific section that they needed. "But, it is as close as you will get. Those of that era would never know the difference." She spared a glance at Roishin. "Made of the same material in the same technique of its time."

"This is absolutely incredible, Enori. Why are we here?" Roishin asked, following.

"Where we are going and what we need to do," she explained, walking over to a section of evening gowns from just about every era known to man. "An intention will not hold up, no matter how good." She almost laughed out loud at the expression on Roishin's face. "Yes, we get to play dress up."

"Wait, we're going as ourselves?" Roishin asked, fingering a red sequined dress that hung from a rack amongst the thousands.

"In a manner of speaking," Enori said. She eyed Roishin then grabbed an emerald-green gown from the rack. It was formfitting and had sequined spaghetti straps. She held it up against Roishin's front, eyeing the look.

"Um..."

Enori smiled, looking up into Roishin's eyes, uncertainty filling their green depths. "Oh, come now," she nearly purred. "Do you not want to be beautiful?"

Roishin quirked a brow. "Aren't I purty enough?"

Enori gave her a look that made Roishin swallow. "Stunning," she murmured, replacing the gown and grabbing another one. "But we must play our part, hmm?" She was amused as Roishin swallowed again.

※ ※ ※ ※

A little tornado of era experts showed up and, with wardrobe, accessories, makeup, and wigs, turned the two into what they needed to be to enter 1931 authentically. When they were finished, Enori was utterly astonished when she saw Roishin for the first time. She no doubt was hiding her reaction much better than Roishin's open mouth and huge eyes.

Enori had to smile. If she had an apple for every time green eyes dipped into the cleavage revealed in her halter top-style dress, she'd never have to visit an orchard again. But, in fairness, Roishin was also absolutely beautiful. The dress chosen for her fit her body like a glove, turning the tall woman into a statuesque beauty.

The deep green dress with thin straps showed off beautiful skin with defined collarbones and the delicate structure of her shoulders and throat. Her hair had gotten shaggy enough that they were actually able to shape it into the shorter styles of the era, whereas Enori had been fitted with a shoulder-length wig of the same color as her own hair.

Her own gown was a light blue that made her eyes look like the waters of the Caribbean. They looked good, and she believed could easily pull off the roles. She had to admit, she so badly wanted to run her fingers down Roishin's sides, feel the texture of the dress, and follow the form it was so lovingly molded to.

"Ready?" she asked, as they'd head out directly from the Warehouse to the Crystal Palace. At Roishin's nod, she led the way.

This was a dangerous mission, and one where the less involved the better. Livia would not be joining them this time, instead just the two of them. They both had a very specific role to play, and they'd play it. Once they reached the familiar darkness with swirling red energy, Enori turned to Roishin.

"Are you ready for this?" she asked. This time, she did place her hands on womanly hips, wanting to be connected to her for this.

"Aye," Roishin said.

"I need you to take my lead, Roishin," Enori said. "Trust that whatever I am doing is for a reason." She lightly squeezed the hips for emphasis. "All right?"

"All right." Roishin blew out a soft breath. Her own hands came up and lightly ran down Enori's arms, sending a little thrill through Enori's body. "I want you to know that you look so unbelievably gorgeous, Enori," she said softly.

Enori smiled. She wore high heels but Roishin, already a tall woman, they'd put in flats unseen from the long length of her gown. They didn't need an exceptionally tall woman to bring any undue attention. They were nearly eye to eye, and Enori leaned forward just the little bit and left the softest kiss on Roishin's lips, not wanting to disturb either of their lipstick.

"So are you," she whispered. Stepping back, she took Roishin's hand in her own. "Ready?" she asked again.

"Aye."

The familiar process began and the door opened…

…into the back hallway of a swank hotel in Manhattan. The patterned carpeting that covered the floors and silk wallpaper that covered the walls cost more than the average person brought home in a year during the height of the Great Depression. But, for the man behind the door of room 301, that wasn't an issue.

Enori stopped them in front of the door after leading the way through the maze of hallways to find it. The gold, oval-shaped plaque on the door had the three precious numbers etched into it. She glanced over at Roishin, who looked nervous but ready.

With a raised fist, Enori let loose three firm raps.

After a moment, footfalls could be heard and a lock disengaged. The door was pulled open to reveal the man of her dreams:

New York, NY—1931
Anthony "Tony" Conway—age 56
Business—arms trade
Weakness—beautiful women

Painted lips smiled as the middle-aged man appeared. His brown hair was thinning on top, the whole lot slicked back from a pudgy face. His nose was large and his eyes were small, colored dull blue. He still wore the tuxedo he'd worn to the dinner party he'd just left.

"Mr. Big?" Enori asked, her words in perfect English, no trace of an accent.

His smile grew, as did his eyes as he took in the two beauties, at the sound of the code name he'd given to the agency. Unfortunately, the two women scheduled to work this client had already been taken out of commission by an earlier team. They would awake the following morning with a nasty headache and perhaps a little stomach issue, but alive.

"Ladies," he said, stepping aside to allow them to enter.

Enori looked around, taking in every detail. The room wasn't large but was well-appointed with everything a well-paying customer could possibly need, including its own telephone and bathroom. She took in the two windows on either side of the bed, as well as Conway's belongings.

There was no suitcase, so clearly he did not intend to spend the night or any time there outside of why she and Roishin were there in the first place. There was no real weapon for him to use should he get the chance. That was good. She turned on the charm, looking back to the man who was visually eating Roishin alive.

"So," Enori said, sauntering over to him. She ran a polished fingernail down his cheek. "Do you want us to call you Mr. Big?" she teased, her eyes dropping down toward his crotch then back up to his beady little eyes.

His pencil-thin mustache grinned right along with him. "Guess I'll just have to show ya." He placed a meaty hand on her behind then looked over at Roishin. "What do I call you two lookers?"

"Well," Enori drawled, bringing up a hand and lightly tugging at the end of his tuxedo bow tie. "I'm Rose, and that there is Betty."

Roishin gave him a saucy little smile but said nothing. Though Roishin had mastered many of the most common languages, her accents weren't as good as Enori's, so they'd decided while she could, she'd remain quiet.

He looked over at Roishin, his gaze instantly going to her breasts. It was clear he very much approved. "Well," he said, looking back to Roishin's face then Enori's. "Tell you what, Rose and Betty, why don't you two gals get started while I get myself ready, huh?"

She smiled at him, all nice and sexy. Getting into his personal space, she murmured a hair's width from fleshy lips. "Don't take too long…Mr. Big."

Her hand slid all the way down his rotund belly until she reached his belt. She tugged playfully at the buckle before turning to Roishin. She looked into her eyes, making sure they were connected on this. They both had to play their parts to perfection to pull this off. The green depths were clear and focused. Enori gave her a small smile, letting her know she was there with her.

"What's your favorite part on a woman, Mr. Big?" she asked, her hands going to Roishin's hips.

"Oh, I like me a good set a' tits," he said. He took a seat in the armchair near the wall. Clearly, he was settling in for a bit of a show.

Knowing there was no choice but to at least get it started, she pulled Roishin's hips into her own, somehow managing to withhold a gasp when their breasts touched through the layers of bra and dress. Her mouth went to Roishin's neck, and she whispered softly into her ear.

"We need to get him to join us..." she said as her hands smoothed around to cup Roishin's beautiful behind, snug in the formfitting dress. Roishin nodded so subtly, it was felt and not seen.

"Jesus H. Christ," he groaned from his chair. "You two is some hot mamas. Take off them dresses."

Enori lifted her head and again met Roishin's eyes. *Stay with me. Focus on me.* She could see that Roishin was nervous, and she understood that. Enori wasn't uncomfortable undressed, so she figured they could start with her. Maybe Roishin wouldn't have to because this idiot would decide to engage. She needed to get him relaxed and make sure neither of them was in danger.

Returning to a soft neck, Enori made it look more like she was kissing it instead of the fact that she was actually paying close attention to what he was doing. She was listening to his every move, every quickening breath. She could hear clothing rustling and figured he was removing his tuxedo jacket.

"Unzip my dress," she whispered into Roishin's

ear. Enori's back was partially to him.

Roishin's hands moved up from Enori's behind to the zipper tab. She tilted her head a bit, as though enjoying what "Rose" was doing, meanwhile Enori knew she was being her eyes.

The zipper was pulled down and Enori could feel the coolness of the night air on her back. For just a moment, Enori's eyes fell closed when she felt the softness of Roishin's hands against her skin. Deft fingers slid up along her spine to her shoulders. Enori was finding it difficult to focus.

She lifted her head and met Roishin's gaze. It was clear to Enori that she wasn't the only one feeling it. Looking into her eyes, she lifted the halter from over her neck, careful not to dislodge the wig, and let it drop. The bust of the dress draped at her waist, exposing her naked breasts.

Strangely, never one to be shy about being naked or even half naked, Enori, in that moment standing before Roishin, felt like it was the first time she'd ever been seen by her. This wasn't messing with Roishin or getting her to blush fourteen shades of red, this was a very real situation of truly life or death.

Yet, she couldn't take her eyes off Roishin's face, her eyes. Those eyes bored into hers before they dropped and took in Enori's naked breasts. Enori could hear the slight hitch in her breathing and see the pulse point in her neck throbbing. She ran her hands down along Roishin's sides again, her thumbs grazing the rounded sides of her breasts still cradled in the dress she wore.

She could feel the softness of the material beneath her fingertips and wanted to know the softness of the skin beneath. She saw Roishin's eyes flick upward and felt the warm, salami-scented breath behind her. *Showtime.*

Enori steeled herself as she felt meaty hands cup her breasts from behind. She kept her expression neutral as he squeezed her like a melon. Nothing he did mattered; she had to get this done. She pressed her behind back into him, able to feel that he was definitely enjoying the show. She met Roishin's gaze and, with her eyes, indicated the bed.

Roishin made her way over to it, careful to touch nothing but the bedding. She pulled back the comforter, blanket, and sheets, Enori watching as she reached back to get an idea of just how much clothing this guy still had on. To her surprise, he seemed to be only in his boxer shorts. She could easily feel his excitement pressed up against her lower back and it made her want to gag. But, alas, they had a job to complete. And honestly, the more excited he was, the easier it was to control him.

Turning, she gave him the look that she knew would make him nearly blow his top right there. From the look of rapture on his face, she wasn't far off. She found him disgusting, but she couldn't allow that to show. Instead, she stepped out of first one high heel then the other, never taking her eyes off his. She stepped out of the rest of the dress, leaving her in panties and garters.

He was putty in her hands. Slack-jawed, he took her in and dutifully followed when she grabbed him by the hand and led him to the bed, where Roishin was already lounging on her side, her head resting in her upturned palm and looking every bit the seductress. Her body looked incredible still in the dress.

If Enori could get through this without Roishin

having to take a single stitch off, she would. She urged him to lie on the bed. She noted his hairy back and shoulders and had to swallow down any expression of any kind. He did as silently bade, lying on his back with his boxers tented in his readiness for her.

She slowly hitched her leg over his body, making a show of it for him. His gaze was locked on her breasts. She watched him carefully as she scooted up just enough so she brushed against the bulge in the boxers. She brushed against him a few times, curious of his reaction. His eyes fell closed and his hips began to move a bit.

That was what she needed. Never taking her eyes off his, and continuing the slow brushing, she reached down into her garter where a tiny glass vial was hidden. She eased it out, continuing the slow movement of her hips against the tented material. She sent Roishin a message with her eyes: *Be ready.*

She held the vial as she used her other hand to quietly pull the cork. It didn't make a sound. She positioned the vial in her fingers as she put a little more pressure against him to increase his pleasure, which made it far less likely he'd be remotely concerned about what she was doing.

His mouth opened wider as he groaned deep in his throat. His head pressed back in the pillow as he became lost in the sensations, his Adam's apple bobbing as he swallowed. Enori looked to Roishin and mouthed the countdown as Roishin slowly got into place.

Three. Two. One.

Roishin placed a hand over his eyes and one on his chest to hold him down at the exact instant Enori stuffed the little bottle into his mouth, the contents quickly draining inside before he could make a sound.

She removed the vial so he didn't bite down on the glass—they couldn't risk anything being left behind.

He struggled for only a moment before it began to take effect. Roishin removed her hands and Enori climbed off him and off the bed. She watched him as she quickly tugged her dress back on. He gagged and his eyes flew open wide, staring blankly up at the ceiling as his body convulsed.

By the time Roishin was rezipping her dress, his upper body slammed back onto the bed and then stilled. His eyes became hooded and his body relaxed. A final long sigh escaped his lips and the smell of urine seeped into the air as it soaked his boxers.

Enori's eyes closed for a moment, relieved it was over. Now, they needed to get out. She recorked the empty bottle and tucked it back into her garter.

She used the material of his jacket to pull out his wallet from the pocket and opened it. Looking up at Roishin from where she squatted, she shook her head. "Empty. He never intended to pay those girls."

Roishin sent a disgusted look his way then shook her head. She looked like she was on the verge of a very strong emotion, and they couldn't afford that right now. Enori pushed back to her feet and walked over to her.

"Can you create the door?" she asked softly.

Roishin looked at her. She was pale and a bit shaky, but she nodded, saying nothing.

Chapter Eleven

Absolutely and completely not sure what she was feeling, Roishin was just glad to have a shower. She'd insisted Enori shower first—after all, she did have that man's stench all over her. She washed her own body and face, so glad to get that makeup off. How did women actually wear that stuff on a regular basis?

She pushed her hair back out of her face, now also clean of all the stiff gook the ladies had put in it. A haircut was on her agenda the next day. She'd ask Enori if she could borrow her scissors again.

Enori.

Her eyes closed as she let out a heavy sigh. It was impossible not to compare Enori and Elsie, not as women, but as situations. With Elsie, it had been so easy in that it had been pretty cut and dried for Roishin. She may not have had the words to put to it early on, but she was attracted to her and she liked looking at her. A lot.

She knew what she felt, and what she felt was attraction. Over time that attraction had turned to like and then to love. But it had never been a mystery to her how she felt, she just had to grow into the words and meanings. It had been almost instant for her as a young girl of ten when Elsie had first come into their service.

It had been a new thing for them both, and though a quiet personality, Elsie was incredibly open—truly what you saw is what you got. It made it so easy for Roishin to fall in love with her before she even knew what that meant. She still loved her deeply, and she knew she always would. But that love was changing, morphing into something deeper, yet simpler.

And then there was the situation with Enori. Roishin had always been attracted to her, that much she knew. What wasn't there to be attracted to? She was stunning, almost painfully so. Even her four-year-old self was aware of that on their first meeting.

But the calm, cool, and aloof way about her kept people at bay. Roishin now understood that was the purpose. It wasn't truly who she was. It had become a protective mechanism over her very long lifetime. Hell, she thought as she stepped out from beneath the warm water of the waterfall to dry off. That had probably been perfected as a child lost on the streets of Brittany.

Now, she had all these massively huge feelings rolling around inside her, and their mission tonight hadn't helped that. She was struggling with the entire thing, and she was struggling with the fact that she was struggling. She'd been part of how many over the past more than a year now? Yes, this one was definitely different in that their sole purpose had been to kill a man. She had questions and definitely needed answers. Needed to set her soul and her conscience at rest.

Still, it was more than that. She wasn't ready to put words to it, wasn't ready to fully admit what had bothered her, but she knew she needed to talk it out. Getting dressed in her simple cotton pants and even simpler cotton shirt, she bundled her dirty laundry into her hands and headed across the hall to her own bedroom.

It was late, but she noticed Enori's door was ajar, the light extinguished inside. She'd learned Enori's very subtle ways of communication over the time she'd lived with her. That was her way of letting Roishin know that, though it was late, if she needed to talk, Enori was more than willing.

Considering for a moment, wondering if this could wait until morning, Roishin decided to take her up on it. She dumped her clothing onto her bed and headed to Enori's bedroom. She pushed the door open just enough to see that indeed the other woman was in bed, but she was awake and met Roishin's gaze.

Roishin didn't bother closing the door and instead headed for the bed. To her surprise, Enori slid over by the wall, holding the covers up in invitation. She climbed beneath them and got settled on her back. She could feel Enori's gaze on her, turned to her side and head cradled in her palm.

As always, Enori waited patiently for Roishin to gather her thoughts in order to express them. Finally, she did. She couldn't look at the other woman, but asked, "Why did he have to die?"

"The purpose of Ankou is to right the wrongs. As the God of the Underworld, he does not like to take those who should not be in his realm before their time."

Roishin nodded. "I understand all that, but we essentially murdered a man tonight, Enori." She looked over at her.

"Tony Conway sells weapons, Roishin," she began, never losing her calm. "But he would have gone on to be one of the biggest weapons dealers for a group of Nazis that would have risen in the United States and led to a second Civil War during the second World War."

Roishin could only stare at her, stunned. "Oh," was all she could manage.

"He had to be stopped before it began. Now," she

added, trailing a fingertip over the back of Roishin's hand that rested atop the covers on her own stomach. "We could have targeted him—not a good person—or targeted one of his parents, who did nothing wrong, to stop him from being born."

Roishin considered for a moment, astonished at who that man actually had been or what he could have contributed to. "Wow," she finally said. Though she still had the horrible images in her mind of that man dying, something else was bothering her. "He touched you," she murmured, feeling rather stupid and childish.

"He did. I knew that the best way to get to him was through his insatiable lust for women"—she smirked—"that are not his wife. And," she added, covering Roishin's hand with her own. "I knew it was a way to get him isolated so nobody else got hurt."

"Did…" Roishin had to swallow the bile down that suddenly rose. "Did you like him touching you? Or, touching him?"

Enori slowly shook her head, a look of utter revulsion on her beautiful face. She quirked an eyebrow. "Did you like kissing that woman to distract her and keep her safe when her boyfriend's car blew up because he had made too many enemies?"

"No," Roishin said easily. "It was creepy, honestly, knowing she thought I was a man."

Enori smiled and lightly tapped the tip of Roishin's nose with a fingertip. "Bingo." Her hand cupped Roishin's cheek as she scooted a little bit closer, remaining on her side. "I wanted you there with me tonight so you can learn. But also," she added, fingertips caressing the skin of Roishin's cheek and the side of her neck. "I knew no matter what, you would never let anything happen to me."

Roishin looked into her eyes, painted nearly silver in the moonlight coming in through the window. The air between them grew heavy as the meaning of Enori's words settled over Roishin, the trust she just conveyed in her with that one simple admission.

Reaching up, Roishin's fingers buried themselves in short, blond strands at the back of Enori's head as she urged her down. As they'd been at the beach, her lips were so amazingly soft as they pressed against Roishin's. It was a tentative kiss, but Enori didn't pull away this time, nor did Roishin.

Their lips caressed and sampled, almost a shy, measured introduction. How was it that everything about this woman seemed so accentuated? Her lips, hair, and skin were softer than any Roishin had touched. Her beauty so otherworldly. Her touch so gentle. Yet, underlying all of it, Roishin sensed a deep well of passion in her that Enori was keeping a very tight lid on. She'd seen it flash through those magnificent eyes a couple times, and it had nearly torched Roishin where she'd stood.

It was more than just her playful, seemingly naturally flirtatious and sensual nature, but something else entirely. She'd seen glimpses of it when she'd played with Isabeau or taught her how to swim. She'd seen it when Enori had showed Roishin the beach accommodations she'd chosen for Roishin's family to visit.

She'd seen it when Enori had held Roishin's own daughter, giving her solemn vow to protect her and love her. It was a passion for those she cared about, such as a precocious young princess from Sursha that, duty or not, she'd never given up on. She'd gone so far as to go toe-to-toe against the formidable future king to make her point.

Yes, Roishin realized. She was lovely, she was loyal, and she was passionate and brave. But, in that moment as their lips touched and lightly explored, she also realized that she was just a woman. A woman who had given so much yet had received so little. She was a woman who, in her tentative kiss, was asking to be loved.

This wasn't about sex. This was about connecting and belonging. It was about needing, and needing to be needed for more than just the sum of her beautiful parts. It was about heart, it was about soul. It was about Enori.

After several moments, the kiss came to a natural end. Looking deeply into Roishin's eyes, Enori murmured, "It is getting late. Sleep."

Roishin nodded, though was loath to go. She leaned up and placed a final soft kiss on Enori's lips when she began to lift the covers to move out of the bed. She stopped at the hand on her arm. With one small, almost shy look, Enori scooted in against her and rested her head on Roishin's shoulder.

Eyes falling closed at the exquisite gift she was being given, Roishin wrapped her arms around her and settled in for sleep.

⁂

The next morning when Roishin had asked about Enori's scissors, she'd been shocked when Enori had offered instead for the two of them to spend the day together at a place simply called Downtown. It was a massive shopping promenade, the stalls outside and packed with wares of every need or want.

It reminded Roishin of a much, much larger version of the shopping square near the harbor back home. People of every color and age wandered from stall to stall, some in groups, some in pairs or singles. From Roishin's many missions now, she recognized clothing and styles from all over the world and time spectrum.

The woman strolling next to her was in what amounted to a white sundress with flowing skirt and sandals. She had never seen Enori look more relaxed, her eyes bright and an easy smile upon her lips. Something had happened to her overnight, a transformation of sorts, and Roishin had a hell of a time keeping her eyes off her.

It had little to do with her outer beauty. It was coming from inside, and she was nearly glowing with it. Enori met her gaze, eyebrows raised in question. Roishin shook her head, unable to keep the smile off her own face.

"You're absolutely stunning today," she said. "Something is different about you."

"So," Enori teased. "I am not stunning *every* day?"

Roishin burst into laughter, absolutely loving the playful twinkle in her eyes and almost lightness in her every step and every gesture. "You love boxing me into those corners where I can get myself into trouble, don't you?"

Enori grinned. "Oh, I think you get yourself into trouble all on your own."

Roishin grinned. "Yeah, maybe so."

"Oh! Come." Enori grabbed Roishin's hand and tugged with her to a stall from which amazing smells were emanating. She smiled at the woman behind the counter. "Two, please."

"What is this?" Roishin asked, watching as the woman dropped something into a large vat of sizzling something. It smelled sweet yet cakey.

"It is called a funnel cake," Enori explained. "She will sprinkle the tops with powdered sugar." She grinned up at Roishin. "Heaven."

Roishin quirked an eyebrow. "You, Miss Fruit Lady, have been holding out on me."

Enori gave her a look that made certain parts of Roishin's body twitch in sympathy. Or, was that anticipation? "You never asked."

"Here you are, ladies," the woman said, holding out two paper plates with what looked somewhat like a waffle but not really. And, sure enough, it was sprinkled with powdered sugar.

"Thank you." Enori took the plates, handing one to Roishin and moving away from the stall to make room for others standing in line.

Roishin studied the huge fried treat on her plate, watching to see how Enori tackled it. She used her fingers to pick little pieces off it. It was then that Roishin realized it was many little pieces of dough that had been tossed in and essentially welded together in the frying process. She followed her example, eyes closing as the first bite melted in her mouth, sweet and wonderful flavors bursting on her tongue.

"Oh my god," she muttered around the bite in her mouth. She opened her eyes to see a very pleased-looking Enori enjoying her own funnel cake. "If Millie got hold of this," Roishin said, pointing at her plate with a piece of the treat that she held between her fingers. "Trouble in Sursha."

Enori chuckled as she nodded, mouth full of food. They began to wander again. "Believe it or not, some version of this has been around for nearly a thousand years." Enori licked a bit of powdered sugar off her thumb. "This is just the most modern version."

"Wow," Roishin muttered. "See, we need to go on food missions."

Enori glanced over at her. "So, instead of stealing clothing or books, we steal recipes?"

"Yes!"

Enori looked at her, amusement in her eyes. She reached over and used a finger to wipe at a bit of runaway powdered sugar at the corner of Roishin's lip. Eyes still on Roishin, she tucked that sugary fingertip into her own mouth before turning back to her own treat.

Roishin wanted to groan. Her body was responding to everything Enori did today, and she felt like a walking, talking livewire. To get her mind off… well, *Enori*, she asked, "Why did you bring me here when I asked about the scissors?"

Enori nodded with her head that Roishin should follow her, her mouth filled with another bite of her food. The wide-open space they'd been walking through, with dirt or gravel at their feet and stalls made of wood, turned off to the right. The dirt gradually changed to what Roishin had learned were called cobblestone streets. None existed in Sursha, but she'd seen some in her missions and had certainly read about them.

The more basic wooden stalls gave way to actual brick-and-mortar shops. Her mouth was agape as they seemed to have literally stepped into an entirely different time in history. In the large plate glass windows she saw modern clothing displayed, some of which she'd had to wear during missions. She even saw a large, lit marquis with flashing light bulbs chasing each other around it. *The Wizard of Oz*, it read.

She looked to Enori with a question in her eyes.

"Movie theater," Enori explained.

Roishin gasped as she stopped and stared up at the tall building nestled in a line of many others along the street. "Judy Garland," she whispered, remembering reading about the movie and the young actress and singer who had starred in it.

"Would you like to go?"

Eyes wide, Roishin looked at her. "Can we?" she asked, feeling like such a kid in that moment.

Enori studied her, head tilted slightly to the side. There was almost a dreamy look in her eyes. Finally, she nodded. "Of course. Let us get you your haircut, then we can. All right?"

❧❧❧❧

"I am the cherry-pop guild, the cherry-pop guild, the cherry-pop guild…" Roishin sang quietly as she creeped into Enori's bedroom the next morning, a large bowl of the other woman's favorite fruit in her hand.

Though reluctantly, once they'd arrived back home after a long, sundrenched day, they'd parted ways and slept in their own beds after a soft good-night kiss. She grinned when Enori peeked an eye at her as Roishin climbed onto the bed.

The other eye opened and an amused-looking Enori watched her. "I knew that movie was a bad idea," she muttered.

Roishin grinned, stretching out on her side as she set the bowl of fruit on the bed in front of her. She plucked one of the succulent little fruits with her fingers and held it in front of Enori's mouth. Leaning slightly forward, Enori took it between her teeth, sucking it into her mouth. Roishin watched, mesmerized.

"Feel better?" Enori asked, reaching over and running her fingers through the much shorter haircut Roishin was sporting.

Roishin nodded, accepting the cherry held to her own lips. "I do," she muttered around the fruit. She chewed then swallowed. "Thank you so much for yesterday," she said softly. "I had so much fun with you."

Enori's smile was easy and free, just like the previous day. She popped another cherry into her mouth and nodded. "I had a wonderful time, too."

"Do you go there that often?"

Enori shook her head, holding another cherry between thumb and forefinger. "It is, however, where I got your percolator for that horrible stuff you insist on drinking." She grinned.

"Well, well," Roishin drawled. "Lookie that. I think we need to go back and check out more appliances."

Enori raised an eyebrow, tossing a cherry into her mouth.

Chapter Twelve

Roishin's stomach was in knots as she wandered around. It was a really beautiful room, all wood paneling and coffered ceilings, all the gorgeous books in the bookshelves that lined the walls. She did, however, avoid those. She had this image in her head of reaching for one and shackles suddenly appearing and forever tethering her to the damn thing.

She smirked at her own musings as she wandered over to the window seat. She'd never seen such a huge stained glass window before and had her neck craned to try and take in the entire thing when she heard someone enter. Turning her head, she saw the Mystic walk to the center of the room and then stop.

He looked as he had every single day while she'd been in the Underground. Except now, as he studied her, hands clasped behind his back, rather than the contemplative scowl that seemed to reside there, he sported a very soft smile. Might she call it…fatherly?

"Um," she said, unable to meet his eyes. When she'd only known him as the pesky librarian whom she could banter with about books, she'd felt comfortable around him, comfortable to pick on him—even though she knew it would earn her another two books to read that day.

He walked in a slow circle around her, seeming to look her over from top to bottom. She stayed put, though clocked his progress visually as she moved her head. Finally, he stopped once he stood before her again.

"I am deeply proud of you," he said, his voice serious and quiet. "You have become all I hoped for and so much more. So much of that, of course, is due to Fallon and Cateline." He smiled. "And, Enori."

She nodded in acknowledgment of what he said. Clearing her throat, she said, "Four and a half years." She shrugged, shaking her head. "Why didn't you tell me?"

"Because you needed to focus on who *you* were, not who *I* was. Am."

That didn't fully cut it for her, but she'd let it go for now. "What do I call you?"

"What would you like to call me?" he countered. He full-out belly laughed at the look she gave him. "Never mind. Ankou is fine." He reached out and lightly touched her arm. "Come. Sit with me by the fire." She followed him to the two large, comfy chairs, taking the one he didn't. "What do you think of this room?" he asked.

She looked around, taking it in again. "It's really beautiful,"

He nodded. "Enori's favorite." He smiled again, that same fatherly smile. "More than once I came in here to find her curled up in the window seat reading." He eyed her. "Not in the past year or so, though."

She snorted. "Yeah, probably because she was afraid she'd come home and I'd have wrecked the house." Again, that wonderful laugh, which she couldn't help but grin at. "You know," she said once he began to calm down. "The look on your face just then, like you really care about her. Like a father."

He nodded, also sobering. "I do. Very much. Took her under my wing when she was but ten years old."

"So," Roishin said slowly. "If you had Enori, why did you create a daughter?"

He studied her as he stroked his grizzled chin. Finally, he let out a heavy breath. "I created you for two reasons, Roishin. One," he said, holding up a meaty finger. "I needed a second who could carry the weight of the Order and all that entails. Two." He added a second finger. "A mate for Enori."

She stared at him, her blood going cold. "What?" She slowly stood from the chair, though had to hold on to it for balance. "What?"

He said nothing, simply remained seated and calm.

"You…" She almost couldn't even think straight to get her words out. "You…manipulated me? This situation, to come here, leave what I know, to move in with Enori?"

"No," he said simply.

"So, *she* did, then," Roishin said, her voice weak as she felt her heart break.

"No," he said again.

"Liar."

She felt the sting of tears behind her eyes as she pushed away from the chair and turned her back to him. She ran her hand through her hair, which made her want to throw up as it made her think of the amazing day they'd shared Downtown. Where she'd visited an actual and real hair salon and got to play with the fun chair.

"Roishin."

She ignored him, about to create a door to get the hell out, when his voice boomed.

"Roishin!"

Her eyes widened as the entire room literally shook. She stopped where she stood and slowly turned to face him. He was standing next to his chair, his gaze laser focused on her.

"Sit. Down."

Without question, she did as told. Her entire system felt out of whack from that, as though her entire skeletal structure had been shaken loose from its moorings. She felt nauseous but sat. He also retook his seat.

"Enori knows none of this, nor did I want her to. She has done her duty as she's been asked to do it thus far. *She* was the one who suggested you stay with her, Roishin. She knew how hard everything had been on you, taking you from your family so young, all of it. She did that because Enori is the kindest, best soul you'll ever find." He smirked. "Even if she doesn't always see it."

Roishin said nothing, unable to truly think, partly because, she assumed, the massive amount of energy he'd loosed in that one word, and partly because she had no idea how to feel.

"She's always cared for you, Roishin. Since the moment she knew of the plan for your being. What is happening between the two of you now is *because* of the two of you." He shook his head. "It has nothing to do with me, other than your existence."

She studied him, looking for any sign of deception or manipulation. "What do you want with us?" she asked slowly, uncertain and a bit nervous.

"What your great-grandmother and namesake should have been doing all this time. For you both, you *and* Enori, to rule with me," he said. "I have been grooming Enori for a very, very long time. You were the final piece."

She sat there quietly, absorbing all that she'd been told. "Am I supposed to tell her this?" she asked. "Enori."

He shrugged. "If you wish. But just know that the two of you are moving toward each other naturally, Roishin. No other force is behind that." He smiled. "It's happened in its own time, just as love should."

Chewing on her bottom lip, she looked into the flames that danced in the huge fireplace. Finally, she gave him a side glance. "I have to thank you for actually giving me full answers on all this today." She smirked. "If you'd done the riddle thing, pretty sure you'd have a door in your head right now." She couldn't help but smile as once again, that belly laugh filled the room.

"Well," he finally said, slapping his hands on his thighs. "I have someone here who is very excited to see you."

Her brows furrowed. "Who?"

The door nestled in with the bookcases was pushed open and a lovely young woman wearing simple jeans and a women's T-shirt entered. Her hair was dark brown and pulled back in a ponytail. The moment she set eyes on Roishin, her dark eyes lit up and she hurried over to the slowly standing woman.

Roishin was nearly bowled over. She caught the woman but had to take a couple steps backward in order not to fall on her behind. Steadying herself, she returned the hug, hoping there would be an introduction and explanation coming forthwith.

"Thank you," the woman said into the hug.

Roishin looked over to Ankou, hoping for a little help. He returned her gaze, amused. Giving a final squeeze, Roishin turned her focus back to the woman who was slowly releasing her from the death grip. Stepping back but keeping her hands on Roishin's arms, she smiled at her.

"It's because of you that I'm here, Roishin." She squeezed her arms before dropping her hands. "I cannot thank you enough."

It took a moment but then Roishin's eyes flew open. "Ava?" The beautiful smile and nod she received sent her gathering the woman back into her arms again. "Oh, man," she said. "*So* glad to see you."

Finally, they parted, Roishin looking the young woman over, stunned at how different she looked. Sure, the clothing and the hair, but mostly, her eyes. The woman she'd seen before in Washington, DC on her very first mission…those dark eyes had been half-dead, the soul within giving up.

This woman before her, she was alive, literally and figuratively. "I've been looking so forward to seeing you again," she said. "I wanted to be able to thank you, Roishin. I would really love to be able to spend a little time with you, talk to you."

"Of course."

Ava absolutely beamed.

"Actually," Ankou said, joining the two women. He placed a hand on a shoulder of each. "I want to send the three of you, you two and Enori, to stay at a location I've selected." He looked at Roishin. "Ava has skills that I want you to learn, and Roishin, you and Enori will be working with Ava on some things from your end."

Roishin nodded. "All right. Does Enori know this?"

"She does." He smiled at both women in turn. "Very soon, you will reunite and begin to train."

Roishin reached the house she shared with Enori, not at all sure what to think. She'd been able to push what she'd been told aside and focus on Ava, who was truly a lovely soul. She'd been glad to spend some time with her and looked forward to training with her and Enori. But, now back at the stone cottage, it all came back to her.

Enori wasn't home, and Roishin wasn't sure if that was a good or a bad thing. She also wasn't sure whether to say anything or not. She'd heard that term *made for each other*, sure. And, she could say with complete confidence that it truly fit her parents. But this—she and Enori—turned that phrase on its head. She truly *had* been made for Enori. What did that really mean? Ankou claimed there had been no manipulation or magic done since her birth, and she had to believe him.

But, beforehand? Maybe he stuck in his magic wand and said, "Abracadabra, she's gonna love ya. Shazam!"

She walked to the kitchen and went to prepare herself some coffee, but the percolator wasn't there. In its place was a more modern coffee maker like the one Roishin had been gawking at in Downtown a few days before. She smiled, caressing the black smoothness of the body and clear glass carafe.

She noticed there was a note atop it. Grabbing it, she held it to read the beautiful, scrawling penmanship:

Yes, I am feeding your addiction for this atrocious stuff. I hope you can learn how to use this, as I do not have a clue. The man at the store said you needed these, what he called filters. I told him this was a good thing, as

you do not possess a filter.
	Enori

Roishin laughed outright at that, her heart swelling. She studied the handwriting, so beautiful and delicate, like the woman who had produced it. She'd loved that woman her entire life, her angel. The woman who had come to her in her dreams, so many times. A woman *she* hadn't been ready for. Yet.

Elsie had come into her life to be that person who could help Roishin bridge that gap and grow into who she needed to be to be ready for Enori at the right time. She'd been the one to hold her hand from puberty on into womanhood, to teach her how to love. They'd been that guidepost for each other, and now it was time to let go and walk on her own.

This new knowledge in her heart, she went into the cold storage that acted as regular storage as well. There, she found the box the coffee maker had come in and the instructions tucked inside of it. Holding them in her hands, she wandered back into the kitchen to find Enori walking through the front door.

Standing there, Roishin looked over at her. She was frozen in place, struck as if for the first time seeing her. Enori looked as she did every day, but something was truly different. When Enori, who was carrying a couple bolts of fabric, stopped and met her gaze, something inside Roishin clicked into place.

Yes. She now absolutely knew she'd been made for Enori—and Enori had been made for her long before Roishin had even been a thought. She absently set the little directions booklet on the counter and walked over to her. Enori watched her progress, looking unsure.

Without a word, Roishin closed the front door.

She walked back over to Enori and took the items from her hands, placing them on the love seat. She cupped Enori's face with both hands. Grinning, she said, "Thank you for the Mr. Coffee. And no," she added, shaking her head. "I do not have a filter."

Enori smiled, looking relieved, though a bit of nervousness had entered her expression. Her eyes closed when Roishin kissed her, her hands lightly gripping Roishin's biceps as her face was still lovingly held. She sighed when Roishin gently swiped her upper lip with her tongue, asking for permission.

It was Roishin's turn to sigh at the first feel of Enori's tongue against her own. Her hand slid into soft blond hair as Enori's hands slid over Roishin's sides and to her back to grip the backs of her shoulders. This pressed their bodies together, which made them both sigh. As the kiss deepened, Roishin knew she was home, even as she stood in the house she'd shared with the woman in her arms for more than a year.

The hand that was still on Enori's face reveled in the softness of her skin as she traced along her jaw and down the delicate structure of her neck, where she rested her hand. The feel of Enori's tongue, the taste of her mouth, the little sighs that escaped into their kiss… It was what she'd been waiting for her entire life.

The kiss slowed and came to a natural end, both of them left breathing heavily. She smoothed her hands down Enori's neck, along her shoulders, and down her sides until she reached her hips. Resting them there, she looked into Enori's gaze.

"Can I ask you something?"

"Of course." Enori snaked her arms up until her fingers clasped behind Roishin's neck.

"Have you always felt drawn to me? Even when I was younger."

Enori's head tilted slightly in thought as the fingers of one hand began to play absently in Roishin's hair, sending a little thrill through her system. Finally, she met Roishin's gaze. "Yes." She smiled. "I used to think it was strange, this child on my mind. Worrying about you."

"That day when I was four…the rabbit."

Enori nodded, smiling as she seemed to call up the memory Roishin spoke of. "You were so upset."

Roishin nodded. "Hey, I had just accidentally shot a bunny."

Enori's smile was beautiful as she looked up at Roishin with adoring eyes. "And you brought it back."

"Did you come to me because Ankou told you to?" Roishin asked, trying to understand all of it. An awkward time, sure, but she needed to know.

"No. He had me pop in on you from time to time to give him a report, but that day, I felt you. I felt how profoundly upset you were." She caressed the side of Roishin's face as if wanting to soothe her even now. "I suspected what you were capable of, so figured it was a wonderful time to try."

Roishin quirked an eyebrow. "And, if you'd been wrong?"

Enori gave her the sweetest smile. "We probably would not be standing here right now."

Roishin grinned. "I was always drawn to you, too," she admitted. "I used to see you in my dreams, called you my angel. I had no other word for you."

"It was the easiest way to check on you," Enori said. "Talk to you, make sure you were okay, and see what you were understanding about yourself."

Roishin smirked. "Still working on that one." She could feel the heat of Enori's body pressed to her and her hands tightened their grip on her hips, gently urging them into her own.

Enori's random combing through Roishin's hair began to slow and become more of a caress. Her fingernails ran lightly along the back of Roishin's neck, making her gasp. Their lips were mere inches apart.

"Roishin?" Enori whispered.

"Yes?"

"Will you come upstairs with me?"

Chapter Thirteen

Roishin said nothing, nothing more to say. Taking her hand, Enori led the way up the stairs and to her bedroom. Once there, she released Roishin's hand and pulled the covers down from the bed. Watching with her heart in her throat, Roishin waited for what would come next. She felt, ironically, impotent in that moment.

Once her task was finished, Enori turned back to Roishin. Looking her in the eyes, she took the hem of the simple tunic shirt Roishin wore and eased it up her torso, Roishin lifting her arms so it could be removed. Garment tossed to the floor, Enori removed the simple, bra-like garment Roishin wore, it too meeting a similar fate to the shirt.

Enori looked over the flesh that had been exposed, including Roishin's breasts. Her hands rested against the warm skin of Roishin's sides as she initiated another kiss. This one was slow and deeply sensual. Her hands found Roishin's breasts and cupped them, garnering a sigh from Roishin in the process. Soft hands massaged her.

Her own hands on the move, Roishin smoothed down the soft, flowing material of Enori's dress, like a spun cloud at her fingertips. She slowly pulled the material up until the skirt portion was gathered in her hands. The kiss broke just long enough for her to ease the garment up and over Enori's head.

The image of Enori naked and standing on the

rock ledge in the Underground waterfall the day Roishin left that place had been burned into Roishin's brain for two years, let alone that day not long ago when she'd walked in on her in the shower. The utter perfection and magnificence that was Enori stood before her, and it stole her breath away.

She stared down at the beautiful breasts, erect nipples rosy and tempting. Her pale flesh looked so soft, Roishin wanting to touch every inch of it and nuzzle it with her face. Her mouth watered and her body ached for her. Her eyes closed when Enori's mouth found her neck, head moving to the side to give her access.

It was strange that they were in the position they'd effectively been in the night of the Conway mission. But this time it was just them, and this time it was *real.* The hot mouth on her flesh made her sigh, Roishin's hands working their way up the softness of Enori's naked back. She could feel the warmth of Enori's front against hers, her breasts pressing against her.

As Enori licked a trail down from Roishin's ear to the side of the neck, she unlaced Roishin's trousers, movements slow and deliberate. The leather was pushed down over her hips and as far down as Enori could reach.

"Sit," Enori whispered against Roishin's lips, getting her turned so all she had to do was fall back onto the bed. Once she did, Enori went to work on her boots and pulled the leather pants all the way off.

Once she was freed, Roishin pushed herself back to lay correctly on the bed, head on the pillow. Enori climbed atop her, both moaning at the incredible pleasure of their full nakedness touching for the first time. Roishin accepted her into her embrace, groaning at the kiss she received. It was fiery and seemed to be loaded with that passion that Roishin had felt within the other woman.

As they kissed, Enori nudged Roishin's legs apart, which opened for her. She settled herself between them, making Roishin groan from both the incredible pleasure of having her pressed against her most intimately, and how wet she was. Enori began to slowly rock against her.

Roishin pulled her knees closer to her body to open herself even more. Her hands trailed down over Enori's back and down to her glorious behind and back up again. The kiss came to an end as they were both breathing entirely too heavily to continue. Enori stayed in her personal space, hooded eyes that held the skies above looking down into Roishin's.

There was so much in that gaze: desire, need, and so much love. No doubt it was all in Roishin's eyes as well, as she felt every single one of those. Roishin's eyes fell closed and her lips fell open as her orgasm began to build and finally, with a loud gasp, crashed through her. She held on to Enori tightly, who groaned into Roishin's neck as she, too, released.

They held each other for a moment as they tried to get their breathing back under control. Roishin could feel Enori's breasts heaving against hers. She smoothed her hands all over her back and shoulders, calming her. Finally, Enori raised her head and looked down at Roishin. She cupped her face and just studied her.

"You have no idea how much it terrifies me to say this," she whispered.

Saying nothing, Roishin continued the soothing caresses of Enori's back. She met Enori's gaze, letting her know she was listening.

"I love you, Roishin. I truly do."

Roishin lifted her head just enough to leave a long, lingering kiss on soft lips. "I love you, Enori," she whispered against them. "I always have."

Something changed in Enori at that moment—Roishin saw it in her eyes. She'd already been opening up to her more and more over the many months, and especially since their time at the beach. But right then and there, Roishin saw the final block fall away from Enori's walls, so carefully built and now broken apart, piece by piece.

The kiss Roishin received was unlike any she'd gotten before from this precious woman. It spoke of a woman freed from chains Roishin didn't understand but certainly had felt over the years she'd known Enori. The restraint was gone, and in its place was a woman free. Unleashed was the true spirit of this magnificent creature who Roishin called home.

Leaving Roishin's lips, Enori explored her neck with her mouth. She sighed into her task, seeming to relish every inch. She made her way steadily down. Roishin's eyes closed and her back arched when her right breast was cupped in a hand and her left was taken into a hot mouth. Her arousal, moments ago spent, was building again as Enori's tongue ran across a rigid nipple.

Roishin was getting lost in the sensations, her hips lightly rocking of their own accord. She could feel Enori's stomach pressed against her and tried to get any purchase she could. Not having any of that, Enori moved away just enough to leave Roishin groaning in frustration.

Chuckling, Enori moved to her other breast, giving her a look that could melt a glacier. "Patience, my love," she murmured before giving the right breast the same treatment as the left.

Roishin tried to just focus on what that talented mouth was doing rather than what her body was begging for. She was a little confused when Enori left her breast and began to continue kissing her way down. Lifting her head, she watched her leave a hot trail down the center line of her torso until Enori moved her body farther down the bed.

She gasped, realizing what was about to happen. She'd read something of the sort in some of the books over those years but had no idea how it was done and certainly not what it felt like. But, as Enori trailed kisses first along the inside of one raised thigh and then the other, her head fell back to the pillow. She was so open, felt so exposed, but oh lord was she pulsing.

It felt like her very heartbeat was located between her legs, and it began to beat even faster when Enori turned her attention there. Almost holding her breath, Roishin had no idea what to expect. It didn't take long to find out as Enori's tongue made a long, slow swipe up through swollen folds in the volcanic wetness that was the very center of Roishin's world in that moment. She gasped when that tongue reached her most sensitive place.

Roishin's hand found its way to the back of Enori's head as it moved and bobbed slowly between her spread thighs. She was lost, absolutely lost in the sensations Enori's mouth created outside and the ones her heart created inside. She almost felt overwhelmed but wouldn't stop it for the world.

As her pleasure began to rise, her hips rolled with the rhythmic licking and sucking. A groan began low in Roishin's throat, not even realizing she was making a sound until it grew louder as her pleasure grew. Her breasts were heaving with her increased breathing. And, when Enori wrapped her arms around Roishin's spread thighs, Roishin's entire upper body left the mattress as she was sucked hard and a tongue batted ruthlessly at her.

Her release pulled a loud cry from her lips as she slammed back to the bed, her neck and back arching with the intensity of it. Desperately trying to catch her breath, Roishin was only vaguely aware that Enori had left a kiss between her legs before moving back up to lie next to her. She cradled Roishin against her, creasing her hair and her face.

She didn't even realize that tears were trailing down the sides of her face until she felt soft lips kissing them away. It took several moments, but finally Roishin fell back to earth and wrapped her arms around Enori. For a long time they just held each other, basking in what they'd just done and what was happening.

Enori brushed back some hair off Roishin's forehead, and Roishin studied Enori's face, just looking at her, taking her in. Her eyes, she couldn't look away from them. Certainly, a beautiful color, but in that moment, it didn't matter. She realized that she'd seen a more guarded version of that look aimed at her several times.

She pushed Enori to her back, moving with her. She held her upper body weight off the smaller woman as she rested on a forearm. As she continued to look into those eyes, Roishin's free hand wandered. She needed to touch her, to bring this angel of her soul into her reality and the very bed she was lying in.

Her hand slid down along Enori's side, her thumb brushing over the rounded side of her right breast as it went. Down over her hip and to her thigh until her fingers slid to the underside of it. She eased that leg to raise, which it did as Enori bent her knee. Her fingernails trailed back up along the side of her thigh and her side, satisfied to see a little shiver run through Enori's body.

She cupped her breast, which felt so right in her hand. Initiating a soft, slow kiss, Roishin brushed her thumb over the hard nipple, loving the wonderful little noises that produced from Enori's lips into their kiss. She felt fingers lazily playing in her hair and let out a little noise of her own. Roishin honestly could have kissed her forever, and once she realized the slick warmth upon Enori's tongue and lips that she felt and tasted was her own desire, it made Roishin want to kiss so many places on this woman's body.

She tugged and lightly twisted on the nipple between her fingers, Enori's back arching a bit in invitation. It was an invitation Roishin gladly accepted. Leaving one final kiss on soft lips, she moved her mouth to explore all that was Enori. Her skin was so soft, so warm, and she loved the taste.

"I'm surprised you don't taste like cherries," she teased as she left Enori's neck and ran a tongue along her collarbone. She smiled at the throaty chuckle that earned her.

When she finally reached the gorgeous breasts with their pale rose nipples, she was in heaven. She'd always found women's breasts entirely too fascinating and beautiful. In her time and in Sursha, they were hidden or even flattened within a woman's garb, so to see them before her, there for her to touch and taste, it was glorious. Especially Enori's breasts.

But, as much as she was enjoying them, and from the noises she was making, it was quite clear

Enori was enjoying it. The amount of wetness that was being painted upon Roishin's lower belly that was cradled between Enori's thighs told her she was needed elsewhere. The scent of Enori's need was far sweeter than cherries to Roishin's nose.

She had no idea what she was doing but wanted to give the same pleasure she had been given. Reluctantly, she left Enori's breasts and continued down, exploring every inch of pale, creamy flesh she came to. The scent of arousal grew stronger, its warm, spicy smell drawing her in like a bee to nectar.

As patient as she was with everything else, Enori showed Roishin the way with gentle nudges of fingers to Roishin's head or her own hips until Roishin was where she needed her to be. The first taste had Roishin sighing in absolute pleasure at what she was doing.

She knew this could easily become an addiction, largely because of the wonderful and deeply erotic noises that sounded from Enori's lips as Roishin made love to her with her mouth. And, once she found her stride, she began to listen with her body: What did Enori need? How fast, or should she slow down? Did she need her to suck or lick?

She read the body beneath her like a book, allowing their connection to lead the way. It was the most beautiful sound in the world as Enori's breathing quickened, little whimpers and moans high pitched and sounding more and more desperate. Following Enori's example from earlier, Roishin wrapped her arms around hips that began to undulate constantly and more aggressively.

Finally, a loud, guttural cry erupted into the room, Enori's passion released and flowing. Roishin hummed in satisfaction as she held on. She didn't stop until a hand weakly pushed at her head. Releasing Enori from her mouth, Roishin's entire being was buzzing as she climbed back up the body which had pretty much become mush.

Enori's eyes were closed and lips were open as she took in long, deep breaths. Roishin sat up just long enough to pull the covers up and over them as she cuddled in next to the woman she'd just made love with. Strangely, she needed to be held, so she rested her head on Enori's shoulder and scooted her body as close to the warm one next to her as she could.

Enori immediately pulled her in, wrapping her arms around her even as she still seemed to be trying to catch her breath. Roishin buried her face in a warm neck, closing her eyes as she inhaled all that was Enori. She smiled at the kiss she received on her forehead.

"I love you," Roishin murmured. She smiled when she felt the strong arms that held her tighten.

"I love you, Roishin."

"Bet you never thought a simple Mr. Coffee would get you here, did you?" Roishin's head popped up as she looked down at Enori. "Did you just giggle?"

Enori shook her head even though she was still grinning.

"Liar," Roishin murmured against her lips, leaving a kiss there.

"Well," Enori said, playing along. "If that is all it took, clearly I was shooting too low with the percolator."

Charmed, Roishin cradled her head in a palm as she looked down at the other woman, her body still snuggled up against her. "Can I tell you something Ankou told me today?" she asked softly, feeling Enori had a right to truly understand just how much Ankou loved and valued her. Roishin understood that now.

"Of course," Enori said, growing serious also. "How did that go, by the way?"

"It went really well." Roishin grinned. "Eventually."

Enori's eyebrows shot up in curiosity, but she remained silent. Instead, she entwined her fingers with those that rested on her stomach.

"He truly loves you, Enori. Believes in you, trusts you." Her gaze trailed over Enori's face, taking in every detail, every feature. "He has plans for you—you may or may not know this."

"For me?" Enori said, brows furrowing.

Nodding, Roishin leaned down and left a small kiss on that troubled brow. "Aye," she whispered against it before lifting her head again. "You see, he wanted to see you happy, to see you loved and to give you a partner to rule right along with him."

Enori stared up at her, so much going through her eyes: confusion, consideration of Roishin's words, perhaps some understanding and shock. "Wait…"

Roishin nodded. She eased her fingers away from Enori's and used them to lightly trail along her jaw. "The night you gave that rose to my parents, you set in motion your own future, Enori. And," she added, seeing anger beginning to bring storms to the beautiful skies that were her eyes. "All this has happened naturally, organically. He didn't make this happen." She grinned, indicating the two of them naked together in Enori's bed. "Trust me, I reamed him on that point."

"All those questions you were asking me earlier," Enori murmured.

Roishin nodded. "I needed to know how you saw all this. But honestly, looking into your eyes, I knew this was about love. Not the musings of a god." She leaned down and kissed her. "We were meant to be together. He just placed us in time where we could find each other."

Enori urged Roishin to move atop her, which she did. As they continued to kiss, slow and lazy, Roishin insinuated a thigh between Enori's spreading legs. Pressed against growing need, Enori's own thigh gave Roishin the pressure she needed. Their hips began to move slowly together as they kissed.

The sounds of their immense wetness and the bed creaking beneath them were the only noises in the small room. It was beautiful and it was a deeper connection than anything they'd done previously. It felt good, yes, but this was about that final tie of body, heart, and soul all bundled into one, supported by two women.

Roishin felt Enori's tongue gliding against her own, their shared tastes in that kiss. She felt their breasts pressed together and the warmth of Enori's stomach against her own. She felt her hot desire against her thigh even as she painted her own upon Enori's. They held on to each other as a slow but powerful release hit them both.

Moans and whimpers were eaten up in their kiss, heavy breathing, and shared pleasure. Finally, Roishin lifted out of the kiss but rested her forehead against Enori's, who cradled Roishin's head in her hands, holding them together.

Nothing was said, no need to. They were one.

Chapter Fourteen

Elsie looked around, making sure everything was perfect. It wasn't that she cared, it was that she didn't want her nor the servants to hear any complaints. The bed linens had been changed since his "be ready"-via-note appearance two months before. Elsie had taken Isla's advice, and it had gotten her out of her wifely duties during that visit. She'd definitely been grateful.

Now, here they were again, though she had no idea how long he planned to stay this time. Sometimes she suspected that he came home at all simply to make his parents happy. He'd make an appearance as Prince Garratt only to head off again as Squadron Leader Garratt, a title Elsie was pretty sure he preferred.

The thing was, she honestly didn't blame him if his heart wasn't in this, but why didn't he just say so? Put everyone out of their eggshell-walking misery, including, no doubt, Garratt himself. She thought it was all just ludicrous, but who was she? Satisfied that the servants had, as per usual, done a wonderful job, she left the prince's chambers and headed to her own.

"Thank you, Agnes," she said, smiling at her lady-in-waiting, who had returned from giving Millie a message regarding dinner.

"Aye, milady." She gave Elsie a little smirk. "She asked if you wanted extra carrots put into tonight's dish."

A bark of laughter escaped Elsie's lips. "What did you say?"

Agnes shrugged nonchalantly. "I told her no doubt Mariota would still appreciate them."

Elsie grinned, shaking her head as she and Agnes headed into the boudoir to get her undressed. She had a fitting for a couple new dresses with Isla coming up before it was time to get ready for Garratt's return. When Elsie had been pregnant, she'd craved carrots so much that it had become the castle joke amongst the kitchen crew—and even the princess herself.

Well, one day Garratt had thrown an absolute fit, commanding the orange vegetable never be served again, that he was sick of them. Obviously, his outburst had not been headed, simply left off his plate and served to him far less frequently than a pregnant woman's predictable cravings after the birth.

They got the princess undressed down to her chemise. It was a bit embarrassing, as not long after giving birth to her daughter, Elsie's body had essentially gone back to pre-baby proportions, all save for her breasts. Still nursing, they were swollen on an otherwise somewhat small-framed woman.

So, the dresses she'd had before Mariota no longer fit in the bust, yet the dresses made for her pregnancy and after no longer fit at all. Yet again, Isla had been called to the rescue. Agnes finished with Elsie's dress then took her leave with a bow, and Elsie was left alone.

She felt so uncomfortable and honestly would be glad once she could stop breastfeeding and allow the milk production to dry up. She loved her daughter dearly, but she was definitely tired of that aspect of things. She'd been told by several of the castle servants who were mothers that a year would be a good time to stop.

For now, Mariota had been fed, changed, and was down for a nap. Any moment, Isla would arrive.

The seasons were changing, and it would start cooling down at night soon. She glanced to her bed, wondering if perhaps it was time to ask the servants to start getting winter bedding out and washed for the season. That thought was pulled out of her head when there was a knock to her chamber door.

"Come in," she called, loud enough to be heard through the thick wood door. She smiled when a moment later Isla appeared, stepping in and closing the door behind her. "Welcome."

"Thank you." Isla gave her a winning smile, all her regular wares with her to perform her job with her usual speed and efficiency. "How's the princess and the princess?" she asked, looking at Elsie then the cradle where the baby slept.

Chuckling, Elsie nodded. "Big princess is fine," she said, indicating herself. "And, so is little princess. She must be growing," she added, moving to where she knew Isla liked to work, where the light was better for her measurements. "Ate like a little beggar."

Isla smiled, setting her measuring rod and parchment on the bed. "She's so precious, Elsie. Do you want to have any more?"

Elsie felt her stomach drop at that question. "Actually," she said softly. "I need to ask you a bit of a favor for tonight."

Isla paused unrolling some fabric as she gave Elsie her full attention. "All right."

Letting out a heavy sigh and unable to meet her friend's gaze, Elsie said, "I know Garratt wants to spend some time with me tonight." She lightly fingered the ell measure on the bed. "I can't put him off forever, Isla. So, I figure just get it over with." When she heard nothing, she looked up to see that Isla was looking down at her hands and the fabric she played with. "Can I ask you to take Mariota for a little bit? I don't...I just don't..."

Isla looked up at her. "Of course," she said automatically. "I completely understand, Elsie." She reached over and took one of the princess's hands. Elsie's fingers curled around hers, their gazes meeting. "Regardless of how young she is, I wouldn't want my daughter in here, either, during...that."

Elsie nodded. "Thank you. I know it won't last long," she said with a smirk. "But, still."

"When do you expect him?"

"My guess is after dinner. That seems to be his time. I guess then after he can go do whatever he does with the rest of his night." She looked away again, feeling...well, she wasn't entirely sure. *Embarrassed* was a word that came to mind.

"Elsie?" Isla said softly, taking a step toward her. When Elsie met her gaze, she said, "It's okay. Unfortunately, regardless of why a marriage happens, this is part of it." She brought up the hand that didn't hold Elsie's and brushed back a few strands of golden hair that had fallen out of Elsie's updo when she had undressed. She gave her a gentle smile. "I guess, think of it this way. If a pregnancy results, you won't have to deal with him for nearly another year."

Elsie grinned. "I like the way you think."

She looked into Isla's eyes, so warm and kind yet filled with a spark of life that could be so engaging. One second the dressmaker was firing off quips and the next being so kind, her voice softening and making everything seem okay, again. She looked down at their joined hands and realized she felt the calluses of otherwise soft hands. Calluses like she'd once had, calluses of a hardworking woman.

She took that hand in both of hers, opening the palm. She held the hand with one of her own while using a finger from the other to lightly trace the calluses. "I see you, you know," she said softly, watching her finger. For reasons she couldn't quite understand, she was unable to look at Isla's face. "You work so hard and you're so kind to everyone you meet." She smiled, finally finding the courage to flick her gaze into brown eyes. "Jumping in to help, even when it's not your job."

Isla swallowed visibly. "I know how hard life can be, Elsie," she responded after a moment. "I am so grateful, daily, that I survived my situation. I almost didn't." She held Elsie's gaze, so much soulful wisdom in Isla's eyes. "And, I'm so grateful for the chance you've given me here." She shook her head. "I'll never do anything to make you regret it."

Touched, and hating that Isla felt she was one bad rumor or misstep away from losing everything, she gently removed the roll of measuring fabric and set it on the bed before taking her into a tight hug. The two women held each other, both having an all-too-real understanding of that very real and valid fear.

Elsie's eyes fell closed as she allowed herself to just feel, to absorb the warmth of another person. She allowed herself to inhale the scent of Isla's hair, her skin. To feel the softness of a woman's body, which sent an unexpected thrill through her that nearly took her breath away.

She heard a little gasp from Isla, which sounded as though she'd tried to hide it with a small cough, but Elsie had heard it. And honestly, she'd felt it, too. She wasn't sure what had happened or what she'd felt but decided perhaps it was a good time to end the hug. Stepping back, she gave the other woman a smile.

"Shall we?" she asked, nodding to the measuring implements on the bed.

Isla swallowed again, seeming grateful to get a little distance. She gave her a shy smile then unrolled her parchment. She made a few notes and grabbed her ell measure. Looking over at Elsie, she seemed to have her professional persona solidly in place as she eyed the princess.

"I think you may need some new chemises, too, Elsie." She gave her a shy smile. "Um…" She placed her hands loosely in front of her own breasts.

Elsie grinned, nodding. "Aye," she sighed, looking down at herself. "I worry about being too close to your straight pins."

Isla burst into laughter, completely clearing the heavy, somewhat awkward air that had gathered between them. She nodded over to the bed. "Need to be careful with my measuring rod. May end up with a black eye."

Elsie gave her a devilish grin. "Bouncy bouncy."

The two giggled like little girls as Isla grabbed the wooden rod and pantomimed accidentally hitting one of Elsie's inflated breasts, tossing the instrument back over her head. She scurried after it, still chuckling as she returned to Elsie.

"Okay, princess." She grinned, eyeing Elsie, who was trying to get serious. "Shall we?"

"I shall assume the position," Elsie said, watching the other woman as she held her arms out from her body. She nearly broke into fresh laughter when Isla blushed and moved behind her.

"Behave," the dressmaker murmured nearly into her ear from behind as she placed her measuring rod horizontally along the middle of Elsie's back.

※ ※ ※ ※

As expected, after dinner Garratt appeared. Perhaps to get his dessert? Elsie had Isla take a cranky Mariota not fifteen minutes before. The baby was beginning to teethe so she was fussy, and Elsie felt guilty. Isla had assured her with a hug that it was fine. She was more than happy to have some baby time.

Now, Elsie sat in one of the chairs before the fire and was knitting a new blanket for Mariota to use this coming winter. She had finally got what Isla had been trying to teach her over the summer. There was a sharp knock, then the door opened. It was Garratt's way, and she was fine with that. She knew in his mind it was his way of giving her respect in her chambers, rather than just barging in.

She glanced over at him as he entered, closing the door behind him. He was dressed in casual clothing for him, which meant no armor or weapons. She knew he'd come in and look around, see if anything had changed since he'd been in the room last. Also, with his predictable behavior, he'd not ask about Mariota nor check on her. He did not disappoint.

He walked up the few steps of the dais beneath the stained glass window, a large rose the centerpiece. There was a large bookshelf up there, filled with all her favorite tomes as well as objects precious to her. He plucked a rose, *Roishin's rose*, from the crystal goblet she kept it in year-round. She hated him touching that but said nothing.

He sniffed it before looking at her. "Where did this come from?"

"Her Majesty ensures I have fresh roses in here," she said absently. She hated to lie, but there was absolutely no way of telling the truth in any form on that.

He twisted the rose stem between his fingers. "My mother? Why?"

"To ensure I always know of her love for Mariota," she said softly, the only truthful words on the matter.

He plopped the flower back where he'd gotten it with a little shrug. Turning to look at the room at large, he placed his hands on his hips and took it all in. Finally, he looked at her, who remained seated, knitting.

"How have you been?" He stepped down the three steps and walked over to the fireplace but didn't sit. "How have things been here?"

"Very well," she said, glancing over at him.

She could see genuine interest in his eyes, though she could feel he was forcing it. Not interest in her, but interest in Sursha, in his role. Which, she supposed, included her. She studied him, such a handsome man. She felt sad for him and wondered why he just wouldn't be honest with Fallon and Cateline.

"Well, uh," he said, suddenly looking shy. "I guess we should…"

Nodding, she kept her sigh internal and set aside her knitting.

❧ ❧ ❧ ❧

The door softly closed behind him and Elsie lay there. She took several deep breaths, trying to will away his ghostly touch she could still feel on her. He hadn't been rough by any stretch, but she certainly hadn't been ready for him. So, not entirely a pleasant experience. She took a few deep breaths then sat up.

Wincing, she threw her legs over the side of the bed. Getting to her feet, she grimaced at the wetness between her legs, and it had nothing to do with her own body. Disgusted, she grabbed a cloth and headed to the garderobe. There, she cleaned herself up, dropping the soiled material through the hole and did her own personal business.

She changed into a fresh sleeping gown and shrugged into a robe before heading out to fetch Mariota. She needed her daughter close to her. The halls were quiet. During her servant days, Elsie had learned the quickest, darkest, and quietest routes to get to the bowels of the castle.

Hiding for a moment as a couple castle guards passed by on their nightly rounds, she waited until they were gone then hurried to Isla's chamber door. Looking both ways down the hall again, she rapped as quietly as she dare in order to be heard inside. As if waiting for her, the door opened within seconds.

The moment Elsie saw Isla, the tears came. She was taken into her embrace and pulled inside the room, the door closed behind them.

"It's okay," Isla whispered, holding her and caressing her back and her loosed hair. "It's okay."

Elsie cried, and honestly, she wasn't entirely sure why. But the moment she'd seen Isla's face, so understanding, the emotion had hit her. After long moments, the emotions eased and the tears dried. Even so, she didn't pull away. Like her, Isla was in her sleeping gown, her long, chestnut hair fallen down her back.

"Are you all right?" Isla asked softly.

Elsie nodded but said nothing. Finally, the hug came to a reluctant end. She looked into concerned brown eyes. "Just glad it's over," she murmured.

"Did he hurt you?" Isla asked, a hand coming up to cup Elsie's cheek.

"No. Certainly not intentionally." Elsie's eyes fell closed as she took a deep breath. "I don't know how long I can do this," she whispered. She hadn't intended to say the words out loud. Opening her eyes, she saw Isla looking at her expectantly.

"Is it him?" the dressmaker asked. "Do you just have distaste for the prince?"

How to answer that? She looked into Isla's eyes. "Have you loved anyone, Isla? Or been with anyone because you wanted to be with?"

Seeming surprised by the question, which no doubt seemed like a non sequitur, Isla looked down at the stone floor. Clearing her throat, she responded. "There was someone, back in Scotland. But..." She shook her head and shrugged. "It was never anything more than just a dream for me."

Elsie nodded, certainly understanding that. "So, you understand wanting to be with another, but your reality is what you have."

Isla nodded. "Very much." She chewed on a full bottom lip before she eyed the princess. "Mariota," she said.

Elsie felt her blood go cold but remained as calm as she could. She said nothing, hoping Isla wasn't going to go where she feared she would.

"And, this conversation will not tread past these walls, Elsie," Isla assured. "But, this other person, the one you love..."

Elsie knew what she was asking, but she also knew that she couldn't tell her the truth. "It's a complicated situation," was all she could think to say.

Isla nodded, her gaze falling. For a moment, Elsie thought she was going to cry, but she seemed to get herself together and asked, "Is this person in the castle?"

Depends on the day. Elsie cleared her throat and said softly, "I cannot be with this person, Isla. I will always love them, through Mariota be part of them, but it must be what it is."

Isla looked at her, her soulful brown eyes expressing so much in that moment. But ultimately, they and her smile conveyed compassion.

Chapter Fifteen

Using the same circuitous route she'd taken to get to Isla's chambers, Elsie carried Mariota back to her own bedchamber. When she entered, she nearly dropped her daughter in shock when she saw the lone figure sitting in the very chair Elsie had occupied while knitting just an hour or so before.

Closing her eyes, she took a deep breath and steadied her breathing before closing the door softly behind her. She headed straight for the cradle when Roishin spoke.

"Can I have her?"

Elsie walked over to the woman who had stood from the chair, wrapped as always in her blue cloak with the gold stitching. "She's teething," she murmured, the two working together to gently transfer the baby from one set of arms to the other. "So, she may wake up and be cranky."

Roishin nodded her acknowledgment of the soft words. "I can't believe how big she's getting," she whispered, looking down at the precious bundle in her arms with so much love.

Normally that look would immediately soften Elsie's heart, but in that moment, it made her feel angry. She said nothing. She felt Roishin's eyes on her as the taller woman gently swayed with their daughter in her arms, rocking her. She met Roishin's questioning gaze.

"What?"

Remaining calm to the single word, bitten out,

Roishin asked, "Where were you? Why were you wandering so late with her?" There was no accusation, just simple confused curiosity in her tone, but again, Elsie felt angry.

"Your brother is home," she said flatly.

Roishin took in Elsie's sleep gown and robe then glanced over at the bed. Her gaze fell before she looked to the fire. "You sent Mariota out with someone?"

Elsie hugged herself, nodding as she, too, took in the flames in the fireplace. "I asked Isla to keep her for me. I didn't want her anywhere near that."

"Why didn't you ask me, Elsie?" Roishin asked, her voice soft but sounding a bit hurt.

"Because you aren't here!" Elsie flared. "What am I supposed to do, Roishin? Send out a homing pigeon and *hope* it can find you, wherever the hell you go? You pop in and out when you want to. I have no idea when to expect you so I can even ask you to do a damn thing."

She could see the stunned expression in Roishin's eyes, but Elsie had held this in for so long now. Now that the dam had broken, it was all coming out.

"It's pretty easy for you, Roishin," she said. "Wander in here in the middle of the night and hold her, cuddle with her while she's sleeping or sleepy. Get the smiles or the giggles then vanish." She snapped her fingers. "Gone. You're not here to deal with her crying and cranky. You're not here to deal with the loneliness of doing this by myself." She turned away, angry all over again but this time at herself as the tears came. "What makes you any better than Garratt?" she whispered.

She buried her face in her hands, trying valiantly to get her emotions under control. She felt completely overwhelmed then had to deal with Garratt, and now Roishin's visit was one thing too much. Sniffling quietly, she wiped at her eyes when she heard Roishin putting Mariota in her cradle.

"Come here."

Elsie wanted to fight her—oh, how she wanted to!—but she allowed herself to be turned around and taken into Roishin's embrace. Her head was urged to rest against her shoulder. Elsie's eyes fell closed as she wrapped her arms around Roishin's waist. For a long time neither said anything. Elsie's tears came back, silent, though Roishin seemed to be aware. She lightly ran her fingers through long, blond hair and rested her head against Elsie's. She held her as the tears kept coming.

"What can I do to help?" Roishin whispered once Elsie's tears had dried. "Where do you need me?"

Elsie lifted her head and pulled out of the hug. She looked up into a concerned face. "I just need to not feel so alone in this, Roishin," she said. "Garratt wants absolutely nothing to do with her, which honestly I'm glad about. And," she added, walking away from Roishin to retake her stance before the fire. "He's so rarely here, anyway."

"Did he hurt you?" Roishin asked gently, walking over to her but not touching her.

Elsie shook her head, not looking away from the fire as her mind went back to the short time he was there. An unpleasant event, so she pushed her thoughts away from it. "I certainly understand why it's referred to as 'duty.'" She let out a long, heavy sigh.

"I'm so sorry, Elsie. What can I do?" she asked again.

"It's been offered to me," Elsie began. "A whole team of servants just to care for Mariota, but I don't want that." She met Roishin's gaze. "I don't want my daughter, *our* daughter, raised by someone else. But there is so much I want to do here. Carthac was a wonderful king, Fallon is proving to be even better. But I see so much more that can be done."

Roishin nodded in understanding. "Aye."

"I want to be able to have that time, that freedom to work on these things, but knowing that our daughter is not with a servant. I feel like my only job here is to sit pretty in this chamber and wait for Garratt to decide to prance in and do his man thing, then head off into the field again." She turned to face Roishin. "I need a purpose," she said, hand splayed out on her own chest. "I am Mariota's mother, and it's my greatest joy, my greatest duty, but I also run this region of the country." She gave her a shy smile. "And I don't really know what I'm doing, nor have the time to figure it out."

Roishin studied her for a long moment, head slightly cocked to the side. The wheels behind that verdant gaze were spinning. "I have a few ideas," she said. "Obviously, I can't be seen here."

Elsie shook her head. "No. Isla already asked me tonight about Mariota's parentage. People see it, Roishin. One look at you, and especially as she gets older, she looks so much like you in some ways." She gave her a small smile. "Some days all I can do is just stare at her and I'm looking into *your* eyes."

Roishin looked down, but not before Elsie saw the massive smile of pride forming on her lips. Clearing her throat, she spared a glance up at the princes. "If I can get this all worked out, will you let me take her? During those times, or whenever you need me to? I mean," she added quickly. "Elsie, I'd literally take her half the time if it was explainable."

Elsie felt her nerves begin to ease, and it made

her smile. Roishin used to have the ability to just look her way and everything fell into place. That had no longer been the case of late, and it had sent Elsie into grieving what was. It hurt so much to know that was seeping away, and it confused her even more to realize that someone else gave her that sense of calm now.

This was not the time to focus on that, as she wasn't ready to explain it to herself, let alone Roishin. She already felt guilt-riddled even though she knew there was little reason to anymore. Clearing her throat and her mind, she refocused on the woman standing before her.

"Thank you, Roishin," she said softly. "I just need to know you care."

Roishin quirked a dark eyebrow before she wandered off toward the dais, trotting up the few stairs before grabbing something and making her way back down and over to Elsie. She playfully stuck the stem of the rose between her teeth, making Elsie smile. Taking the rose in her hands, Roishin held it out to her.

Taking it, Elsie couldn't help but remember this very rose being handled by Garratt little more than an hour before. She remembered how it had burned her for him to dare touch something so precious to her. She looked down at it, noting that the large, red bloom seemed to be lightly pulsing, almost like a heartbeat.

"I told you," Roishin said. "As long as this rose blooms, you'll know that I love you and I love Mariota." She shook her head. "That will never change, regardless of our respective life changes."

Elsie's eyes closed in relief as she held the rose to her chest as once upon a time she would have held Roishin. Nodding, she looked up at her again. Her eyes once again closed when Roishin cupped the side of her face to steady her as she left a lingering kiss on her forehead.

"I'm sorry I failed you," Roishin said. "I am no Garratt, and I will do everything in my power to change your impression of me in that way."

Elsie nodded. "Thank you. And, I'm sorry, I didn't mean to hurt—"

"No," Roishin said, taking a step back out of Elsie's personal space. "I earned that. So, now it's time for me to *un*earn that." She grinned.

Elsie smiled, nodding. "I think you can." They shared a long look, a look that spoke of two people who had been through a lot together and who would always be connected. "Well, I need to get to bed. *Your* daughter wakes up awful early."

Roishin grinned. "Hey, if she wakes up awful early on purpose, then that part is *your* daughter."

Elsie smiled and nodded. "Fair enough."

She studied Roishin for a long moment, stunned at the beautiful woman who stood before her. It amazed and saddened her how little she recognized in the face of the woman who she once knew so well. Identical twins physically, but that was where it ended. This woman was an entirely different person now.

In her eyes, however, she did see glimpses of that little spitfire. She knew that woman was still in there, that soul that she loved so dearly, but she also knew Roishin would never again be the little girl and then teenager who had stolen the heart of a lonely young servant. And maybe, just maybe, that was okay.

❧ ❧ ❧ ❧

"Now," Roishin said, holding the tapestry back so

Elsie could push open the door to the secret passageway. "Since we spoke last eve, I've done my due diligence and am taking you to the best person for this job."

"What job?" Elsie asked, holding the door open for Roishin to follow her into the dark tunnel.

"The job of helping you accomplish all that you want to here in Sursha. She's smart, she's feisty, and most importantly she loves this country as much as you do," she said, standing before the door to their cave. "She believes in what you do, wants what you want for Sursha's people." She took Elsie's hand. "Especially the women."

They took a step forward...

...into their cave. A lone figure stood, lit by the light of the eternal flame. Elsie gasped, her eyes growing huge. She looked to Roishin, not sure if what, *who* she was seeing was truly there. By the grin on Roishin's face, she had to assume she was.

"Livia?"

The older woman and Fallon's longtime adviser when she'd been alive smiled brightly at her and stepped up to her to take her into a tight hug. "Hello, my dear."

Elsie allowed the hug and heartily returned it. She couldn't keep the tears from falling as that horrible, horrible day came back to her from so many years ago. "How is this possible?"

"Where I live now," Roishin explained softly. "Where I'm from, boundaries aren't what they are in your world, Elsie."

The hug ended with one final tight squeeze and Livia's dark eyes showed compassion as she wiped away Elsie's tears. "The dead and the living coexist there," she said, expanding upon what Roishin had said. "I work with Roishin now. Live a normal, happy life that I never could have lived in Sursha."

So confused, Elsie turned to Roishin. "Are you… are you *dead*?" she whispered, nauseous at the very thought.

Roishin grinned and shook her head. "No. And in Duras, neither is Livia. That's more of an earthbound thing. In Duras, it's about a state of being."

Elsie didn't really understand but was thrilled to see her. "I'm just shocked," she said, shaking her head, taking in all of the lovely woman who stood before her.

She looked to be the same age she was when she'd died, a woman of not quite thirty. But, much like Roishin, there was a maturity about her, the essence of an ancient soul, just like Enori. "So…" She looked from one woman to the other. "I don't really understand."

"I want to help you," Livia explained. "Roishin has filled me in on what you want to do and what you need." Her smile was brilliant. "I want to step in as an adviser for you, Elsie. Help you achieve all you wish to."

"But," Elsie said slowly, looking to Roishin then back to Livia. "How? Do I come meet with you here?"

Livia shook her head. "No need. I can come to you. But," she said, holding up a finger for emphasis. "My energy is no longer compatible with that in your world. I need to use your energy essentially as a pathway."

"She will be your reflection of the other world, Elsie," Roishin explained. "She needs your permission."

"Aye," Elsie said, nodding vigorously. "You have it." A bit of relieved and nervous laughter burst from her lips. "I don't understand any of this, but you definitely have it."

Livia gave her another tight hug. "Good. And," she added, pulling out of the embrace but holding

Elsie by the arms. "I cannot wait to see this beautiful daughter of yours. This one," she added, nodding toward Roishin, "Does nothing but talk about her."

Again, that smile of absolute love and pride on Roishin's lips as she looked down at the ground. That made Elsie immensely happy. Perhaps Roishin hadn't walked away or forgotten about them as much as she'd feared she had.

"Well," Livia said, pulling Elsie's attention back to her. "I must go. I'll be by to see you tomorrow evening once the baby is put to bed. Will that do?"

"Aye!" Elsie was overjoyed as she accepted another hug. She knew how much Fallon and Cateline had adored Livia and trusted her. In fact, she had been Fallon's most trusted confidante next to her wife. No doubt had she lived, she'd still be the right hand of the king of Sursha.

A tight squeeze and Livia released Elsie then gave one to Roishin. "See you soon," she said to her before vanishing as she stepped through the door Roishin always used.

Elsie stood there feeling absolutely shell-shocked, but in a good way. She almost felt giddy, as she had a newfound hope for so many reasons. Looking to Roishin, who looked rather smug, Elsie could only smile and shake her head in amusement.

"Thank you," she said.

Roishin nodded and gave Elsie a deferential bow. "Of course, Your Highness."

Elsie rolled her eyes. "Come on. You wanted to see the baby."

They returned to Elsie's bedchamber where the baby had been left napping, Roishin promising her they wouldn't be gone long. True to her word, they had returned.

"Tell me about this place," Elsie said, watching as Roishin walked over to the cradle. "Duras, you called it."

Roishin nodded, pushing back the curtains. She smiled down at the baby, who was breathing deep and even on her back. "It's Ankou's realm. Those like Livia can choose to go there or Yewa." She looked back to Elsie. "The land of the dead." She smiled. "No pesky living people coming and going."

Elsie crossed her arms over her chest, watching Roishin. So much tenderness came over her as she looked down at Mariota. She was absolutely wearing her heart on her sleeve in that moment, and it made Elsie smile.

"Why did she choose Duras instead of Yewa?"

"She heard I was going to be there," Roishin explained, shrugging. "She found out from Enori who I was and that I've be returning home, as it were, so she asked to stay." Her smile was blinding. "There, she met her husband and their son."

Elsie's breath caught. "She's married?"

Roishin nodded. "She's very happy, Elsie. I've known Livia all my life, and I adored her. But who she is with Gerald and Mattia…" She nodded, looking back to Mariota. "Who she was always meant to be." Roishin got serious for a moment. "I like Isla."

Elsie stared at her, stunned. "When did you meet her?" She racked her brain but couldn't think of a single time Roishin had been around her.

"I didn't. Well, not technically." She met Elsie's gaze and held it. "I can tell you care about her. That you need that sort of a friend." She looked away. "Because I can't be that."

Elsie had no idea what to say, or if there was anything for her to say. She did, however, feel that stab of guilt that she'd felt the previous night again, though she knew Roishin's words were true.

"Elsie," Roishin said softly, allowing the curtains to fall back into place around Mariota's cradle. "Today, before I came here to you, I watched her for a bit." She held up a hand to forestall the tirade of violation Elsie was about to unleash. "She had no idea I was there. I watched her around the servants, got an idea of her energy, the kind of person she is." She smiled. "I think she's lovely. And, if she's going to be around *my* daughter and you, I wanted to make sure."

Elsie looked down at her feet, no clue what to say. She felt that Roishin's simple, straightforward words were loaded with hidden meanings. Or, was that just her own secret hopes?

"She is a good person," she finally said, meeting Roishin's patient gaze again. "She understands a lot of what I'm dealing with, Garratt and all that. She's a comfort to me. And aye, she's very good with Mariota."

Roishin gave her a beautiful smile. "Then," she said softly. "That's all that matters."

Chapter Sixteen

The irony was, as much as she had no real understanding of why Roishin enjoyed her coffee so much, Enori had found a use for the Mr. Coffee coffee maker she'd picked up for her. Once in a while, she enjoyed a nice cup of hot tea. And, since a pot of water could be heated in the carafe, it worked out well for the both of them.

Currently, she cradled a mug of the fragrant hot drink as she wandered the rooms of the stone cottage. She'd lived there for a very, very, very long time. It was small, spoke to her want of simplicity, but also spoke to something else. This house and the village where it sat was nearly an exact replica of the place she and Mariota had spent their stolen moments together.

The place where they'd made love for the first time and where they'd professed their love to each other for the first time. Choosing to live here had been a comfort for a long time, and then it had just become home. Well, certainly where she kept her meager belongings and where she slept when she actually *was* home.

She often slept in her cave in the Underground, the same space she'd first met Fallon—certainly a moment that had changed her life forever. She honestly had begun to spend more time here when Roishin had moved in. She'd wanted her to have a space to feel safe in, comfortable in. A place to call home that wasn't hidden away underground. Roishin had already had enough of that during her four and a half years of isolation.

Now, as she wandered the rooms carefully sipping from the hot beverage in her mug, she made sure everything was perfect for the very special guest that would be arriving home soon enough.

But also, she was considering. Roishin had never said one word, not complained nor made any sort of suggestion about the house or its furnishings and decorations. It was all Enori—rightfully so for so many years—and her touch was everywhere. This house had once represented something to her, had been the physical embodiment of love, of a profound loss and profound guilt. Perhaps, she thought as she stood in the open doorway of the bedroom Roishin had used. Perhaps it was time to move on to something she and Roishin wanted together.

She walked in and took a seat on the bed, which Roishin had not slept in since they'd finally made love for the first time several days ago. After that, it had been unspoken and mutually accepted that it was now about *them*. If she were honest with herself, which she was becoming more and more by the day, Enori had never been happier or more fulfilled.

There was no hiding, there was no secret rendezvous, it was just them, in their home, being true to themselves and each other. Still, she questioned. Living in this house and the reasons she'd chosen it... was that her being true to them and what they were literally created to be? Was it being true to Roishin?

She wanted to talk to Roishin about that. For now, they had plenty of space for the precious gift that was coming. Enori smiled at that thought. She knew it bothered Roishin in no small way to see so little of Mariota. So, today, they were going to try this. Ava had instantly jumped in to help.

She had uniquely useful skills for what they had planned. Roishin had met with Elsie in their cave to discuss it, and she was on board. Now, they just had to get the pieces together to make it work. She also knew of a grandfather who was mighty excited to meet his granddaughter, and they were all curious as to what gifts she'd received.

Granted, a lot of that would come out over time, as Roishin's had. And now that Roishin spent the majority of her time in Duras, they were becoming stronger, more defined, and frankly, awesome. The longer she was there, the more her gifts grew. The same would be true for Mariota.

She needed time in Duras for that part of her to mature. In the earthly realm, her powers would be slow and sluggish to develop. She needed the pure energy of Duras for her Ankou blood to truly realize its potential.

Pushing up from the bed, she turned and looked at it as she took another sip of her tea. Setting the mug down on the dresser top, she went about pulling the covers off the bed and tossing them out into the hall. It was time to disassemble it and make room for the crib they were bringing in.

"Baby love!" was belted from downstairs.

Amused, Enori glanced over her shoulder toward the doorway as she was finishing up with the frame. Shaking her head, she smiled. "Up here!"

A moment later, loud footfalls were heard tromping up the stairs until they ended in the appearance of Roishin in the hallway looking in. "My goodness," she said. "You've been busy." She entered, squatting down next to Enori. "So, now that you've taken my bed apart, does this mean I'm out?"

Enori met her gaze, giving her a look that she knew would melt Roishin's undergarments. "No," she purred. "I would say it means you are *in*."

Roishin gave her an absolutely devilish grin. "Gonna hold you to that," she murmured before initiating a deep but short kiss. "Gerald is downstairs to help me bring the crib up." She grinned. "Lucky for us, they kept Mattia's."

Enori looked into Roishin's eyes, so beautiful. In their depths she saw a deep and profound happiness. She truly hadn't realized just how devastated Roishin was to not be able to see her daughter often or spend any real time with her. How had she not seen that? Known that? She cupped the side of Roishin's face.

Only one thing to say in that moment, and she meant it with all she was. "I love you, Roishin."

The sun that was already shining through those eyes amped up a million watts at those softly spoken words. "And I love you," she whispered back, resting her forehead against Enori's for a moment. Their kiss was soft but lingering before Roishin pushed to her feet.

The two cleared out the rest of the frame and got everything moved out of the way and into the hall. They headed downstairs to see Gerald waiting. Enori gave him a sweet smile in greeting. She stayed out of the way as the two moved the piece of furniture up into its new space. With Mattia in his "big boy" bed, there was no longer a need for it.

Though Duras held no real boundaries between the living and the dead, the dead could not conceive. However, the wonderful thing was that Mattia's little body had lived for only an hour before birthing traumas too great for him to survive had sent Ankou for him.

Livia and Gerald, already happily married, had gladly taken the newborn, effectively becoming his parents from birth.

Mattia knew no other parents and could have known no greater love. He was utterly adored and cherished by two souls who had been given a second chance after losing their lives and all they'd built through their deaths. It amazed Enori, as it had when she'd seen it in Livia, truly finding her real happiness only because she lost the chains the living world had put upon her.

Once the pair had made it upstairs, Enori followed, watching from the hall as they carefully moved the crib into place. It was gratifying to see it, she had to admit. Enori loved children and would have been thrilled to have Mattia or Isabeau come and stay with them.

But, as she watched Gerald show Roishin how the crib worked, it hit her what a drastically different situation this was. This was for Roishin's own child, and one that changed their situation. It was no longer about Enori and Roishin the couple, but Enori and Roishin *and* Mariota the family.

The realization stole her breath. She literally had to stand there for a moment and allow her heart to stop racing and her body and mind to calm. She blinked tears away at the magnitude of just how precious the situation was. She walked into her bedroom for a moment to try to gather herself.

She wasn't sure how long she stood there, so lost in her own emotions and feelings that she didn't even know anyone had stepped up behind her. It wasn't until she felt arms ease around her waist from behind and a warm body press against her that she knew Roishin was there.

She felt so much coming off the woman behind her: love, worry, hope, and uncertainty. Turning in the circle of her arms, Enori said nothing. She simply snaked her arms up around the taller woman's neck and pulled them together. She held her, face buried in a warm neck and fingers buried in soft, dark hair.

The relief coming off Roishin was in waves, like heat. "I was so worried you'd changed your mind," she whispered into the hug.

Enori shook her head. "No." She left a kiss on Roishin's neck before lifting her head to look at her. "When you lock yourself away for so long," she explained softly. "You do not honestly know what you needed so badly until you are presented with the key."

Roishin said nothing.   All she was thinking and feeling was expressed in her kiss, which was slow and absolutely worshipful of the woman she held. Never had Enori known love like she had from Roishin. Never had she thought it could be so pure, so true, and so utterly and completely conveyed in so many different ways every minute of every day.

As Roishin undressed her and then herself, Enori saw so much of Fallon in her. The way she'd dedicated herself, heart and soul, to Cateline, Roishin had taken those cues of how to love to heart. It wasn't a type of love that was overwhelming or suffocating, but all-encompassing and just truly who they were.

With every look, every touch, every kiss, lick, and suck, Roishin made it known how she felt. Enori's eyes closed and her back arched as Roishin took her into her mouth. She held Enori's thighs open with strong arms as she demonstrated her gratitude and love through her passion.

It didn't take long before Enori's body exploded, her cry loud and breathy as her breasts heaved and mind shattered with the impact. Vaguely, she was aware that a moment later Roisin was holding her, raining kisses all over Enori's face and murmuring words of love against her lips.

Finally, Enori had enough wits about her to hold Roishin to her. She took a deep, centering breath and murmured, "Please tell me Gerald left."

Roishin grinned, a twinkle in her eyes. "Nope. He's waiting downstairs for lunch."

Enori burst into laughter.

❧ ❧ ❧ ❧

"Welcome," Enori said, opening the door for Ava, who gave her a bright smile.

"Thank you." She entered the stone cottage with the bag she carried slung over her shoulder.

The door was closed behind her and a freshly showered and dressed Roishin trotted down the stairs with a nice big welcoming smile for the newcomer. "Hi there!"

The two shared a quick hug, clearly a bond forming after Roishin had made the abrupt decision to bring the young woman back to Duras with her from that tiny, shabby boardinghouse bedroom.

"Okay, ladies," Ava said, walking over to the couch and dropping her bag. She looked to them both. "With the notes you gave me on your time, Roishin, and a little shopping spree at the Warehouse, I think I was able to come up with something that will really work."

Enori could tell Roishin was nervous so moved

in to stand near her, their shoulders nearly brushing. She watched as Ava opened up the bag and pulled out a very plain long-sleeved dress and then a sleeveless tunic to go over it. Very familiar to her from her years wandering through Sursha.

Roishin stepped forward and fingered the garments, looking approvingly at them. "Absolutely," she finally said, sparing a glance to the other woman. "I could imagine this on anyone I'd pass in the halls."

Ava grinned. "Excellent." She gathered everything up. "All right, where can I go to change?"

"Bedrooms are upstairs," Enori said. "Whichever you wish." Left alone, Enori looked to Roishin. "So, you're satisfied that her outfit won't be questioned?"

"Definitely," Roishin assured. "She did a wonderful job. She won't have a problem at all passing as a caretaker for Mariota." She met Enori's gaze. "What?"

"Just wait," Enori murmured, knowing what was to come.

Roishin kissed Enori's lips before she wandered to the kitchen to make some coffee. Enori stayed where she was, standing near the fireplace. It wasn't ten minutes later when there were footfalls coming back down the stairs. She watched in utter amazement. She knew what Ava's skills were, so was thoroughly curious to see what Roishin's reaction would be.

The young woman in her twenties with dark hair and eyes had gone up the stairs, but who came down was a woman in her late thirties. Her long, auburn hair was pinned up, and somewhat dull brown eyes met Enori's. Her bearing was not sweet and excited like Ava, but almost regal, and certainly more sedate.

She gave Enori a small nod of her head in

acknowledgment before moving on to the kitchen. Enori waited with nearly bated breath as she watched as the woman approached Roishin, who's back was to them both.

"Might I have a cup?" she asked in perfect Gaelic, accent spot on.

Roishin turned her head and her eyes widened as she jumped back in startled surprise. Mouth open, she looked over to Enori, almost as if to make sure she was still in the right house. Enori was no longer able to keep her smile under wraps, and it began to slowly spread across her lips.

Turning her gaze back to the woman who stood before her, Roishin set the coffee carafe down, beverage forgotten. "Ava?"

"Touch her," Enori said, walking over to them.

Roishin studied the woman before her. She was hesitant for a moment but brought up a hand and lightly touched the auburn strands and even lightly ran her fingers over the slight laugh lines that were beginning to form at the woman's mouth, those which the much younger Ava did not possess.

"They're actually there," she murmured. "I can actually feel them."

"Ava is a chameleon, Roishin," Enori explained. "As you know, no matter how good an intention is, it only goes so far and can only last so long. This," she said, indicating the woman before them, "is total."

"Am I crazy, or does she look like the actress we saw on stage in Washington, DC that first mission?" Roishin dragged her eyes to Enori.

"Not crazy. As long as a chameleon has known the person, been in close proximity of their energy, they can replicate it."

"Wow," Roishin whispered.

"Ava," Enori said, turning to the woman who met her gaze. "Please create a mirror pocket." Nodding, the woman stepped over by the kitchen table and, for just a moment, she dimmed, nearly vanishing before she reappeared, but over in the living area. Enori looked to Roishin. "Watch."

She walked over to where Ava had been standing and, based on Roishin's loud gasp of shock, Enori successfully took on the likeness of the auburn-haired woman as she walked through the area created by Ava. Stepping out of it, she returned to herself. She walked over to Ava, looking back to Roishin.

"And," she added. "She can change at a moment's notice."

On cue, the redhead slowly faded, an even older woman with dark skin and black hair pulled back in a tight bun appeared, wearing the same outfit. Every detail was on point, from the dark skin that covered her face and hands to the lines and wrinkles on her face to the tired look in her light brown eyes.

"Forgive me, Ava," Enori said softly as she removed the outer tunic, tossing it to the couch before she unbuttoned a couple buttons of the dress. The dark skin tone continued beneath the garment.

Roisin walked over to them as if in a daze. "This is extraordinary," she whispered. "And, you can come back into yourself?"

Taking a deep breath, the woman standing next to Enori centered herself and the older black woman slowly vanished, leaving the woman they knew as Ava in her wake.

"Could you do my energy? Or Enori's?"

"Only if I was in a different time than you," Ava

said. "The energies can't cross."

"No twinsies then, huh?" Roishin muttered.

Enori smirked. "The first woman, based off the actress from 1865, will be the character she will portray for this."

Ava nodded. "Nobody there in Sursha has seen her before, and I feel she has the age and bearing to be believed."

Roishin nodded. "I agree. And, the mirror…?"

"Mirror pocket," Ava supplied. "So it doesn't seem like she just vanishes, when anyone happens to walk through the random mirror pocket, others will get a glimpse of this woman around the castle, giving her credibility."

Roishin rubbed her face as if in deep contemplation. Enori looked at her. "What do you think?" she asked softly.

Finally, Roishin met her gaze. "I wanna know how to do that."

Chapter Seventeen

Dressed in her flowing gown and cloak from the Order, Enori was escorted into the throne room by castle guards. She saw the woman who had also been escorted in, who was there to be introduced to Princess Elsie as her new caregiver for Princess Mariota. The two women didn't meet eyes, as after all, they didn't know each other.

Elsie was formidable and impressive in her royal duties, Enori thought. She was mighty impressed at whom the young woman was becoming. She couldn't help but feel pride as she watched her dispatch one issue after the next, all of which she listened to thoroughly, and with kindness and compassion where needed— and a spine of steel when required.

Enori knew Mariota would be so very proud of her great-granddaughter. And, for the first time, that thought made Enori happy and didn't gut her with grief. Finally, it was her turn, and she was announced to the Court.

"Your Majesty," the Court Cryer called out. "Enori, High Priestess of the Order of Ankou, has arrived upon your request of spiritual counsel."

Elsie looked to Enori, recognition upon her lovely face but nothing of the friendly nature the two women shared. All of this was for public spectacle, announcing both Enori and Ava in this way. It gave both women legitimate reason to be seen there, as well as to garner talk around the castle that Elsie had brought in a caretaker. She wouldn't have to say a word, as gossip would do it for her.

"Aye. Welcome, Priestess," Elsie said. "Please escort her to my private chambers."

Enori gave her a deep, sweeping bow of respect before she was escorted from the large throne room. Obviously she knew where to go but stayed with the guard until he opened one side of the princess's bedchamber doors for her to enter.

Inside was a young woman with dark hair who was sitting at the table where the princess took her meals. She was bent over a piece of parchment sketching with a whittled piece of charcoal. Glancing up when Enori entered, she smiled before putting the charcoal down and pushing back from the table.

She wiped her hands on her tunic, leaving black smudges from the charcoal on the material. She bowed her head a bit as Enori walked over to her. "You're Enori."

"I am." Enori gave her a smile as she eyed her. The young woman was lovely, her chocolate-brown eyes open and friendly. "And you are?"

"Isla." She indicated her parchment on the table. "I'm the dressmaker here, and I help the princess watch the baby at times."

Roishin had mentioned Isla to Enori. She'd also mentioned her observations that perhaps the two ladies were more than friends—or wished to be. Enori studied the young woman and tried to look deeper than just her adorable dimples and somewhat awkward demeanor. She could tell she had a wonderful spirit to her. A good heart.

But, was there more to her than met the eye? Did she have it in her to love a woman, or would Elsie end up hurt? She wanted to see them together. For now, Enori bestowed on her a smile.

"It is truly nice to meet you, Isla." She quirked an eyebrow with interest. "I have been interested in learning how to weave. Perhaps you can teach me?"

Isla's smile was nearly blinding, the love for her textile work shining through. "Aye! As long as the princess has no need of me, I will be honored."

They shared a smile when the bedchamber door opened again. Elsie stepped through with Ava. Enori let out a quiet sigh of relief. The woman near forty with auburn hair and brown eyes stood next to Elsie. Their gazes met for just a moment before Enori looked to Elsie. She still had to play her role in front of Isla.

"Milady," the dressmaker said, bowing in deference.

"Isla," Elsie said, walking over to her.

She placed a hand to her arm, which initially one would do to get a person's attention, but Enori noticed the hand remained, and Isla didn't react. It was as though it was commonplace affection. Certainly odd for a dressmaker and her princess, she thought with an inward smile.

"This is the woman I told you about, who would be caring for Mariota while I have my meetings during the days." She looked to Isla, who was already looking at her. "So I don't have to constantly pull you from your duties." The two women shared a small smile. Clearly, this had been discussed already.

Again, Enori took note, pleased. For any normal and curious onlooker, Isla was there to do as she was bade, be it creating a masterpiece of silks and fabrics or caring for the royal daughter. Why on earth would the princess of Sursha worry herself with the schedule of her dressmaker? *Interesting, and delightful.*

"Aye." Isla turned her beaming smile to Ava. "I'm so pleased to meet you. I think it's a wonderful idea for Els—Her Highness to bring someone in for this. Mariota is such a wonderful baby."

"Thank you," Ava said, her voice that of the stage actress from centuries away. It never got old for Enori. So incredible.

Elsie turned to Isla. "I know you have work you need to do this afternoon, Isla," she said softly to her. "Thank you so much for all you do." The two women shared a quick look before Isla bowed.

"Aye, milady." She nodded at Enori and Ave before leaving.

The three left alone, Elsie let out a long, shaky sigh. She looked at Enori. "You're sure this will be okay?" she asked, nervousness in her voice.

"Of course, milady," Enori said, taking a hand in hers and giving the princess a warm smile. "Roishin is so excited to spend time with her. She was like a little kid getting her room ready for her."

"So," Elsie said, eyeing the priestess. "She's still staying with you, then?"

Enori knew Elsie and Roishin needed to talk, and it wasn't Enori's place to speak for Roishin. So, she simply nodded. "She is."

"And, you're sure it's all right for Mariota to be there?"

Enori took her other hand so she held both. "Elsie," she said softly. "Mariota is Roishin's daughter, with you. That will *always* be." She smiled and squeezed her hands with affection. "I made the vow to love this child and protect her, and I will. So, her having a crib in a room in my house does not bother me one bit. She is very welcome."

Elsie took her into a hug. "Thank you," she whispered. Getting a tight squeeze in return, Elsie turned to Ava after the two women separated. "Thank you, as well," she said, taking Ava's hand. "I appreciate your help in this."

"It's truly my honor, milady," Ava said, giving her a reassuring smile.

Nodding, Elsie blew out a breath. She certainly looked like a mother who was leaving her baby for the first time. She walked over to the cradle and pulled back the curtain. Enori followed her, smiling when she saw the sleeping babe within.

"I did as you asked me to," Elsie said, glancing over at Enori. "That pump and the jars you left for me in the cave. I used them and there is breast milk left there for her."

Enori smiled. "Wonderful."

Elsie picked up her daughter and left a kiss on her cheek before she and Enori exchanged the precious bundle between them. Cupping the back of her blond head for a moment, Elsie finally dropped her hand from the little one.

"I promise," Enori said softly. "She will be fine." She held the baby with one arm while once again taking Elsie's hand with her free one. "Do what you need to do as ruler of this region. Worry not about Mariota. Just be the princess of history that you are meant to be."

༄ ༄ ༄ ༄

Enori got home, baby bundled in her arms, and Ava, now returned to her normal self, carried the jars of breast milk along with one of the clay bottles

Mariota was used to using. If she hadn't been able to feel Roishin's anxiety personally, she would have found her incessant pacing amusing. It made her think of an expectant father.

As soon as the two women stepped in, Roishin stopped, so much passing across her beautiful face: relief, happiness, love, and almost a look of wonder. Enori immediately walked over to her.

"Here's your daughter, my love," she said softly.

Roishin took her in careful arms. As she always did, Mariota looked up at Roishin with wide, happy eyes. "Hi, baby girl," Roishin murmured. It looked like everything in her world had righted itself in that moment.

Enori wanted to give them a moment so turned to Ava, who was nearly swooning. She took the jars from her and gave her a one-armed hug. "Thank you so much," she said quietly into the hug, which was returned.

Ava smiled. "I'll see you two soon at training."

With a nod, Enori watched her turn and leave, easing the front door closed behind her. Though Mariota knew Roishin and had done well with Enori, this was still new surroundings for the baby, so she didn't want to make any loud or startling noise by closing the door too hard. She carried the breast milk jars to their cold storage and left them on a shelf there before returning to the living space.

"I can't believe you two did this for me today," Roishin said, looking over at Enori.

"Why?" she asked, stepping up behind Roishin and hugging her around the waist. She rested her chin on Roishin's shoulder to look at the cradled little one.

"I don't know, I..." Roishin seemed genuinely lost

for words. She turned her head enough to get a kiss before returning her attention to Mariota, who was looking around with wide, deep green eyes. "I can't believe she's here. How did it go?"

"Really well. Elsie was nervous, of course, but what good mother would not be?" She smiled as she looked into the precious face. "But, I could tell she was grateful." She reached up around Roishin's body and playfully tapped Mariota's nose, smiling when she got a little grin in return. "She has your smile."

"She's so beautiful," Roishin whispered, a bit of emotion in her voice.

Enori nodded. "She is."

"I can't believe how big she's gotten. Soon enough, she'll be wanting her own place."

Enori smiled at that. "Well, I hope this place she wants is a castle of her very own," she teased.

"That's right, little one," Roishin said. "Someday, you'll be Queen Mariota."

"Speaking of which," Enori said, leaving a kiss on Roishin's neck before she moved away from her to sit on the big couch, plenty of room for Roishin and the baby. She was pleased when they joined her. "I am so impressed with Elsie."

"Why?" Roishin asked, placing the baby in her lap, back against her front. Enori chuckled, watching the wonder on her little face as she took everything in. A whole new world for her, literally.

"She is just so poised," Enori said, thinking back on the day. "So decisive. A true leader." She made a silly face at the baby when she looked up at her, her smile instant when the baby stared wide-eyed as if trying to decide how to respond. When Enori did it again, she giggled. So of course, Enori had to do it again. She'd leaned over so she was more on the baby's eye level as she continued their silly face game. She spared a quick glance up to an amused Roishin. "She is no longer the scared servant girl, Roishin."

"No," Roishin said, gently caressing the soft hair atop her daughter's head, Elsie's exact same color of golden blond. She grinned at the big belly laugh Enori got from her. "She's grown up. I see it more every time I see her."

Mid-silly face, Enori met her gaze. "You both have."

She glanced at the door when there was a knock. She leaned forward and gave first Mariota a kiss to the head then one to Roishin's lips before climbing off the couch as she shrugged out of her cloak. She draped it across the love seat as she made her way to the door, white gown flowing around her with every step.

She was surprised to find Ankou on the other side. "Well, hello," she said, stepping aside to allow him in.

Roishin chuckled. "Waited a whole five minutes, huh?" She gathered the baby in her arms and stood. "Ankou," she said softly as he walked over to her. "I'd like to introduce you to your granddaughter, Mariota."

Enori was pretty sure she'd never heard Roishin speak one sentence with such pride in her voice, in her eyes, and in her smile. She also was pretty sure she'd never seen Ankou look so much like he was going to melt. She watched as he took her in his hands, holding her up to inspect every aspect of her.

She hadn't fully understood at the time, but Ankou had asked Enori to be his eyes and ears with baby Roishin. She had thought it was because he didn't want to get too close, in case it didn't work. Once the girl was ready to understand her lineage at age thirteen, he'd taken an unsuspecting Roishin under his wing for all those years in the Underground.

Recently, she'd come to suspect he'd wanted Enori in charge of much of Roishin's early life to cement that soul bond between them. And now, with the baby he cradled in his large hands, the look upon his grizzled face soft and filled with wonder, she knew he had other intentions for this little one. Certainly other intentions for his place in her life.

⁂

Later that night, Mariota had been fed, burped, changed, and was now tucked into her crib for sleep. She'd had a lot of play in her time there, between Roishin and Enori and Livia, who had arrived after Ankou left. The little one was wiped out. The wonderful thing about the doors was, in Duras time, they could enjoy an entire day and night with her and take her back to her mother in the morning, at whatever time Elsie expected her back. For the princess, only a matter of a few hours had passed.

They'd made love quietly, now lying on their sides facing each other with legs entwined. Enori studied Roishin's face. She looked so at peace. She smiled, running her fingers over a soft cheek.

"I cannot tell if the peace and calm in your eyes is from the orgasms or the little one sleeping in the room next door."

Roishin grinned. "Aye." Her grin widened when she received a little smack to a naked behind beneath the covers. She let out a long, slow, contented sigh. "Did you ever want children, Enori?"

Enori considered the question and shrugged the shoulder that wasn't pressed into the mattress. "I never was in any sort of situation to have them. I knew very early on that I was not attracted to men." She smiled. "I did not exactly have someone like you around to make it work."

"And now you do," Roishin quipped.

She looked deeply into Roishin's eyes. "You want a child?" she asked. "A second one?"

Roishin used a fingertip to trace Enori's features, light blue eyes closing as the gentle touch swept over her eyebrow and down along her cheekbone. It traveled down her nose then across her lips, which left a kiss as it passed, until finally that hand settled on the side of her neck.

"You're so beautiful," Roishin whispered, almost as if she hadn't meant to say it out loud.

Enori's eyes slowly opened and she smiled. "So are you."

"As for your question, I don't know, honestly. Would it even be conducive with what we do? If you even wanted such a thing," she added quickly.

"I do not know, either," Enori said. "It hasn't ever been anything that has been on my mind or any part of what I saw for myself. Now, I am not saying no. Just that…" She shrugged that shoulder again.

"I understand. For *normal* people," Roishin said, eyeing the other woman. "They get to think about it, decide if it makes sense."

Enori smiled. "I know, and I am sorry. For that particular one, I was just the messenger."

Roishin snorted. "Yeah, whatever." She grinned, then asked, "Did you see Isla today?"

"I did. I agree with you," Enori said. "There is

something between them. I like her." She studied Roishin's face for a long moment before asking quietly, "Does it bother you? That perhaps Elsie has interest in another?"

"No," Roishin said without hesitation. "I mean, is it a bit strange, how things have changed between us? *For* us? Absolutely. I'd be lying if I said it wasn't." Her smile became so beautiful as she studied Enori. "I'd loved her my entire childhood, Enori. So, it took some getting used to the fact that first, that wasn't going to happen as I'd once hoped it would, and second, I was completely fine with that. There's a lot of guilt associated with that."

"Regret?" Though it wasn't pleasant to ask these questions and hear the answers, Enori needed to. She wanted Elsie in their lives for a whole host of reasons, mainly because of Mariota. She needed full understanding of Roishin's heart.

"No," Roishin said. "We never lied to each other, I didn't cheat on her or anything like that. My place is with you, Enori. My heart and my soul, with you." She rested her hand on Enori's hip. "I made sure my business in that way with Elsie was finished first." She shook her head where it lay against her pillow. "I wasn't going to do that to Elsie or to you."

Enori smiled and leaned forward, leaving a kiss to her lips. "I love you for that," she whispered against them.

"I want her to be happy," Roishin whispered back. "And, if it's Isla that makes her happy, I will do absolutely everything in my power to help them."

Chapter Eighteen

A re you really going to suck on those all day, little one?" Roishin chuckled when she got a completely unapologetic look in return, the ties to her cloak connected from the garment to Mariota's mouth. "I guess so." Amused, she began to extricate the ties. "Now, we talked about this…"

"Try having long hair."

Roishin glanced up, watching an amused Elsie walk up to them. "Oh, I do not even want to think about that one." Finally, the excitement of seeing her mother was reason enough to release the ties.

Mariota began to squeal and wave her arms and legs. Roishin was charmed as mother and daughter were reunited. Elsie's eyes fell closed as she held her daughter tightly to her, leaving noisy kisses on a warm, soft neck.

"How's my girl?" she asked at length. Both parents chuckled as the little one babbled on and on about it. "Really?" Elsie said dramatically, though of course she could not understand the unintelligible ramblings. She glanced at Roishin. "My goodness, what a day."

Roishin smiled. "Well, let me fill you in on the highlights. Let's see here." She ticked them off on her fingers. "We played, we had us a bottle, we played some more. We put *everything* in our mouth, then we had another bottle and a nap." She gave her a large grin. "Oh, and diaper changes along the way."

Elsie was laughing by the end, which made

Roishin smile. For just a moment she saw that beautiful young servant that she'd visually stalked for two years. Elsie gave Roishin a genuine smile, clearly convinced her daughter was fine and had been treated well, loved, and taken care of.

"Thank you so much for taking her," she said.

"Why are you thanking me?" Roishin asked, truly perplexed. "It's my duty, too," she said quietly. Though they were in the princess's bedchamber, they couldn't chance being overheard. "She's my baby as well, and I so want to be part of her life. I'm sorry I didn't say this before." She shrugged, feeling foolish as she looked down at her booted feet. "I honestly wasn't sure that it was my place to say that. That's why I'd show up in the middle of the night," she explained. "I could see her, maybe change her or whatever so she wouldn't wake you up. Let you sleep."

Elsie met her gaze and her own softened. "Oh, Roishin," she said. Roishin wondered what she saw in her eyes in that moment, because Elsie looked downright like she was going to cry. "I'm so sorry." She shook her head. "No. I've always wanted you involved, regardless of us."

Roishin gave her a sheepish grin. "Guess we should work on our communications skills a bit."

That beautiful smile returned, and Elsie nodded. "Aye." She placed another kiss on Mariota's cheek. "How did she do?"

"She did extremely well. She was with me the entire time, so I'm sure that helped. But, Livia was around, Enori, of course, and even Grandpa Ankou." Roishin grinned.

Elsie nodded at her to follow as the baby was getting restless. The parents walked over to the space in front of the two chairs near the fireplace, which was warm and inviting. A thick rug had been placed there, along with a veritable nest of pillows. Roishin helped her stack them to make a sturdy little wall for the baby to sit up against. She already had her favorite toys spread out there, so it was clearly a favorite spot for Elsie to put her.

Elsie's entire energy had changed, and Roishin sensed she wanted to talk. She felt a bit nervous. Where was this going? The two women got seated and settled. Elsie watched Mariota for a long moment as the infant reached for the smattering of little carved animals and a couple small rag dolls that were perfect size for her little hands.

"You still live with Enori," Elsie finally said, her gaze never leaving the baby.

Here we go. Roishin swallowed, then nodded. "I do."

After a moment, Elsie glanced over at her. "Is that part of why you and I can never be?" There was hurt in those sapphire eyes, but her tone indicated more of a need to understand.

"Yes and no," Roishin responded. "Enori had nothing to do with the fact that you and I had to go separate ways romantically. All those reasons are as true today as they were then. The doors you've used with me, to get to our cave, for you to see my parents?"

Elsie nodded, meeting her gaze. "Aye."

"I use those for my work, to get to all over the world and different places, but the hub of what I do is in Duras. I have to be there. It would be like my parents ruling Sursha yet living in Spain near Laigen and her family."

"Ah, I see now. Thank you for explaining. That I

can understand." She looked back to the baby, a small smile on her lips as Mariota looked at one of her toys as though it were some unknown species and not just a horse. "Do you love her?"

"I do," Roishin said easily. "And, we had no idea, but Ankou told me that had always been his plan. He had literally created me as a partner for her."

Elsie pursed her lips but said nothing for a long time. Roishin could tell she was trying to get her thoughts and feelings together before she spoke. Roishin wanted to take her hand, as she cared and always would, but she was sure that wouldn't be welcome at the moment, so she remained quiet and kept her hands to herself.

"How long has it been going on?" Elsie finally asked, her voice very soft.

"Not even two weeks," Roishin said honestly.

Elsie looked over at her, studying her. No doubt she was trying to read Roishin, see if she was telling the truth. Roishin kept her expression as honest and open as she could. She had nothing to hide and nothing to feel guilty for, but she had no desire to hurt Elsie further or unnecessarily. She'd been hurt enough in her life.

Finally, she turned away. "But it's been building. Hasn't it?"

"Aye," Roishin admitted. "I know I've loved her all my life, Elsie. My soul was literally programmed to. I just wasn't in the right place to love her as I was ultimately supposed to." She then did reach across and lightly touch Elsie's arm to get her to look at her, which she did. "I was supposed to love you first." She gave her the smile that had always been *just* for Elsie. "And I did. Do. I always will, Elsie."

Elsie returned the smile. "I love you, too, and I

always will."

Roishin took her hand in that moment, feeling like a true understanding had passed between them. A new level of love, yet it had changed once again. "I want you to be happy. If there is anything I can do, I want you to let me know." She quirked an eyebrow. "Special door for just the two of you? From the bottom level of the castle up here?" She smiled as Elsie blushed and looked away.

"I do feel something growing between us," Elsie admitted, her voice almost shy. "I honestly don't know how to proceed." She shrugged. "If I should."

"Kiss her."

Elsie gasped and looked at her, eyes wide. "I couldn't."

"Why?"

Elsie looked like an uncertain schoolgirl in that moment as she gazed down at her lap, where her hands rested now. "What if she doesn't want me to?"

"According to Enori, that isn't likely." She held Elsie's gaze when wide blue eyes met her own. Nodding, Roishin continued. "She was watching the two of you. Do what you need to do to be happy, Elsie. You deserve that." She shrugged. "And, from what you've told me about her life prior to coming here, so does she."

⁂

"Okay," Ava said, her hands holding firmly to Roishin's. "Feel my energy. Tell me the first thing you see."

Roishin nodded, doing as she was told. Her eyes were closed and she focused on what she was feeling. She turned her thoughts away from the feel of soft hands held within her own, as she'd been told to not focus on the physical sensation, to push that out of her mind. She tried to close her ears from the birds lightly chirping and singing in the myriad trees that populated the property she, Ava, and Enori had been sent to.

Much like the beach house, this one was near nothing, surrounded by mostly empty expanse of land and open sky.

"I see the color purple," she murmured, her mind filled with the color.

"Good," Ava said quietly. "I'm sending you more energy, Roishin. Each one should have a distinct look to it, okay?"

Roishin nodded, too focused to even speak. The purple slowly began to vanish, only to be replaced with neon orange shooting across her mind's eye like a comet. She gasped, it was so bright. "Really bright orange." That was followed by the yellow of a banana that morphed into a bright yellow bird. She was in awe. "Yellow," she murmured, sounding like she was half-asleep or in a daze. "Fruit, banana then a bird."

"You're doing really well, Roishin. Now, I want you to tell me when you feel something against your hands that are holding mine. Okay?"

"Aye." She took a deep, steadying breath and refocused. The hands holding hers began to grow warm, and it seemed more than just the skin-against-skin contact of the last several minutes. "Warm. No, almost hot."

"Good."

"Good lord!" Roishin cried out, wanting to pull her hand away from the sudden iciness that literally gripped her but held firm.

She heard the soft chuckle from a foot away. She

cried out again, this time she *did* pull away and her eyes flew open. She was shaking her hands out from her body, still able to feel the thousand little insect legs crawling all over her hands. When she looked, there was nothing there, nor on Ava's hands. She turned her hands palms up and down, nothing.

Looking at the grinning woman, shocked, she asked, "What was that?"

Ava nodded over to Roishin's left. Glancing that way, Roishin saw an ant hill on the ground. No big deal, just the tiny little buggers going about their business. "I sent that energy to you," she explained.

Roishin could only stare, still creeped out as she rubbed her hands on her pants. "That's incredible," she murmured, truly stunned. "I know what you said, but *how did you do that*?" Roishin demanded, making the other woman laugh.

"It's all about the energy. Harnessing it. Which, I might add, you already do." She pinned confused green eyes to the spot with intense dark brown. "You shouldn't be able to create doors, Roishin. Nobody can," she added. "Other than Ankou."

Giving her a sheepish grin, Roishin shrugged. "Yeah, well…"

Smiling, Ava squeezed her hand. "So, I want you to try something." At Roishin's nod, she continued. "I want you to focus on something here in this field. Doesn't matter what it is. Can be a tree, cloud in the sky, whatever. Focus on it, okay?"

Roishin nodded. She saw a tree about thirty yards away from them, just out there a bit by itself. She thought it could use a friend. Taking a deep breath, she tried to do as Ava had suggested. She thought again about what Ava had just done not long before, from sending her the colors to the changes in temperature to the damn ants all over her hands.

She studied the tree, took in its every feature, every branch, bare from the cool temperatures of approaching winter. She saw the tree begin to shimmer, almost reminding her of a door beginning to form. Then she felt a weight, almost as if her mind were literally lifting that tree.

The shimmering solidified and she was able to move it to the right of the original tree. It took a moment for her mind to release the second tree, but when she did, it landed on the ground ten feet from the original one with a soft but deep thud that Roishin literally felt radiate through her.

She walked up to the tree, neck craning as she looked up its height, marveling at the rough bark beneath her fingertips. She tried to wrap her mind around it, looking to Ava, who had also walked up to it.

"Is this real? Like," she asked, looking back to the beautiful creation of nature. "Could I chop it down?"

"No," Ava said. "Once you try and make any permanent alterations to the energy, it will dissolve. For instance, if I'd tried to change the hairstyle of the women I became in front of you that day in your house, it would have dissolved."

"But you were able to put different clothing atop it than the original woman was wearing."

Ava nodded. "Yes."

Nodding in understanding, Roishin looked back up at the tree. Chewing on her bottom lip for a moment, she reached down and pulled her dagger from her boot. Looking to Ava, she placed a hand lightly against her middle.

"Step back, please," she said softly, no clue if what

she wanted to do would work, and if it did, she didn't want Ava to get smacked in the head. Ava did as asked and stepped out of Roishin's periphery. "Okay," she whispered, blowing out a nervous breath.

Taking her dagger with the rose etched into the blade, she winced as she slid the edge across her palm, blood squeezing out in thin streams between her closed fingers. Opening them, she looked down at the blood-covered palm and fingers. Looking back to the tree, she took another deep breath and visualized in her mind what she wanted to happen.

She whispered her intent, almost as if to the tree itself, as she gently ran her hand down along its trunk. A perfect bloody handprint was left, which smeared downward. She wasn't sure if it would work, since this was the replicated energy. Stepping back, she squeezed her hand closed to stop the cut from continuing to bleed.

She stood next to Ava, and the ground began to rumble, almost as though the earth had just gotten a huge tummy ache. The bloody handprint began to seep into the bark as though it were absorbing it. With what Ava had said about the hairstyle, she expected the whole tree to vanish with that, but it didn't.

Instead, it was as if the blood had been sucked through the tree and up into the branches. Slowly it began to seep out the tops, the thick fluid oozing down to cover the branches. But, as it did, it began to change colors. From the deep red of the precious life's blood it turned purple in some places, the exact same purple that Roishin had seen in her mind. Then, on other branches, it was yellow and the bright, neon orange.

Roishin heard a sharp intake of breath next to her but didn't take her gaze from the tree, continuing to focus. The branches now looked as though paint had been spilled along their bony lengths. Roishin clapped her hands together in one loud rap of noise. The color exploded into huge leaves covering the branches, purple and yellow and orange. At another sharp clap and cry of surprise and delight from Ava, the leaves flapped away like colorful birds, leaving the tree exactly as the twin it stood next to.

"Oh my god."

She turned to see Ava shielding her eyes as she watched the "birds" fly out of sight into the blue sky above. Grinning at the other woman, Roishin felt eyes on her. She glanced over her shoulder and saw Enori watching from the house where the women were staying. She had a look of total satisfaction on her face.

When Enori saw Roishin was looking at her, the beautiful woman blew her a kiss. Roishin's attention returned to Ava when she began to speak.

"You animated the colors I sent you," she said, grinning. "Thank you for not creating giant ants crawling on that thing."

"Oh, good idea!" Roishin brought up her dagger, only for Ava to bat it away with a dramatic scream, both giggling.

Chapter Nineteen

Roishin glanced over at the young man who stood next to her. He looked to be about seventeen or eighteen. He was a bit scrawny as a lot of young men are before they fill out as they head further into adulthood. He wore black jeans with a thick chain looped down one leg for his wallet and a black T-shirt that hung from a frame that held little to no real muscle. His shaggy brown hair had a dark blue knit beanie tugged down over the crown of his head.

"I will never, ever, ever get used to this," she said.

He gave her a toothy grin. "Yeah," he said, voice somewhat deep. "So says the chick who friggin' makes trees bleed colors and birds and shit."

She burst into laughter. "Creepy, Ava. Creepy."

"Nick, yo."

Shaking her head, Roishin was still chuckling as they entered the Crystal Palace. Today, theirs was a fairly straightforward surveillance mission. It wasn't normally something Roishin would be part of, but Ankou asked her to personally assist Ava for her first mission.

The young actress had become a good friend to Roishin and Enori, so she was more than happy to help. Plus, as creeped out as she was by Ava's incredible gift, she was fascinated by it and wanted to learn more. Roishin found that she could easily replicate—and animate—inanimate objects, but she wasn't so sure she had the ability to do so with living things. That talent seemed to be relegated to bringing them back from the brink of death.

The normal swirls of energy met them and Roishin focused on her intention. Today she was a man in his sixties, extremely plain and innocuous. Very easy to blend in and be essentially ignored by their targets. Yet, it would allow her to stay close by and keep an eye on Ava—Nick—while she joined in with the group.

She glanced to her right, barely able to see her companion. "Ready?" she asked. At the soft *yup* she got, she grabbed Ava's hand and stepped through…

…and into the dark, dingy hallway of an abandoned building. It looked as though it had once been an apartment building, the last tenant having moved out long ago. The hallways were narrow and the walls were filthy from years of wind and dust blowing in through the cracked window at the top of the stairs. It was a three-story building, and they were on the second floor.

Roishin was all eyes and senses as they walked. She glanced into every doorway they passed. Some were closed, but most were open to some degree. What had once been very small living units for working families or, word was, single women back in the nineteen fifties, sixties, and seventies was now a squatter's paradise.

Bare mattresses were flopped down on the floor in some while others contained sleeping bags, and one actually had a folding cot. There was broken furniture shoved around some of the rooms, empty bottles or food trash. She also saw some drug paraphernalia. Yes, this needed to be a short trip. She absolutely didn't want to see Ava get hurt in the role the talented actress was about to play.

They heard voices coming from the end of the

hallway. Roishin glanced over to see that Nick was already looking back at her. Nick was in full control now, so Roishin drifted into a nearby apartment as Nick continued on to meet with the owners of the voices. It sounded like there were about four of them: three young men like Nick and a female voice, also young.

The irony was, these teenagers weren't a whole lot younger than Roishin's chronological age, but to her, they seemed eons younger. She wondered how she'd feel when she reached Enori's age. Not even wanting to consider that thought, she took in her surroundings in the apartment she'd chosen. She was loath to touch anything, as it looked like someone had taken care of some bodily business in the corner, but she couldn't tell which end it had come from.

Thoroughly grossed out, she looked away and took in more of the space. It wasn't much more than a large room that was likely used for both bedroom and living area. A tiny kitchen was tucked into the corner, though only the stove remained to show the room's intended purpose. A large rectangular shape drawn in years of dirt and grime showed where the fridge had once stood.

Another small room off to left when entering the apartment was the bathroom. It was tiny, a shower stall taking up most of it, no room for a bathtub. The toilet was missing, only the hole in the ground where the pipes had once been. The porcelain sink was cracked and absolutely filthy. If not for a few spots of white on the outside, it would be impossible to know what color it had originally been.

"Dude!"

Roishin's attention was grabbed by the exclamation. She walked away from the small bathroom and back to the kitchen. That space shared a wall with the apartment Nick had just gone into.

"What's up, bro?" one of the boys asked.

"I heard you guys are doin' some cool shit," Nick said, his deep voice resonating. Roishin just shook her head in wonder. Ava's voice was normally so sweet and *very* female—it was wild. "My buddy told me about it," he continued. "Like, Ouija board and shit."

"Who's your buddy?" one of the other guys asked, suspicion in his voice.

"Daniel Mendoza," Nick said.

"Fuck, dude," the first guy said. "Dan has been dead for, like, two years."

"Exactly," Nick said, amusement in his tone.

Roishin nearly burst into laughter at the heavy quiet the fell over the group.

"That's not funny," the girl said.

"Who's laughing?" Nick responded. "You're Kayla?" When there was nothing but silence, Roishin had to assume the girl had nodded or given some sort of affirmation, as Nick continued. "Yeah, he told me your mom was crazy nice to him and made him lunch a few times."

Soft crying began, and murmured words of comfort followed. "Dude, who are you?"

"I'm Nick," was said simply. "And Daniel told me you guys are trying to do some crazy shit with this thing." There was a tapping sound. "Trying to conjure up some demon or something." He paused. "I want in."

"He's not a demon," another boy said, his voice not heard until now. His had a quality to it that sent a shiver down Roishin's spine. "It's a god."

Nick burst into laughter. "What, like fuckin' Zeus or something?"

"It's not funny!" the boy yelled.

Roishin had to stop herself from storming over there. Something about that kid did not sit well with her. But, she had to let Ava do her thing. A strong sense of unease was slithering through her as she stood there, listening.

"All right, all right," Nick said with contrition. "Who is it?"

"Have you ever heard of the God of Chaos?" the boy said, his voice deadly serious.

Roishin could almost see him sitting on the floor, partially leaning over his own lap of crossed legs, dark eyes boring into Nick, the lit candles all around the small group reflected in them. Roishin had to shake the image loose, as she felt herself getting lost in it.

"No," Nick said, his voice serious now.

"He's been lost to history, Nick. He was banished hundreds of years ago, locked away by some Druid bitch and her curse on his tomb," the boy explained, his voice filled with quiet reverence.

Roishin felt her blood go cold. Though a slightly off take on events, it sounded too damn familiar to her. Immediately, her mind went to Elsie and the trunk. Was she the "Druid bitch"? She knew she'd helped Enori seal the trunk before it was dropped into the ocean. And, was the trunk the so-called tomb?

"How do you know this?" Nick asked.

"He told me. Seems I'm not the only one getting messages. He came to me in a dream."

"That's totally cool, bro," Nick murmured. "Who is it?"

"His name is sacred," the boy said, extremely serious. "I'm only gonna say it here with you guys."

"Is he going to talk to us with this?" one of the

other boys asked.

"Yes. He told me to bring the Ouija board and he'd talk to us, bless us."

"What's his name?" the girl asked.

"Bāhūthā. And he wants revenge."

Roishin felt the floor drop out from under her. Covering her mouth with her hand, she stared off into space. They'd gotten a message that some kids were up to no good and perhaps it needed to be nipped in the bud before they could act on it. That was the sole reason for this mission, just to watch and listen. But now…

Was it possible? Had he escaped that watery grave, or was he somehow communicating with this kid from within? *My god.*

"Holy fuck!" Nick exclaimed. "Bro, I am so fucking in."

Roishin knew Ava was just keeping the game going as she had to, but this had to be stopped. Even if it was just some kid hyped up on what he'd read on the internet, they couldn't take that chance. She cursed under her breath for not bringing Livia, who could get a message to Ava to find a way to stop this.

She'd have to use her own acting chops as a stumbling, bumbling drunk old man to spoil their fun. Taking a deep breath, she focused fully on her intention and let out a loud groan, knowing she sounded like the old man she was portraying.

"Did you hear that?" the girl whispered.

"Who the hell…?" Roishin growled, almost unintelligible. "Who's in here?" She purposefully bumped into a wall, muttering angrily afterward. Making as much noise as she could, she stumbled from the apartment into the hallway. "Who's in here?" she called out again, words deep, grumbly, and slurred.

"Who cares about him?" the dreamer boy exclaimed. "We need to finish this. Everyone, put a hand on the thingy, and I'll call for him."

Roishin ping-ponged her way through the hallway to the open door. To her shock, sure enough there were candles everywhere, the group of five, including Nick, sitting cross-legged with the spirit board on the floor at the center of their circle. She met Ava's gaze, hoping like hell the quick look she gave her told her all she could impart in just a few silent seconds.

Without a word, Nick grabbed the Ouija board and hopped up, kicking over a candle in the process. He booked it after Roishin, who sprinted down the hallway toward the stairs.

"Fuck! Put that out!" someone yelled from inside the apartment.

Roishin focused on getting out, the rubber soles of Nick's sneakers slapping against the floor as he followed. They pounded down the stairs, shouts sounding behind them. Heart pounding, Roishin looked both ways as she burst out into the evening. The sidewalk was empty in the neighborhood containing other empty buildings or shuttered houses.

Down one way she saw a large truck stopped in an alleyway. It was used to collect trash, and two men were dumping metal trash cans into the back. Down the other she saw a street, perpendicular to the one they were on.

"Let's go that way," she said to Nick, who nodded.

They took off toward the busy street, which would be a lot easier to blend in with and then disappear than the quiet darkness of the current one. Also, it would give them a place to ditch the spirit board, as it was not a good thing to bring back with them through the door, that kid's intention already seeped into it.

Roishin knew her intention had evaporated as she felt her cloak fanning out behind her like a cape as she ran. She silently cursed again, but right now it didn't matter. She had other things to focus on as she heard someone giving chase behind them. She and Ava took a left turn at the corner, running along the street as traffic zoomed past them at dizzying speeds along the busy street.

"Over there!" Ava called out, Nick's voice gone.

Roishin saw what she was indicating—an alleyway. Putting more power behind her sprint, Roishin pushed herself to get there before they were seen. She could hear Ava not far behind, her breathing just as heavy. She nearly threw herself around the corner to the left and into the alleyway.

It was empty, dark, and narrow. Buildings and houses butted up to it on either side, nowhere to go except the street beyond, far down the tunnel-like thoroughfare. They stopped about halfway down the length of the alley, hopefully out of sight. She was relieved when she saw two of the boys run by, shouting to each other as they went.

Pressing herself against the wall as she tried to catch her breath, Roishin looked to Ava who stood bent over, hands on her thighs as she took deep breaths. The spirit board was leaning against her leg on the ground.

"We need to get rid of that."

Ava glanced down at it and nodded. "Yeah," she panted.

Roishin met her gaze. "Holy cow, did you do amazing."

Ava looked up at her and grinned from ear to ear.

"I won't lie, that was fun. Good thing Dan gave me a few little tidbits before we left." She cackled.

About to say something, Roishin looked back over her shoulder toward the opposite end of the alleyway. Headlights suddenly appeared at the other end, and it was clear they were headlights to something large. The rumble of a powerful engine came next.

"Oh boy," Ava muttered. "Think we should go."

Nodding, Roishin pushed away from the wall. Something in her gut was niggling at her. She reached down and snagged the Ouija board from where it leaned against Ava's leg. With a grunt of exertion, she held it in both hands and brought it down, snapping it in half over her raised thigh.

The truck began to move, and the size and other lights along the top over the wide windshield told her it was the trash track. It began barreling down on them, and they had a matter of seconds to get out. Looking at the two pieces of spirit board, Roishin growled.

"Run!" she exclaimed, tossing the two pieces to the ground, as she'd need her hands.

They booked it back the way they'd come. Roishin's heart was racing as she could hear the engine growling behind them like a monster ready to eat them. She and Ava would simply take a sharp left to the sidewalk once out of the alleyway, but then it hit her.

The truck would plow right into the busy traffic along the street. No doubt lives would be lost, certainly destroyed. There was no choice. She plowed on, legs pumping, as she sent her hands out in a wide arc. The air at the entrance of the alleyway began to shimmer.

"Grow, damn it!" she yelled through clenched teeth.

She was running out of alley before she would

be in the street herself. Using every bit of focus she had, she let out a loud shout as the door exploded in a massive expanse. Reaching the end of the alley, she grabbed Ava, yanking her with her as she threw herself to the left moments before the trash truck overtook them. The loud engine raged on before silence replaced the noise, the entire truck vanishing through the door.

Roishin cried out in pain as she landed hard on her left shoulder on the cracked, jagged concrete of the sidewalk. She lay there, trying desperately to catch her breath as the white-hot pain rocketed through her entire arm. Taking several deep breaths, she finally rolled to her back, crying out again as a fresh wave of pain hit her.

Nauseous, she slowly sat up. It was then that she saw Ava lying a few feet away, and she wasn't moving. She lay partially on her side and partially on her stomach. A pool of blood was forming around her head, and a nasty spatter of it was on the brick of the building at the base of which she lay.

"Ava?" Roishin said, doing her level best to ignore her pan as she gritted her teeth to push to her knees. Nothing. "Ava?"

Feeling nausea for a whole new reason, she scrambled over to the other woman as quickly as she could without throwing up on herself from the pain. She flipped her cloak back over her shoulder to get it out of the way as she eased the other woman to her back. Hooded, sightless dark eyes stared up into the night sky.

"Oh god," Roishin whispered. "No. No, no, no!" She pushed up to her knees to kneel next to her, looking down at her. "Don't you dare, Ava! Don't you *fucking* dare." She felt the tears coming from both her physical and emotional pain. They were pricking the backs of her eyes but had yet to fall. "Come on!" she yelled, desperation in her voice.

She tried to push the emotion to the surface, her gaze studying Ava's face, which was growing pale. Cupping the side of her face, Roishin stared into her eyes, willing them to blink, willing them to focus. *Willing* them.

The wound at the upper left side of her forehead looked like a skull fracture. Likely, she'd died instantly upon impact. Suddenly, Roishin couldn't breathe, the tears nearly overwhelming her. They were hot and powerful as they flowed down her cheeks. She was sobbing, remembering the lost young woman in that boardinghouse bedroom, begging her to take her home.

"Come on," she whispered. "Please, Ava. Please come home with me again."

She lowered her head until it was mere inches above Ava's. She let the tears fall, her sobs racking her whole body as she prayed the precious moisture would work yet again. She watched as her tears fell into the awful wound, and nothing happened. She caressed Ava's cheek, her eyes scanning her face, her eyes, anything.

"Please."

Sitting on the sidewalk next to her, Roishin covered them both with her cloak, the two vanishing from the sidewalk even as they remained. She grunted in pain as she pulled Ava's limp upper body into her lap. She cradled her head against her chest as she began to cry harder. Her sobs were loud.

Roishin gasped when she felt warm breath against her neck. It was slow and not consistent, but it was there. Lifting her head, she saw that Ava's eyes had closed. Sniffling, Roishin brushed bloody dark hair away from Ava's face.

"Yes," she whispered. "Yes, yes, yes. You can do it."

Ava took a long, deep breath before it was exhaled, though shaky. "Whoa," she murmured.

Crying for a whole new reason, Roishin laughed and hugged her to her.

Chapter Twenty

Law three-one-six would apply here, Elsie," Livia said.

"Are you sure?" Elsie asked, looking down at what she'd written in her petition to the king. It was a formality, as she knew Fallon agreed with her, but it was still necessary, and Livia was helping her to make her case by citing existing laws that either upheld her petition or that needed to be recast.

"Yes," Livia assured.

Finishing what she wanted to write, Elsie scanned it over again. Then she glanced at the mirror to see the other woman looking back at her as if she were standing just beside where Elsie was sitting. To many, the added mirror would seem oddly placed, and no doubt it was. But, during these incredibly important meetings with Livia, the princess wanted to be able to speak directly to her closest adviser and not just hear her.

"From the bottom of my heart, Livia, thank you. You are so utterly brilliant."

Livia's smile was equally brilliant. "You are most welcome, fanciulla," she said with affection in her tone. She looked pointedly at her. "You let Roishin bring that little one back soon, because my little Mattia is in love." The two shared a motherly smile before Livia was gone.

Sometimes Elsie had to shake her head to clear it. She'd just sat there for more than an hour having a discussion with a woman whom she had seen killed with her own eyes. Even still, over the weeks Livia and her wonderful counsel and advice had become as real to her as Mariota was. She could hear her cooing and beginning to blabber to herself in the nearby cradle.

Her whole life she'd known about her great-great-grandmother Mariota. She knew of her immense power as the high priestess of the Druids, and of her death at a very young age—only in her twenties. She'd been proud of that heritage and had love for a woman she'd never met. She knew she had abilities of her own, ways of knowing things she had no way of knowing, and a way to sense things in people at their core that had helped her greatly in her life.

But since coming to live in the castle with Fallon and Cateline and their children so long ago, she'd been introduced to a world she still struggled to wrap her mind around. The woman who had been her first love was at the center of all of it, and their daughter carried such an intensely strong bloodline between her two mothers. It might be a bit frightening to consider who Mariota would grow up to be.

She smiled at that thought, and then again when she pulled the curtain back away from the cradle and received a huge smile and happy squeal from that very infant. Elsie opened her eyes wide and gasped dramatically, earning her another squeal in return.

"Mamaí's little princess," Elsie said, reaching in to pick up the excited little bundle. She left noisy kisses on a soft little neck. "How's my girl?" She laughed at the babbling and raspberries she got in response. "Are you hungry, little one?" she asked unnecessarily, as her own breasts were already aching in anticipation of a little pressure release.

She would go to the cave after Mariota was down for the night and pump breast milk into the jars for

Roishin, who would be taking her the following day. She was amazed at how well it had all worked out. And honestly, since she had gotten long-dwelling anger and resentments out, her relationship with Roishin had gotten even better.

Now knowing and understanding that Roishin wanted to be a parent every bit as much as Elsie did, it made the princess love her even more as a person. Yes, she thought, getting situated in front of the fire as she released the flap on her dress to give the baby access for feeding. Having a child with Roishin had been the greatest joy of her life. She knew, absolutely knew, if anything should ever happen to her, no matter at what point in Mariota's life, Roishin would come through for her in a heartbeat.

This of course brought her to the knowledge that Roishin and Enori were now a couple. Had it hurt that day? You bet. But, after Roishin's explanation and after Elsie had given it a tremendous amount of thought, it made sense. Whether she wanted it to or not, it did.

Roishin and Enori literally lived in the same world, but both were clearly part of something Elsie could never understand. They both held that bearing, that mysterious understanding of things that Elsie had no idea even existed. Roishin had always had it, ever since she was a kid.

It was a look in her eyes of someone lost because she wasn't with "her own" kind. Enori *was* her kind, whatever that even meant. Roishin needed someone who truly understood her, truly lived the same life on the same level. *That* was Enori.

A soft smile graced her lips as she watched Mariota feed. Her little hand rested against Elsie's breast as she did. She thought of what Roishin had suggested to her regarding Isla. *Kiss her.* Funny thing was, that's exactly what she'd done with Roishin. Was that what she wanted with the dressmaker?

She saw her beautiful face before her mind's eye—those twinkling brown eyes, either filled with kindness, compassion, mischief, or that light that was uniquely Isla. It made Elsie smile to think of it. She'd truly never met anyone who was so incredibly open as her friend. All you had to do was look into those eyes or catch a glimpse at those dimples threatening to come out, and you'd know exactly how she was feeling.

She was a few years older than Elsie, but at times Isla seemed like an awkward teenager. Elsie chucked at that. She thought it was adorable and was charmed by it every time. But then, five minutes later, an incredible wisdom entered her eyes or fell from her lips.

"What do you think, love?" she asked softly, gently brushing at some blond locks with gentle fingertips. "Should I kiss her?"

If she were honest with herself, there had been something there from the first day when Isla had come to measure her for her wedding dress. Certainly, she conceded, it could have just been an easy way between them that led to a fast friendship. But somehow she didn't think so.

So busy trying to deal with what she'd thought at the time was losing Roishin, dealing with beginning her marriage to Garratt and then her pregnancy, Elsie hadn't allowed herself to focus on it. Now, things with Roishin were finally becoming comfortably settled into a wonderful and loving friendship of two women who cared deeply about each other and would always be bound by their daughter and her needs.

Her marriage to Garratt was essentially

something she dealt with on a quarterly basis, and the pregnancy was certainly complete. Now, aside from a very demanding schedule that she was creating for herself and the Office of the Princess of Sursha, she had time to consider. And, now that Roishin was taking her daughter more and more, she wanted to make time for...

That thought scared her. She couldn't even bring herself to be fully honest with herself, let alone Isla at this point. She was so terribly afraid it was all in her head. On the other hand, Roishin had said that even Enori had seen it. But...

She growled in frustration as she studied Mariota, trying to get an idea of where she was in her feeding. Another ten minutes or so and she'd be done. She hadn't felt like this shy schoolgirl in a long time. It was a strange feeling, if a bit exhilarating. She wasn't fond of the unknown, though. She'd had too much of that in her younger life. It had been Fallon and Cateline who had finally given her the most stability she'd ever had.

And now, more than a year into her marriage, she felt she was getting a good, strong hold on everything. She felt safe and secure in her position and was finding her purpose, a purpose outside of being mother to Mariota. She smiled as she realized she was beginning to love her life. She was fighting every day to make a difference for the women of Sursha. She wanted to make it the most progressive country for women since the era of the ancient Egyptians.

She glanced to the door when she heard a knock. "Come in," she called out across the large space. Her smile was instant when the door opened and the very woman she'd just been pondering appeared. "Well, hello there."

Isla gave her a bright smile. "Hello, milady," she said, a bit of teasing in her voice as she no longer used the title at all anymore in private. "Uh-oh," she said, closing the door behind her. "Supper time. Shall I have brought a bib?"

Elsie quirked an eyebrow. "Are you planning to stay for supper?" She just barely managed to hold in a full laugh at the look on the other woman's face as though she just realized what she'd said and what it meant. "I'm sure there's plenty."

"Uh!" Isla's eyes grew huge. "I…uh…well…"

This time, Elsie did burst into laughter. She got a very shy smile from a very blushing dressmaker. Deciding to let the poor woman off the hook, Elsie said, "She should be done here soon. You'd mentioned a fitting tonight?" She raised her eyebrows in question.

"Aye," Isla said, rubbing the back of her neck, seeming unable to meet the princess's gaze. "I have two I'd like you to try so I can see if I need to make any alterations."

"Well," Elsie suggested. "How about while she finishes up here and then I get her burped and changed, you bring them up? Then I can leave her on the floor with her toys. I can ask Patrick to help you."

Isla brightened, seeming to bring herself out of her embarrassment from moments before. She nodded. "All right, I can do that."

❧❧❧❧

Mariota was fully taken care of with a little playtime before Elsie would put her down for the night. Isla had returned with Patrick, who had helped her carry up the two dresses from her rooms down below. Once Patrick took his leave, Elsie and Isla stood at the bed with a direct eyeline to the baby, who had a fortress of pillows around her to ensure she didn't get anywhere near the fire, as Elsie knew any day now she'd be successful at rolling over.

"All right," Isla was saying. "You picked out this material yourself." She placed her hand on the blue dress and gave her a bit of a shy smile. "I think it'll really bring out your eyes."

"Thank you." Their gazes held for a moment before Isla looked away.

Clearing her throat, the dressmaker said, "And this one I just thought was truly lovely." She lightly fingered the second dress, the lavender material beautiful.

"Oh, Isla," Elsie said softly. "I love this."

"Phew," Isla blew out.

Elsie smiled, reaching out and taking Isla's hand in her own. "You know me well by now, and other than my ever-changing body," she said, indicating her enlarged breasts, "you could easily make me a dozen dresses without a single word of input, and I'd love every one."

Isla squeezed her fingers. "I hope so. I took some liberties on these, so I'm a wee nervous."

Elsie squeezed her hand before releasing it and turning back to the garments on the bed. Without preamble, she began to unbutton the ill-fitting dress she currently wore, one of the ones made for her during her pregnancy. Isla turned away, busying herself with the blue dress, the color an exact match to the sapphire of Elsie's eyes.

The princess shrugged out of the garment, which fell around her feet, leaving her in a chemise with the handy little flaps like the dress had. She stepped out of the pile of material before picking up the dress and tossing it across the bed.

"I think two of me can fit in that dress now," she said, chuckling.

Isla grinned. "Well, technically, two of you *did* fit in that dress." She nodded toward the baby, who was happily babbling to herself as she gnawed on the rag doll Isla had made for her.

"True enough."

She stepped into the garment Isla held for her, her hand resting on the dressmaker's shoulder for balance. Once she was in, Isla pulled it up and over her body, making sure she wasn't pulling the chemise up with it. Isla moved around back to hold the sleeves for Elsie to slide her arms into before she eased it onto pale shoulders.

"Is it comfortable?" Isla asked softly, adjusting the garment in the back as Elsie began to fasten the many buttons up the front.

"Very."

Isla ran her hands down along Elsie's sides, and while Elsie knew she was purely in dressmaker mode, feeling and looking for issues in the fit, she still felt her breath catch a bit. "You can button it over your bosom all right?"

"Aye," Else said, surprised at how weak her voice sounded.

Isla moved around front, eyeing the fit of the dress critically. Her gaze landed on Elsie's breasts, which fit comfortably in the bust but were still quite swollen and hard to miss. When she looked up and met Elsie's gaze, for just a moment, that professionalism was gone and a fire burned in those warm brown eyes that Elsie had never seen before. At least, certainly not one so blatant.

Quickly, Isla looked away, kneeling before the princess as she messed with the skirt of the dress. She was looking at the hem, making sure it was even and that the dress hung correctly. Elsie's eyes fell closed as her heart raced. And, to her shame, her nipples hardened, almost painfully tight.

"I think it fits well," Isla said, pushing to her feet. Her voice was a bit deeper than its regular timbre, and that sent another little thrill through Elsie, who could only nod. "Shall we try the other one?"

Elsie nodded again. She brought her hands up to the buttons on the bodice, but they were trembling so badly that she was struggling.

"Here," Isla whispered, gently brushing Elsie's fingers away.

She began to unbutton the many little buttons efficiently, but Elsie could see the pulse in her throat was pounding. The proximity between them was not even half an arm's length, and as Isla's fingers worked their way down the front of the dress, they accidentally grazed over Elsie's extremely sensitive breasts more than once.

Finally, the torture was over and the dress was fully unbuttoned. Isla met her gaze for only a moment before she hurried over to the bed. She seemed to need to get some distance between them, and Elsie was grateful for it. She had to close her eyes for a moment to center herself so she could get through the fitting of the second dress.

Finally, she shrugged out of the blue one, allowing the garment to fall off her shoulders and down her arms. She stepped out of it and carried it to the bed to lovingly lay it back down upon the quilt covering the mattress. She glanced over at Isla to see that she was struggling to unbutton the lavender dress, her own fingers trembling now.

It looked as if the poor woman were about to burst into tears, which Elsie understood all too well. She stepped over to her, placing a hand on her arm. "Stop," she said.

Isla glanced over but didn't look into her eyes. Elsie could see so much turmoil in that beautiful face. "Sorry, milady," she whispered.

Elsie was surprised to hear her title but truly wondered if it was to impose a little distance, for Isla to remember her place, as it were. Taking a step closer, she urged the other woman to face her. She gave her a soft smile, a hand coming up to lightly brush away a few tendrils of dark hair that had fallen from her updo.

"I'm Elsie to you, Isla." She looked deeply into those eyes, which held so much of what Elsie felt.

Roishin's words echoed in her head, and she knew she needed to heed them. Placing a hand on Isla's soft cheek, Elsie held her steady as she leaned in just a bit. Isla's lips were so soft, and to Elsie's great relief, she didn't pull away or slap her, or even tense up. Instead, she seemed to relax into it, even if her uneven breathing still told the story of a woman who was nervous, or perhaps even scared.

Elsie wanted Isla to know she didn't have to do this based on status. This wasn't about a member of the royal family taking advantage of a woman who was seen by others as just a step above a servant. So, she began to ease back, to let her know she wasn't going to force her to continue.

But, to her relief, Isla followed, her hand taking Elsie's arm as if to keep her in her personal space. Elsie stopped pulling away. Their kiss was extremely gentle, shy even. Elsie was pretty sure Isla had never kissed another woman before, as she seemed as unsure as she was eager. Her heart was racing, and Elsie knew she needed to pull back before she took them both in a direction neither of them was ready to go.

Cupping Isla's face with both of her hands, she left several soft, lingering kisses on incredibly soft lips before she pulled away. She looked into warm brown eyes as they slowly opened.

"I think perhaps we should make sure the other dress fits," she said softly, fingers lightly caressing Isla's cheek.

Swallowing and letting out a long, shaky breath, Isla nodded. "Aye. Probably a good idea." She gave Elsie a little smile, letting her know she was okay.

Chapter Twenty-one

Fallon was furious, and it wasn't hard for Elsie to see that. They were in Elsie's bedchamber, and as she watched the king pace, she worried she'd erode the stone in her constant path. The king glanced to the mirror where Livia waited patiently for questions. Elsie was so grateful she'd joined them, as Livia understood the bylaws that Fallon was talking about in context with the problem.

"I honestly think you need to remind him of bylaw four-sixty, Fallon," Livia was saying. "Garratt could legally be arrested for being away from Surshan lands more than eight months out of the year." She looked at the king, concern in her dark eyes. "The bylaw states that's desertion and dereliction of duty."

Those words hit Elsie hard, and she felt them like a punch to the gut. Glancing from Livia to Fallon, she could see the king was hit the exact same way. She hadn't seen this amount of worry on her beautiful face in all the time she'd known her.

The long raven locks of Fallon's hair, in their perpetual warrior's braids, were just beginning to show streaks of gray, no doubt from a lifetime of such heavy burdens upon her very capable shoulders. But alas, she was only human. Elsie hated this for her and wished that Garratt would just be the man he'd been raised to be.

The profound disappointment in Fallon's eyes upon her arrival for an official visit at Caisleán Thiar had been a dagger to Elsie's heart. She and the advisers had met Fallon's entourage, and when those violet eyes had not seen Garratt standing next to his princess, it had been written all over her face.

Elsie was so glad that Mariota was with Roishin right now, because she had a feeling it was going to get very ugly and sparks would fly. Word had come the day before Fallon had arrived that Garratt was on his way home. This, however, had been a planned visit with meetings between king, prince, and the nobility in the region. Garratt had known this well, and much in advance.

"What are our options?" Fallon asked, standing at the fireplace, hands on her hips.

"Well," Livia drawled. "Either he can stop acting like a petulant little boy and focus on his new role, or he can abdicate. Or, worst case, if he is arrested he will have no choice in the matter."

Elsie's eyes widened as she looked from one woman to the other. Fallon stood there for a long time, stroking her chin as she looked into the flames. Elsie felt in her heart that Garratt didn't have it in him to stay home and learn the laws, let alone understand the regular people and their needs as Fallon had done

"If he abdicates," Elsie asked quietly. "What does that mean, exactly?"

"It means he walks away from the throne," Livia said simply.

Elsie nodded. "Right. And, if he walks away from the throne, or if it is taken from him, what does that mean for Mariota and me?" She looked from Fallon to Livia and back.

Fallon and Livia seemed to have a private, silent conversation for a moment before Fallon turned to

Elsie. "Roishin would technically be the next in line as the next sibling. Laigen is married to Reinaldo and part of that nobility now. But," she added, looking from Elsie to Livia. "We all know Roishin cannot do this. I suggest it go to Mariota."

Elsie's breath caught. She knew what Enori had said during the baptism of the baby into the Order of Ankou, but she figured that would be something far down the line, after Garratt's death while king of Sursha.

A heaviness fell over the room as it seemed to hit home to all three that this could very well happen. Finally, Livia broke the silence. "That is legal, Fallon. Since the child was born while Garratt was the heir apparent."

Fallon looked to Elsie. "That would make you the Regent Queen, Elsie," she said quietly. "Depending when that time comes, of course." She gave her a smile.

❧ ❧ ❧ ❧

Later that night, Fallon arrived at Elsie's door to escort her down to the gala that had already been planned for the king's arrival. It was essentially for the local nobility to come to suck up to Fallon and the prince, though of course Garratt wasn't there, so they'd be dealing with Elsie as per usual. The queen wasn't with Fallon, as she'd gone to Spain to spend the month with Laigen and her new baby.

Fallon was dressed in all the finery of her status and station. Many in Fallon's position had grown soft over years on the throne, no longer out in the field or as active. Fallon in her mid forties, however, was as powerful as she'd been as a warrior at twenty. She was a sight to behold.

"Milady," the king said with a twinkle in her eyes as she held her arm out to Elsie.

She grinned at her. "Milord."

Her hand tucked at the bend of Fallon's arm, the two made their way down to the great hall. Agnes and Isla had taken great pains to turn Elsie into a true princess. She felt conspicuous in her finery and the beautiful new dress Isla had made her for just this occasion, but the way the dressmaker had looked at her was what made Elsie feel beautiful.

They had not shared a kiss again after the night Elsie had tried on the two dresses, but something had changed between them over that stretch of time. *Was* changing between them. It felt nice. Like the warmth of the sun spreading across the skin after a cold night, Elsie felt like slowly life was pouring back into her heart and her body.

Their kiss that night hadn't been platonic by any stretch, but certainly not passionate. It had been the beginning of creating a more definitive line in the sand, as their employer/employee relationship had been blurred long ago. But, this new line was still being defined. Elsie felt a buzz in her body that she hadn't felt in a long time, and it felt wonderful.

"You know," Fallon said, pulling Elsie out of her thoughts. "You have outdone yourself, Elsie. As a mother, as a daughter to Cateline and me, and as the leader of this region." She looked down at Elsie as Fallon stopped their progress. "I just wanted you to know that. Garratt has disappointed me greatly, but you have more than made up for it." She gave Elsie a beautiful smile. "I know no matter what he chooses, everything will be fine because you are here."

Elsie's heart melted at that. "Thank you, Daidí," she said softly. "That means the world to me. Livia has been so helpful, and I'm truly finding my footing now."

Fallon leaned down and left a motherly kiss on Elsie's cheek. "I just wanted to make sure you knew how loved and appreciated you are by both Cateline and me. And if you need anything, and I do mean anything, you let us know and you shall have it."

"Your support has meant everything to me," Elsie said.

"You'll always have that." Fallon covered the hand that still rested at the crook of her arm, giving it a small squeeze before releasing it. "Now, shall we go meet some pompous, groveling nobility with far too much jewelry on?"

Elsie chuckled and nodded. "Aye."

☙ ❧ ☙ ❧

Blue eyes popped open at the loud voices that suddenly sounded in the hallway outside the closed doors of her bedchamber. Elsie lifted her upper body to rest on her elbows as she tried to figure out what was going on. It took a moment, but she realized it was Fallon and Garratt, their voices ebbing and flowing in volume. It sounded as if the argument was moving from Garratt's bedchamber closer to hers and back again.

"You have a duty!" Fallon roared.

"And, it's not a duty I ever asked for!" Garratt bit back. "Why can you not understand that?" Something was slammed, making Elsie start. "I never asked for this, Daidí. *Never*."

"You're the oldest child, Garratt. And, when my father died, there was no other choice because you're the male—"

"And that law has been changed, so throw Roishin to the wolves," Garratt fired. "What does she do all day anyway? School? She's almost twenty-goddamn-years old. When is it enough school? If she's not learned everything she needs to by now, she never will," he said with a sarcastic snort.

"That's not the point Garratt," Fallon said. Though still clearly angry, it seemed as if she were trying to sound more reasonable. "Cateline and I talked to you about this, to make sure this was what you wanted."

"Aye, and I was a fool to accept. I accepted because I knew that's what you wanted me to do." Elsie could hear the anger and hurt in Garratt's voice. "You know I have always looked up to you," he continued. "Man, when I first saw you when I was a boy, standing there proud and tall with your two swords on your back..." It grew quiet for a moment until he spoke again. "I wanted to be just like you. Big, strong, and respected in the military."

"And you've done that, son," Fallon said softly. "But—"

"*That* is who I am. I am not a goddamn fat cat sitting on the throne, Daidí. I never will be. And in fact, when you walked away from the military, the goddamn *leader* of the elite guard, the most feared and respected special military team on the planet, I lost respect for you that day."

"Oh, Fallon," Elsie whispered, knowing that had to have gutted her.

"Duty isn't just about fighting, Garratt," Fallon said. "Duty isn't about ego, and it's not about the fight. My duty has always been to this country, and then it became to your mamaí and then you and your sisters.

Still is, always will be. Duty is about love, Garratt. And, that love isn't of yourself."

"Yeah, well it's not for me." A heavy silence fell at his declaration. Elsie could almost see the two standing toe-to-toe in a standoff. "My duty is to my men."

Clearing her throat, Fallon finally spoke. "Well, then we need to talk."

Elsie heard footfalls heading toward Garratt's bedchamber, followed by the crack of a slamming door. She sat there, heartbroken for Fallon. She'd seen her and Cateline as parents for so many years. Yes, Garratt was an adult by time she'd come to serve in the household, but Laigen and Roishin had not. And then of course, Isabeau.

Never had there been children more loved or cherished than the children of Fallon and Cateline. And, she had no doubt that had included Garratt as he grew up. She had no idea what she was supposed to do. Go talk to them? Stay put? Was Fallon safe? She knew the king was more than capable, but it seemed Garratt was a bit unstable, and what happened when she—assuming she was going to—told Garratt what his options were?

Letting out a long, nervous breath, Elsie lay back down. She was trying to decide whether she should just get up, perhaps read or knit until she grew tired again. Right now, going back to sleep wasn't going to happen, that much she knew. Her attention was drawn when she heard Garratt's bedchamber door open then close.

Booted footfalls stepped up to Elsie's door. A moment later, there was a soft knock. Elsie pushed the covers off her body and climbed out of bed. She shrugged into her robe as she made her way over to the door, pulling one side open. An extremely tired-looking Fallon stood on the other side.

"Are you all right?" Elsie asked softly.

"You heard?"

"Aye."

Fallon ran her hand through her hair before letting out a heavy sigh. "I'm sorry, Elsie," she finally said. "I need to leave. Much I need to take care of for the abdication." She placed her hands on her hips and looked down at her booted feet for a moment. Elsie honestly thought she was about to burst into tears. But, after a moment, she seemed to pull herself together. "I just wanted to let you know I was leaving tonight."

Elsie nodded, allowing herself to be pulled into a tight hug, which she returned. "I am so sorry," she whispered. "It never should have happened this way."

Fallon kissed the top of her head before letting her go. "No, it should not have." She gave her a sad smile. "I'll talk to you soon." With that, Fallon headed out, making her way quickly down the hall and the stairs.

Elsie leaned her head against the door for a moment, still looking at the space where Fallon had disappeared from sight. Finally, she stepped back into the room and closed the door. No, she thought. This never had to happen at all. She glanced over at the cradle where Mariota would normally be sleeping.

Again, she was so grateful Roishin had taken her. It was her first night away from her child, and she missed her terribly, but it had been such a timely thing. Mariota would have no doubt been awakened as Elsie had and frightened out of her mind by the angry voices.

She brought her hands up to push her loosed hair back from her face. For not the first time she was envious of Roishin and Enori and their short hair. If only she could get away with it. She was headed toward her bookshelf on the dais to decide what she wanted to read when her bedchamber door was opened again.

Looking over her shoulder, she fully expected to see Fallon, but instead it was Garratt. He stepped in, never taking his eyes off her as he closed the door behind himself. She met that gaze, turning fully to face him.

"Garratt," she said. "It's late."

He smirked. "Truer words…" He took a deep breath and wandered away from the doors. He looked around, taking in the room which was held in the grip of shadows as the fire was burning down.

"Would you mind moving that log around?" she asked. "The fire is burning down." Garratt, who stood near the fireplace, just stared at her. "Since you're closer," she finished weakly.

"You just couldn't keep your mouth shut, could you?"

She looked at him, baffled. "About what?"

"About how often I was or was not here."

"Garratt, I never said anything about that," she said honestly.

He smirked again, clearly not believing her, or perhaps not even really hearing her. "You told Fallon to do this," he said, voice quiet but anything but friendly. "You wanted the throne for yourself. Didn't you?"

"Garratt," she said reasonably. "I think you know better than anyone that once your father decides something—"

"*She's* not my father!" He glared at her. "She's not my mother, either."

"No," Elsie said evenly. "But she is your king."

He snorted at that. "Do you honestly think you'll

see that throne?" he challenged. "Or your brat, for that matter?"

"I don't particularly care, Garratt," she said, doing her level best to stay calm. "I'm doing my duty, nothing more."

He shook his head, sardonic laughter on his lips. "There's that word again." He glared at her. "Why is my duty to my *men*, to protecting this country in the military not seen as *my* duty?" He pounded himself in the chest with his fist. "Why does that not count, Elsie?"

"I don't know. I didn't make the rules. All that was done long before any of us were born." She walked down the three steps of the dais, hoping to appeal to his plight. "You should be very proud of what you've done in the military. Not everyone is strong enough to do it."

He eyed her as he began a little tour of the room. She felt like prey. She didn't think he'd hurt her, but there was clearly something very different in his eyes than she'd ever seen. She hoped he'd just yell and vent to get it out and then leave.

"Does Fallon and Cateline know about you and Roishin?" he challenged.

Elsie felt her blood go cold but did her level best to hide any reaction. "What about us?"

"You know," he said, voice turned conversational. "I honestly thought you were so bad in bed initially because you were a virgin but figured over time you'd thaw." His laughter was bitter. "I don't even think you were a virgin on our wedding night." He pinned her to the spot with a hard gaze. "Were you?"

Elsie was beginning to feel a little icy trickle of fear worm its way down her back. "Garratt, this was never a marriage either of us entered out of love, and we both—"

She gasped when he was on her like a feral cat pouncing on a mouse. Pinned to the wall by her throat, all she could do was stare wide-eyed at him. She could feel and smell his hot, ale-scented breath on her face.

"You let her touch you," he growled. "Didn't you?" When she said nothing, his grip tightened. "I saw how she used to look at you when we were younger. She'd follow you everywhere with her eyes. At first, I thought it was just that crazy little runt. But then," he added, voice deepening, eyes growing small. "But then I saw you watching her, too. I'd sit in this very room, watch the two of you as you served us our meals. You'd watch each other like two little bitches in heat."

"Garratt," she cried, desperately trying to pull his hand away from her throat. "I can't breathe…"

"Should have thought of that before you got me kicked out of this family," he said, leaning in mere inches from her face. "Now, I can't even go back to my squad. All because of you!"

He yanked her away from the wall, nearly carrying her over to the bed where he threw her down.

Chapter Twenty-two

A handsome man, muscular and capable-looking. Long, light brown hair pulled back from an angular face. Piercing blue eyes and a stance at attention. Dressed in a tunic belted at the hip with sword belt. The short sleeves of his shirt beneath visible over well-developed biceps. Leather pants ending in boots.

Sursha—1385
Garratt—age 28
Occupation—warrior

Enori gasped as her eyes popped open. She was staring at the ceiling of the bedroom she shared with Roishin, who lay sleeping next to her. Blinking several times, she took a moment to get her heartbeat back under control. She squeezed her eyes closed.

No, no, no, no! She could hardly breathe. Glancing over to Roishin, she saw that she was still deeply asleep. As quietly as she could, Enori slipped out of bed, gathered her clothing, and carried it with her before slipping out of the bedroom. Dressing in the hallway, she checked on Mariota, who slept deep and peacefully, then scurried downstairs.

She had the most horrible feeling. She desperately needed to speak to Ankou, but as she whipped her cloak around to slide onto her shoulders, she knew that had to wait. She hurried to the door Roishin had made to the cave that would connect to the castle. From cave to secret passageway, she finally opened the door to Elsie's bedchamber.

She stilled when she stepped inside the large space, the door still held open by her hand. It was dimly lit, the fire nearly embers in the large fireplace. Listening, she heard not the deep, even breathing of sleep, but instead a very faint and quiet *drip, drip, drip.* Easing the door closed behind her, the tapestry fell into place.

Enori walked farther into the room with catlike stealth as she took in everything. As her eyes adjusted to the dimness, she saw nobody populating the furniture, and a glance to the bed showed no form lying beneath the covers resting peacefully. In fact, the covers were halfway pulled off the bed.

She hurried around the other side of the bed. Eyes widening, a hand went to her mouth for a moment. Walking over to the slumped figure, she eased herself down to squat before her. She was partially lying, partially sitting against the bed. It was too dark to see any features, but from the light color of her hair, and her own gut feeling, Enori knew it was Elsie.

The sound of the dripping was with her, also. It took a moment to realize that it was blood dripping from some injury, unseen due to the darkness, onto the floor. Terrified of what she'd find, she gently took one of Elsie's hands in hers. Her eyes squeezed shut in relief when she found her skin still warm. She placed her fingers on her wrist, searching for a pulse and finding a faint one.

"Oh, Elsie," she blew out in further relief. "If you can hear me, hold tight."

Gently placing the hand into the lap of the naked woman, Enori shot to her feet and ran to the bedchamber door. Her gown and cloak fluttered behind her as she didn't stop in the quiet castle until she reached the bottom level. Finding Isla's door, she didn't even bother knocking. The key inserted into the lock on the other side was released when she waved her hand, the key clattering to the stone floor.

The door was pushed open and she hurried inside. As expected, Isla was in her bed, asleep. She gently shook the sleeping form. "Isla."

Sleepy brown eyes blinked a few times before their owner gasped in startled surprise. "What…Who?"

"It's Enori," the priestess said softly. It was dim in the room, and they'd only met the one time. "Come with me. Now."

Isla stared at her for a moment, but clearly she heard something in Enori's voice that concerned her as she quickly sat up and pushed out from beneath the covers. She grabbed a robe and was still belting it as they hurried from the room and back upstairs. When she saw where they were going, Enori could feel a bit of panic set in the other woman.

"What's wrong?"

Enori didn't respond, knowing soon enough she'd know. They entered the bedchamber and Enori led the way to the slumped figure, which hadn't moved. Isla's gasp was loud, a cry of shock and fear muffled behind her hand.

"Stay with her," Enori said. "I am going to get a fire started."

Tears in her eyes and beginning to trail down her cheeks, Isla nodded.

Enori lit several candles along the way until she got to the fireplace. There wasn't a lot left of the logs within, but one had rolled away enough to be lit and provide at least some heat and light for a bit—certainly long enough for them to care for Elsie.

The fire started, Enori shrugged out of her cloak and hurried back to the women. Isla had grabbed part of the linens that had been pulled off the bed and was using them to wipe at Elsie's face. Now that there was light, it was clear she'd taken a horrible beating. And, given the fact that she was nude, Enori suspected the worst.

"Who did this?" Isla whispered through her tears.

Enori said nothing, but she was sure she knew. "I need you to go wake Millie," she said. "Get her to get water brought up here. We need to get her into a warm bath." When Isla looked up at her, confused, Enori explained. "I have something that will help with the pain. I'll be back very shortly." She squeezed Isla's shoulder with her hand before she hurried to the passageway door to head home.

She was doing her best to stay focused, but all she could think about was Mariota. What if she'd been there? What would that monster have done to her? Could they go back and change this? Stop it before it ever happened?

Enori angrily swiped at a tear as she entered the house. She was squatted down in front of her cabinet in the bedroom sorting through her pouches when she heard Roishin's voice behind her.

"Baby? What are you doing?" she asked, her voice sleepy and words a bit slurred.

"Roishin," Enori said, never taking her eyes off what she was doing. She couldn't chance grabbing the wrong mixture. "I need you to stay here with Mariota."

"What?" The bed squeaked a bit as Roishin moved to sit up or stand.

Finding the right one, Enori grabbed it and shut the cabinet door. She pushed to her feet and turned to see a very concerned Roishin looking at her. Enori almost smiled at her sleep-tousled hair. It made her look like a little kid.

"Enori," Roishin said, her voice all adult. "What's wrong?"

Reaching up, Enori placed a hand on the side of Roishin's face as a tear slid down Enori's cheek. "I need you to stay here with Mariota," she said again. "Promise me."

Roishin nodded dumbly. "Sure. What's—"

Enori leaned up and left a lingering kiss on soft lips before she breezed by her and headed back out.

⁂

The look on Isla's face when Enori suddenly appeared through the door behind the tapestry would have been amusing if the situation weren't so incredibly dire. As she'd requested, the doors to the bedchamber were pushed open, and Millie and a veritable army began bringing in bucket after bucket after bucket of steaming water.

As soon as Millie had dumped her two in the bathing tub that was always in the boudoir for that purpose, she hurried over to the side of the bed where Elsie had been carefully laid down upon her back. The older woman met Enori's gaze, deep concern in their depths.

"That little bastard did this," the cook said quietly. "Didn't he?"

Enori said nothing but didn't lose Millie's gaze for a long moment. Finally, the tub was filled. "Help us move her?"

"You bet." Millie turned to those who had brought in the water and stood waiting for further instructions. "All of you keep your traps shut," she warned, pointing a finger at each one. "If I hear one single whisper of this in this castle, I'll know who it came from. And if that happens, you get to deal with *me*." She stared them all down until she got promises from all of them. "Go on back to bed."

The servants were dismissed, not one of them allowed to see Elsie or the situation, though no doubt they'd come to their own conclusions. The three women worked together to get the unconscious woman up. It was a struggle as she was dead weight, but Millie was strong as an ox and, with the help of the other two women, they got her carried as gently as they could.

Enori sprinkled some of the mixture from the pouch into the water, as it held healing properties and would help ease the stinging of delicate places as the princess was eased into the warm depths. When her body became submerged up to her breasts, she gasped, a cry of pain escaping her lips.

"It's okay," Isla said, pulling the lady-in-waiting's stool close by. The dressmaker had tears in her eyes as she dipped her fingers into the water and gently began to wash the blood away.

"My baby," Elsie whimpered. "Where's my baby?"

"Shh," Enori said, lightly cupping a part of her jaw that wasn't cut or bruised. "She is with Roishin, sweetheart."

Elsie relaxed just a bit at that, but she was crying. Isla cradled her head gently against her chest. She looked to Millie and Enori. "Can we have a moment, please?" she asked, her own voice thick with emotion.

Enori pushed to her feet and handed the pouch to Isla. "Make a paste and put it on the worst cuts," she advised.

With that, she and the cook left the boudoir, closing the door behind them. Blowing out a long breath to try and center herself, Enori glanced over to Millie. She could feel the rage coming off the woman next to her in waves.

"Come," Enori said. She wanted to give them both a task so Millie didn't run out into the night hunting. That would be taken care of in time.

She walked over to the bed and began to gather the linens, bloody and torn. Millie helped, the two women working in silence. As if by unspoken agreement, they carried them to the fireplace and loaded them into the hungry flames. Millie stood there for a moment, hands on rounded hips.

Enori could feel the storm of emotions in the older woman. There was more to do, but she stood there with her, feeling the woman's growing need for comfort. She waited her out until finally Millie spoke. Her words weren't much more than a whisper.

"Fallon is going to be absolutely devastated," she said. Swallowing hard, the welling tears in her eyes were reflected by the flames she stared into. "Cateline—" Her words were choked off by her emotion.

Enori took her into an embrace, holding the cook as she cried. Of anyone alive, Millie had known Fallon longest, since she'd been a mere child. Millie had been the young wife of Burke, best friend and comrade in arms of Ailfred, Fallon's beloved oldest brother. Both had been killed while off on a secret mission when Fallon had been but seventeen.

"Fallon will tear off his testicles," Millie muttered

into the hug.

Enori smiled, rubbing soothing patterns on the woman's back. "I assure you," she said, "Garratt will be taken care of." She gave her a tight squeeze before releasing her.

Stepping back from Millie, Enori looked back to the bed. She knew there was no way they could expect Elsie to go back to it, even with fresh linens. They needed to get her down to Isla's chambers, and carrying a beaten princess through the hallways wasn't an option.

Turning back to Millie, Enori said, "I need you to talk to Isla and Elsie, let them know the plan is to get Elsie downstairs, all right?"

Millie nodded. "Sure. But how are we going to do this without a castle guard seeing her?"

Enori gave her a little smile. "Through a door, of course."

⁂

Roishin was standing at Mariota's crib when Enori arrived back home. She was just staring down at the sleeping baby, a deep crease of concern between her brilliant green eyes when she glanced over at Enori. She gasped when she saw the blood on the white gown Enori wore.

Using a finger over her own lips, Enori stepped backward across the hall…

…and into the small cave bathroom. She knew they would be able to talk there without waking the baby. She had a feeling Roishin was going to get loud.

"What is going on?" Roishin asked.

"I need you to come with me to Caisleán Thiar,"

Enori said, one hand resting on Roishin's shoulder, hoping the contact would help keep her calm. "We need a door from Elsie's bedchamber to Isla's. Do you think you can carry Elsie?"

"What? Enori, what the hell—"

"Shh, my love," Enori murmured. Her hand moved to cup Roishin's jaw. She looked deeply up into Roishin's eyes. "I need you to focus and stay calm."

Swallowing, Roishin nodded. She looked like she was either on the verge of tears or rage. "All right."

"Elsie is alive, but she is hurt. She was attacked."

Roishin swallowed again. "By who?"

Enori said nothing. Instead, she leaned up and kissed Roishin's lips softly. "Come help us," she murmured against them.

⁂

Millie, who had been remaking the bed with clean linens, looked as though she nearly had a heart attack when not only did Enori emerge from the secret passageway door, but she had Roishin with her. She just stared for a full twenty seconds.

Finally, shaking her head, she returned to her task muttering, "I always knew there was something about that damn kid."

Enori walked over to her. "Millie," she said, noting out of the corner of her eye Roishin was creating a door out of the line of sight of the older woman. "Take this," she said when Millie turned to her. "Make a tea." She held out one of her small leather pouches. "It will help her to rest."

Millie nodded. "Bring it back up here?"

Enori shook her head. "Bring it to Isla's chambers

down below."

Nodding, Millie stepped over to Roishin, who had finished, giving her a tight hug and kiss to the cheek before she hurried from the bedchamber. Left alone, Enori met Roishin's gaze. They held it for a moment, as she knew Roishin needed it for strength. Finally, they went to the boudoir.

Knocking lightly on the door, Enori said, "Isla? May we come in?"

"Aye."

Enori looked to Roishin, a hand squeezing one of Roishin's in warning before she pushed open the door. She heard a gasp behind her, but that was all. Roishin managed to keep most of her reaction and emotion in check.

Elsie looked almost worse with all the blood washed away. The horrible bruising and cuts were visible in stark relief against the paleness of her skin. As had been instructed, light patches of the paste had been applied to the worst areas. Isla looked up at Roishin in confusion, as she'd never met her.

"Roishin," Elsie managed, her voice not much more than a whisper.

"Hey," Roishin said softly, kneeling next to the tub. She took the hand that was held out to her. Roishin gave her the bravest smile she could, even as it was obvious she was struggling mightily not to show what she was feeling. "I'm here to help get you downstairs, okay?"

Isla watched the interaction of the two women with partial curiosity and clear confusion. It was obvious the two women had a deep connection.

Roishin turned to Isla. "Isla, would you mind getting Elsie dried off so we can get her into a sleeping gown?"

Isla nodded. "Uh, of course."

"Isla," Enori said quietly. "This is Roishin, Fallon and Cateline's second daughter."

"Oh!" Isla said, a relieved smile upon her lips. "I've heard about you. Awkward time, but nice to meet you."

"You as well." Roishin gave her a small smile before she got to her feet, giving Elsie's hand a light squeeze before she released it.

It was a group effort, but Enori and Roishin largely left the more intimate tasks to Isla. Elsie cried out more than once in pain, as no doubt everything hurt. Incredibly, it didn't seem anything was broken, but still Enori wanted to bring over a healer from Duras to give her a thorough examination once they got her settled.

Chapter Twenty-three

The last thing they needed in that moment was for Isla to drop dead of shock as they shepherded her through the door Roishin had just made. So, Enori took her the normal way, claiming Roishin, having grown up in the castle, knew a quicker way and could get there far more unseen with just she and Elsie, who had to be carried.

So now, Roishin held Elsie in her arms, cradled against her chest with one arm behind Elsie's back and the other beneath her bent legs. She sat on Isla's bed, just holding her, the tears slowing trailing down her cheeks. Elsie held on to her the best she could. Nothing was said, no need.

Leaning down, Roishin left a soft kiss on Elsie's forehead. "Everything will be okay," she whispered. "I promise."

Elsie looked at her, her own cheeks wet with tears. "Mariota," she said, her voice barely heard.

"Safe," Roishin assured her. "Do you want to see her?"

Elsie slowly shook her head. "Not like this."

Roishin nodded. "Okay." She gave her a little smile, bringing up a hand and tenderly wiping the tears away from Elsie's cheeks as gently as she could so as not to hurt her more. "They'll be here soon, so, ready?"

Elsie nodded, grunting in pain as she was jostled a bit when Roishin pushed to her feet with her precious bundle. She eased Elsie's body around until she could lay her down upon the mattress. Isla's earlier quick leave had left the blankets already pushed out of the way.

"I'm sorry," she whispered, Elsie wincing as she was set down.

Elsie said nothing, simply closed her eyes as she seemed to be trying to work through the pain. After a moment, she relaxed and opened her eyes. She met Roishin's concerned gaze. "Thank you. You and Enori. For everything."

Roishin gave her a winning smile. "Why, of course." Her smile grew when she received a very small one in return. She sobered. "Who did this?"

Elsie looked away. She said nothing, and then Enori and Isla entered the chamber outside of the bedroom. Roishin wasn't going to push it and instead focused on tucking her in. Truth was, she was absolutely terrified she knew the answer to her own question. The fact that Enori wouldn't tell her, either, cemented her suspicion into her heart, which was becoming heavy with dread.

But right now, that wasn't where her focus needed to be. She glanced over at the other two as they stepped inside the chamber. She gave them a weak smile in greeting before standing erect again and taking a step back from the bed.

"Thank you so much, Isla," she said. "For being willing to take care of her."

Brown eyes grew wide. "Of course. I would have insisted."

Roishin gave her a sweet smile. In that moment, she saw a flash of...what had it been? Territorialism, perhaps? She was glad. Elsie deserved a woman who could and would fight for her, would be there for her no matter what, for better or worse. And it didn't get much worse than this.

"Tea time."

Roishin looked to see Millie entering with the hot tea Enori had asked her to brew. She stepped over by Enori, needing to feel her close. In that moment, she would have done absolutely anything to take her in her arms and just…*be*. It wasn't an option, so brushing her shoulder against hers would have to do.

Seeming to understand, Enori trailed her fingertip along the underside of Roishin's arm for just a moment before dropping her hand back to her side. Together, they watched as Isla took careful measures to get Elsie as comfortable as possible in a more reclined position so she could accept the tea.

Millie murmured quiet words to her as she sat on the side of the bed and held the mug as Elsie took careful sips. "Good girl."

"Do you need anything else?" Enori asked Isla and Millie. "Anything at all?"

Millie glanced at them over her shoulder. "She needs to see a healer."

"Aye," Roishin agreed.

"I am going to send someone in to see her," Enori said. "Not the castle healer. A woman."

Millie nodded, looking rather pleased with that idea. "Aye."

Isla looked at her, eyes huge. "There are women healers?"

Roishin wanted to smile but simply let Enori take care of it. "Oh yes, Isla. She is wonderful."

Elsie looked up at Enori, holding her gaze as she held her hand out to her. Roishin watched as Enori walked over to the bed, sitting where Millie had been when the cook stood to give her the seat. Roishin stayed back where she was, as it was clearly a moment meant for them. Enori took Elsie's hands in her own, tucking them against her chest as she spoke softly to her.

Elsie nodded, the tiniest smile upon her lips, the full bottom lip sustaining an ugly cut. "Aye," she said softly to whatever Enori had whispered to her.

Enori reached out and gently brushed long, blond hair back behind an ear. "You rest," she said a bit louder. "Isla will take care of you until the healer comes, all right?"

Again, Elsie nodded. Her eyes seemed to be growing heavy already from the tea. Enori leaned over and kissed her forehead before squeezing Isla's hand as she stood. She met Roishin's gaze, a look of peace in their cerulean depths. *She will be fine,* Roishin easily read.

❧ ❧ ❧ ❧

They headed back upstairs to grab Enori's cloak and have a good look around. Roishin stroked her chin as she took it all in. The attention and focus had been on getting Elsie taken care of, so she'd paid little mind to the bedchamber. It had been trashed, and clearly a horrible struggle had taken place.

Something caught her eye, and she walked over to the fallen bookcase, brought down upon the dais where it had stood. Amongst the broken and scattered items was the rose she'd given Elsie the night she'd told her about the baby. It was crushed, one of the petals hanging on by a tiny piece.

Squatting down, she carefully gathered the flower. Though it may have been one made of magical properties, it was still very much a real rose and just as delicate. Holding it in one hand, she used the other to infuse every ounce of love she felt for her daughter, all the love and caring she held for Mariota's mother, and her renewed devotion and dedication to protect them back into it.

The rose glowed softly as it began to mend itself. The petal eased back home to join its mates, and the crushed blossom slowly retook its former shape. Finally, as if taking a deep breath, the petals eased open to fully extend the beautiful flower to its glory. Cradling the rose, Roishin pushed to her feet.

"What happened?" she asked. "Who did this?"

Enori let out a heavy sigh as she was picking up Elsie's latest knitting project off the floor and placing it lovingly on the chair where it had likely been left. She glanced over at Roishin. "I think you know the answer to that."

Jaw muscles bulging as she was doing her level best to keep her emotions under control, Roishin ran a hand through her hair. "We need to tell the king," she said, specifically noting the title as this was a crime against the legal Surshan princess.

Enori walked over to her, deep concern etched upon her face. "Roishin," she said softly. "I agree, Fallon needs to know, but you need to know something else as well."

Roishin met her gaze and held it. Her stomach was a knot of emotions, feelings, and flat-out hatred in that moment. Nodding, she managed tightly, "All right."

"I was given my next target."

Swallowing, Roishin said, "Who?"

"Garratt."

Roishin could only stare at her. Enori gently removed the rose from her hands as Roishin was in danger of crushing it all over again. She set it aside before looking back to Roishin. A very pregnant silence fell between them as Enori waited her out.

"Put me on your team," Roishin finally managed, the voice not her own. It was flat and deadly calm.

"No," Enori said coolly.

"Put me on your team, Enori," she nearly growled. "I'm sure he's a target not because he needs protection. So, put me on your team, or you know I'll go after him on my own."

Enori walked up to her, cupping her face in her hands. "My love," she said softly. "It is never a good idea to be part of a mission out of revenge."

"Put me on your team," Roishin whispered, her voice faltering with her grief.

Enori brought Roishin's head down until their foreheads were touching. She caressed the side of her face. Finally, she nodded. "All right."

❧❧❧❧

An announcement had been made about the attack, but no details were given. Elsie, along with Isla, had secretly been moved to the king's residence at the insistence of Fallon the moment she'd been told what had happened. Now, Roishin stood back out of the way as Fallon wandered through the bedchamber, which had not been touched save for the few things that had been done the night of the attack.

Roishin watched her, noting the silent tears that fell down Fallon's cheeks even as she had said nothing. She rubbed her chin, eyes wide as she took in everything. Taking a shaky breath, Fallon shook her head.

"Why?" she whispered, seeming not to be speaking to Roishin. "Why did I leave her that night?" She blew out a breath and shook her head again. "Why? I knew he was upset."

"Nobody thought he'd ever do something like this, Daidí," Roishin said.

"I'll send an entire regiment of men to find him—"

"Actually," Roishin interrupted. "I need to talk to you about that."

Fallon stopped her wandering and looked at her, half the expanse of the bedchamber between them. "All right."

Roishin perched on the edge of the bed, still made up with the fresh linens Millie had put on it the night Elsie was hurt. "You know when you and Mamaí and Isabeau were in Duras, the night Livia and I told you about the missions we do?"

Fallon nodded, putting one of the overturned chairs that went to the table right side up and sitting down. "Aye."

"You see," she continued, hands sweating. She ran them along the thighs of her trousers. "We get our missions, our targets, through dreams. Information." At Fallon's nod of understanding, she took a deep breath and continued. "The night this happened, Enori got her next target."

Eyeing her, Fallon's jaw began to move as though she were trying to keep emotions under wraps. "And it was?"

"Garratt."

Fallon swallowed but held her composure. "And,

what is he the target for?" she asked, emotion tinging her voice.

"Assassination," Roishin said softly.

Fallon sprang to her feet as if launched. She turned her back to Roishin, a hand running through her hair. "Because of what he'd done to Elsie?"

"That would have earned him arrest and imprisonment and whatever punishment you'd ultimately decided to wield as king, Daidí." She continued, voice a bit louder to ensure Fallon really heard her. "But the reason he must be taken out is because if he is not, he will raise an army and Sursha will be at war."

Fallon turned to look back at Roishin, a stunned expression on her face.

"And," Roishin concluded. "We will not win."

Looking like she'd literally been punched in the gut, Fallon took two full steps backward. Her back came into contact with the side of the cold fireplace. She swallowed again. "Is this because of what I did?" she asked, voice barely above a whisper. "The choice I forced him to make?"

"I think that may have lit the fuse, but the bomb has always been there." Roishin shrugged, feeling so sad. "None of us realized it."

Fallon nodded. "Aye." She pushed away from the stone of the massive fireplace surround and walked back to her abandoned chair. "Do you know where he is?"

"I know how to find him."

Fallon pushed to her feet and walked over to where Roishin sat, pulling her to her and then into a tight hug. Roishin squeezed her eyes shut as she held on, almost unable to breathe from the intensity of the physical and emotional hold. After several moments, Fallon pulled away just enough to look into Roishin's face. She had tears in her eyes as she looked deeply into Roishin's gaze.

She placed her own forehead against Roishin's, lingering for a moment. Then, the king turned and walked briskly out of the bedchamber.

❦❦❦❦

Her head bowed, Roishin rested her hands on the warm stone of the wall as the water from the waterfall in their bathroom massaged her back as it fell. Her eyes were closed and the tears slipped out, mixing with the millions of tiny diamonds of water that rained down. She cried for Elsie, she cried for Enori and what she'd had to find, but mostly, she cried for her parents.

Fallon had been a warrior for half her life, and she understood what must be done. But that didn't mean it wasn't going to tear out her heart, let alone Cateline's. The heart of a mother. She'd never seen Fallon look as defeated as she had that day in Elsie's bedchamber.

She sensed her before she felt strong arms wrap around her from behind. The warm, naked skin of Enori's front pressed against Roishin's back. A kiss was left at the nape of her neck before the softness of Enori's check rested against her upper back.

"You do not have to do this," Enori murmured. "You know that."

Nodding, Roishin sniffled and covered the hands clasped at her stomach. "I know. But I *do* have to." She let out a heavy sigh and turned in the circle of Enori's arms. "I want to take this mission from you, Enori."

The beautiful woman looked up at her, head

slightly cocked to the side "Do you not think that if Ankou had wanted you involved, he would have given you the mission?"

Roishin shook her head. "No. I think he knew if I'd gotten that that night, I would have been focused on that—the emotions of it rather than the bigger picture."

"Which is what?"

"Vengeance," she said simply. "Justice." She shook her head. "This isn't just about stopping him from a horrible plot that could get thousands of innocent people killed." She brought up a hand and brushed back short blond hair that the steam that filled the space was beginning to make damp. "Not anymore."

"This is not a burden you should have to carry, Roishin," Enori said, her fingers running over the slick skin of Roishin's back. "You do not have to."

Roishin nodded. "I do, though. He attacked Elsie, Enori. He *would* have killed Mariota had she been there." She snorted. "That night, he had nothing left to lose. He'd been hurt and betrayed, in his mind. Why not hurt and betray on the way out?"

"What is this going to do to you, my love?" Enori asked. "To kill Garratt, the man who has been your brother your entire life?"

"Isn't that the price we all pay?" she asked. "I have to live with essentially getting Ava killed. Yes, I brought her back, but…"

"There is no 'but,'" Enori said, cupping Roishin's face. "How many did you save by sending Bāhūthā out of there?" She nodded. "Yes, the man he had taken over who drove that truck likely died in that, but you know as well as I do you would not have been able to save him without another being killed or taken over." She gave her a sweet smile. "You stopped those stupid kids from inadvertently welcoming him inside them, Roishin."

Roishin nodded, knowing she was right, but it was still hard to let what had happened to Ava go. Yes, Ava was fine. Yes, she'd forgiven her or, as Ava put it, "Nothing to forgive." But still, it weighed on her. And Roishin would never be able to handle it if something happened to Enori during this

"Please," she said again. "Let me take over this mission." She shook her head. "I don't want you there." She left a soft kiss on even softer lips. "I'd never survive it if he hurt you."

Enori said nothing for a moment, simply hugged Roishin painfully tight against her. She buried her face in Roishin's neck, clinging to her. "You come back to me," she whispered.

Chapter Twenty-four

All was quiet as Roishin headed down the hallway on the second floor that led to her old bedroom. She pushed open the door and stepped inside. It was so strange to be in there, a room she hadn't been in since the day Enori had told her the truth about her parentage. That had been years ago, but it felt like a lifetime. In so many ways, it was.

Looking around, she saw that the bedchamber had been maintained by servants sweeping, dusting, and such. Everything was where she'd last left it, including what she'd come for. Walking over to it, her gaze moved up the long, lean, curved lines. Reaching out her hand, she ran her fingers down along the curvy, smooth wood.

Just to the right of it hung its mate. One wasn't much use without the other. She tossed her cloak off her right shoulder before she grabbed her quiver, still stocked with arrows, and slung it over her shoulder before grabbing her bow. She ran her fingers down along the tight bowstring made of flax. She had been careless and should have removed the bowstring. She'd been taught better than that.

She took the time to quickly restring it and made sure it was ready to fire. Both items in hand, she stilled her mind and allowed her soul to reach out. She had no need of the Crystal Palace for this. This wasn't the business of the Order. This was personal.

Turning to face the room again, she took a deep

breath. She could feel him, his energy like a stench that she could, and would, follow. She began to create a door, slowing growing it as she felt him stronger and stronger. She had him zeroed in as finally the door was large enough for her to step through.

Bow in hand, she took a step…

…into a very dark and smelly alleyway. She looked around, trying to get a feel for where she was. She knew she was in London but needed to get her bearings. It was then that she heard a very enthusiastic coupling taking place on the other side of the door in the wattle-and-daub house she was standing next to.

Quirking an eyebrow, she decided it would be wise to get out of there before attention drawn by the groaning rested upon her lurking silhouette. She focused her senses on where Garratt was. Her head whipping to the left, she knew he was in that direction, so she took off. The city was a maze of twisting paths and lanes.

Lucky for her, the moon was but a sliver so there wasn't a lot of light to spotlight her activities. Like a bloodhound sniffing out its prey, she followed his energy. Finally, she stopped at a small house that was made of wood with a thatched roof. Looking up, all she could think of was that it was quite the tinderbox.

She felt he wasn't alone inside there, so she would do nothing to the structure. Besides, the entire city would go up in a matter of seconds. Taking a look around, she saw nobody was watching her or even in sight, so she created a door to…

…step inside the tiny structure. It was essentially a bed pallet on the floor and a table with two benches. A couple shelves attached to the wall acted as storage. Turning her attention to the bed pallet, she saw two figures entwined on it.

The woman was partially covered by a blanket while the man, Garratt, was not. They were both naked. It absolutely incensed her that he *dare* be lying there with this woman, asleep next to her, after what he'd done to the woman he was married to. This didn't feel like a prostitute situation. It looked more like there was a relationship here, time spent together more than this one romp.

But then, he was gone so often, why wouldn't he have a woman somewhere? Perhaps several of them. It would be easy, she thought as she looked down at him. In fact, she felt the dagger in her boot like it was a hot coal singeing her flesh. She could stab him, slit his throat, or gut him, all without touching the woman. She had done no wrong, and Roishin would not hurt her.

Deciding it made more sense to lure him out, Roishin set her intention. As she looked at him, she felt the process begin. She morphed into an ordinary man dressed in the basics made of wool. She locked in her intention before falling to her knees next to him.

"'Ay," she said, voice deep and gruff. She jostled him with a hand to his shoulder. "'Ay," she said again.

Garratt's eyes opened and he looked up at the man kneeling near the bed pallet. He looked panicked. "What are you doing in my house?"

"Sorry, lad. Need your help, I do." Roishin pushed to her feet. "Got me a wench out there. Felled off her wagon."

Garratt shot up. "Aye." He looked to the woman next to him, who was stirring. "Be back," he murmured to her with a gentle kiss before he got to his feet and pulled on his clothes.

Roishin watched, disgusted by everything about him. The brother she'd once loved, had been close to, and once had looked up to was nothing more than a wolf in sheep's clothing. There he was, so gentle with this woman, so willing to lend a hand to a complete stranger in the middle of the night.

Who are you really, Garratt? Once he was dressed in his basic civilian clothing, he grabbed his sword off the table and followed Roishin out into the night.

"Come on, then!" Roishin took off running, Garratt's booted footfalls following after.

As she went, Roishin created another door and, making sure he was right behind her, ran…

…into an open, arid landscape that looked like it belonged more on the moon than London. It was a desert with not another soul around. She didn't want anyone else to get hurt, and she never wanted him found.

"What in the gods?" He stopped, eyes wide and face showing his shock.

Roishin had never seen him look truly scared before, but in that moment, oh, he was scared. He still saw the common villager, but as she reached up and pushed her hood back, the intention vanished, leaving her staring back at him. His mouth fell open and his eyes widened even more. It would have been amusing if she weren't filled with such utter hatred in that moment.

She smiled at him. "Hello, brother." He said nothing, looking as though he were truly unable to speak. "Didn't think we'd find you, did you?"

"What is this?" he asked, beginning to get his bearings back, even if it was clear he was still deeply shaken.

"This would be called revenge," she said simply.

She reached behind her and pulled an arrow from her quiver. She nocked it and pointed it right at his chest, nothing but a simple shirt to protect him. "You never did like the fact that I fancied archery over swordplay," she muttered absently.

"I haven't done anything to you!"

She quirked an eyebrow. "No?" she pulled the bow back, eyeing her target.

"Roishin! Damn it, I haven't—Ah!"

The arrow hit its mark, dead center of his left hand. She wanted to make him suffer first. He brought it up, staring down at it with huge, stunned eyes. It was already beginning to bleed, the drops dripping on the sand.

She lowered her bow for just a moment. "You know," she said. "A little poetic justice right there. The way you cut Elsie's face so badly that the blood literally dripped onto the floor." She pulled another arrow, nocking it. "That's what Enori said." She loosed the second arrow, making him cry out again as that one sliced through the muscle of his left arm, slicing it open.

"I'm sorry!" he cried.

She lowered her bow for just a moment, a third arrow already nocked. "Too late."

As she raised it, he ran toward her, voice erupting into a battle cry as he raised his sword. She grunted as his sword pierced through her gut to the hilt. They were standing face-to-face, almost as if they were about to kiss. The rage and hatred in his blue eyes would have been terrifying if she were even a tiny bit afraid of him. Which she was not.

"Know what?" she said, her voice breathy as the blade was preventing her from getting a full breath.

"What?" he growled.

"I'm going to tell you a secret." She looked into his eyes, her brother no more than two inches taller than she was. "For one, you were right to not want anything to do with Mariota."

"Why?" he asked, a look of pure pleasure on his face as he began to twist the blade inside her.

Roishin grunted a bit. "Because she's not your daughter."

His snarl turned his normally handsome face into that of a monster. "I knew it. I always knew she was a whore—"

"She's *my* daughter." She grinned when she saw his eyes widen. She reached down and took hold of the shaft of the arrow in his left hand. With a vicious tug, she pulled it out, and much of the meat of his hand with it.

He screamed, dropping his hold on his own sword as he staggered backward in excruciating pain. Pieces of flesh dangled from the terrible wound in his hand. He cradled it with his other hand, staring at her.

She stood there, his sword still sticking out of her body. It wasn't that it felt good exactly, but it certainly wasn't what it would have been seven years ago. He watched, horrified, as she slung her bow over her shoulder and used both hands on the grip of his sword to slowly pull the blade from her gut.

She bared her teeth at the sickening sound it made, plus the blood that was turning her tunic shirt crimson. Sparing him a glance, she asked, "Scared?"

He was growing pale, no doubt from pain and loss of blood, but also she could see the terror in his eyes.

"I strongly suggest you run, Garratt," she grunted

through gritted teeth as she pulled the sword out as far as she could reach before she had to continue with her hand on the blade. She met his gaze as he hadn't moved. "Now!"

He was whimpering like a child as, still cradling his hand and his arm bleeding profusely, he took off. The sand swept up with every footfall. She watched him go, deeply satisfied. The sword was finally out and she took several deep breaths. She was in pain, but that would wait.

Holding the sword in her right hand, she looked down at the sand at her feet to see that a pool of her blood was slowly seeping into the millions of grains. Her eyes flicking up to watch his sluggish progress again, she grinned.

Stomping her foot with a loud cry, she watched as the desert groaned and shuddered, then, like a massive wave of water, rippled and churned, cruising from her to him as the tide went out to sea. He was tossed into the air with a cry of shock then a grunt of pain as the wave of sand disappeared from beneath him, leaving him to fall back to earth.

Roishin took her time to walk over to him, his sword shouldered. When she reached him, he was sprawled out on his back, which was arched in pain. It looked as though he'd broken his leg in the fall. She had no sympathy for him but instead felt like an animal on the hunt. He looked up at her, face distorted in pain.

"Please," he whimpered. "Roishin, please…"

"What did you do when Elsie begged you?" She slowly slid the flat of his blade across the leg of his pants to wipe off her blood. "Hmm?"

"I'm sorry," he panted, clearly trying to work through the pain. "So…sorry."

"I don't think you are," she said. "I think you're sorry I found you, nothing more." Using all her strength, which admittedly wasn't to full par because of her wound, she used the pommel of his own sword to crack him in the jaw.

Blood began to dribble out of the side of his mouth, and a moment later he spit something out. She looked to see that a tooth had landed on the sand. She used the pommel again and cracked him square in the stomach, where he'd run her through. His body jerked up into nearly a sitting position, the air completely knocked out of him.

She took that opportunity to kick him in the face, which sent him flying back into the sand again. He lay there unmoving. She watched him, looked for any signs of life. He was bleeding badly from what looked to be a crushed nose, and more teeth had been knocked out.

"It didn't have to be like this," she whispered. "You selfish bastard." She spit down at him. "Guess you're not so different from your blood father after all."

She grabbed the grip of the heavy sword with both hands and, with a mighty grunt, sent it flying off to land in a cloud of disturbed sand. Bringing her bow back around, she grabbed another arrow, the other one dropped when he'd charged her. She nocked it and aimed it at his chest.

Suddenly, with a roar he launched himself at her, knocking them both to the sand with him on top of her. His hands were instantly around her throat, squeezing as hard as he could. She grabbed at his hands, which were slippery with his blood from the wound. She knew he couldn't kill her, but he could render her unconscious and do some real damage.

She clawed at his face, managing to land a blow

to his mouth, which was already bloody. For just a moment his grip loosened, but then he moved his face out of her reach and put his upper body weight into his grip on her throat. She felt something pop in her neck and worried he was crushing her windpipe.

Baring her teeth, she focused, feeling the sand all around them, the breeze that swept the surface and over them. She looked up into his face even as her vision was beginning to dim around the edges. She blinked rapidly, forcing herself to stay conscious. She felt the energy around them begin to shift.

The breeze began to strengthen into wind, and the subservient sand that cradled their bodies began to draw up, up and up, lifted by the increasing winds. A column soared five, ten, twenty feet into the sky, turning and turning and turning. A massive wall of sand grew as the column unfurled itself. The wall began to shift yet again, curving itself into a massive hand. With the howling of the wind, it scooped down and enveloped Garratt within its deadly fingers.

Pulled off her like an insect off a log, Garratt was lifted high into the sky, the hand closing in a fist around him. Then, with no more trouble than a child throwing a ball, he was hurled high into the sky and out of sight. Roishin watched, gasping for air as she desperately tried to stay conscious.

Within moments of his disappearing, the wind died down and the massive amount of sand fell harmlessly back to the earth half a mile from where she lay. She closed her eyes, taking in as much air at a time as she could.

She sat up, coughing as her body tried to return to normal. She turned over and lifted herself to her hands and knees. She was hurting and still bleeding, though it was slowing substantially. Finally, she lifted herself to her knees and slowly, oh so slowly, to her feet. She was exhausted and just wanted to get home to Enori.

❧ ❧ ❧

Roishin pushed open the door to the stone cottage, closing it and leaning back against it after dropping her bow and quiver at her feet. Her head rested back against the wood as she took deep, steady breaths. Her wound had already begun to heal, just in the time it took her to create and walk through the door.

She could feel things knitting themselves back together and bones realigning. It was a strange feeling—pretty unsettling, really. It was almost as if your insides were moving around on their own, like little burp bubbles working deep inside. She wondered if that was what it felt like when a mother felt her baby move.

"Roishin?" The voice came from upstairs.

"Yeah," she managed, though her voice sounded weak and strangled, no doubt from the broken hyoid bone that was working to mend itself.

Quick footfalls sounded on the second floor, then Enori flew around the corner and down the stairs. She looked frantic as she took in Roishin's pale form. She slowed when she reached her, eyes large as she took her in.

"Oh, my love," she breathed.

Roishin grinned weakly. "You should see the other guy."

"Is he…?"

Nodding, Roishin brought up a hand and lightly brushed her fingers along Enori's jaw. "The entire time," she murmured. "All I wanted was to be home with you."

She let out a tired sigh. "But, I got justice for Elsie. For what this will do to my parents, and for what he would have done to the people of Sursha."

Enori smiled, nodding as she took Roishin's hand and cradled it in both of her own against her own chest. "I love you."

"And, I love you."

Enori took a step closer, ever so gently leaving a kiss on bruised lips. "I'm so proud of you. All that you are, all that you will be."

Roishin sighed in contentment. "With you?"

Nodding, Enori said, "Always."

Epilogue

A small stream gurgled its way past large rocks that littered the path along the waterway. On this day, chunks of metal, a massive rubber tire, and plastic bags filled with trash acted as additional obstacles for the water to find its way around, over, and through.

A bald man lay face down in the water, his denim-clad legs partially on the rocky shore, one leather work boot still upon his foot. The other lay downstream when it came off as he crashed through the windshield upon impact.

Farther downstream another man lay partially submerged, face up. His left hand and arm were covered in blood, and fresh blood trickled from his mouth. Sand caked his body except for what had been washed off by the gentle stream. His chest was moving, but just barely.

On shore, a slow-moving black mist oozed along just above the ground. Like whisps of smoke it swirled around rocks and over the little beachhead. It made its way to the new man, slowly oozing around his body as gently as the lapping water. It moved over to his badly wounded hand and, like a lover's caress, began to move over and through the wound in the palm.

Slowly, it began to close up, the gristle and muscle and flesh stitching itself back together. Next, the mist made its way to the man's head, circling it and lightly teasing across the bloody mouth and nose, lips just barely open to reveal teeth, broken and jagged. The bleeding began to stop and a sweet kiss upon the badly cut lips eased the wounds.

After one more pass, the mist gathered and rose like a snake and then slowly curved down and eased itself into the open mouth.

About the Author

Kim has spent her life in Colorado and can't imagine living anywhere else. She's been writing since she was 9 and stumbled into her first book being published in her mid-20s. She's worked in the film industry as a writer, director and producer, but now enjoys the quiet, happy life of a professional author. She can be reached on Facebook and on her website at,

www.kimpritekel.com

If you liked this book...

Share a review with your friends or post a review on your favorite site like Amazon, Goodreads, Barnes and Noble, or anywhere you purchased the book. Or perhaps share a posting on your social media sites and help spread the word.

Join the Sapphire Newsletter and keep up with all your favorite authors.

Did we mention you get a free book for joining our team?

sign-up at - www.sapphirebooks.com

Check out Kim's other books.

1049 Club - ISBN - 978-1-939062-97-0

Almost two hundred souls, one plane, six survivors, endless heartbreak.

When flight 1049, headed from Buffalo, NY to Italy falls from the sky, a firestorm of drama, pain, angst and sorrow ensues. Can an author, a business owner, a teenager, good ol' boy, veterinarian and ruthless lawyer survive? Better yet, can those left behind?

1049 Club is a story of survival, love, deep regret and miracles. Can the living make peace with the presumed dead? Can the presumed dead make peace with the lives and loves they thought they had before?

Blinded – ISBN – 978-1-943353-53-8

After a horrible explosion sends local television news reporter, Burton Blinde reeling both physically and emotionally, she walks away from her life and the dream job she was about to start at a major news network.

For six long years she hides out in a small mountain town, working at the local library, though is haunted by the life she had, including mysterious messages and gifts she was receiving before her life was turned upside down, a veritable bread crumb trail leading to the unknown.

Unable to resist, Burton begins to follow the clues,

which will lead her into the darkest places of human nature that she may not be able to return from.

Damaged - ISBN - 978-1-939062-45-1

Family. A group of people you are related to by blood or love.

Nora Schaeffer has come home to her family after twenty years working around the world as a photographer for National Geographic. She's welcomed into the open arms of her father and siblings.

Family. A group of people who support you, lift you up when you fall.

Shannon, the youngest of the four Schaeffer siblings, has vanished, leaving her five-year-old daughter, Bella, terrified and alone. To help find Shannon, Nora has no choice but to turn to the dark-haired specter who has haunted her for twenty years. Along the way, she finds her own long-dead heart and uncovers chilling family secrets beyond imagination.

Family. A group of people who will stick together to hide the rotten soul at its core at any cost.

Who will live? Who will die? Who will be the most damaged? And who will learn to love again?

The Gift - ISBN - 978-1-948232-47-0

The dead do speak. You just have to listen. Homicide Detective Catania "Nia" d'Giovanni is the only daughter in a large Italian family of six children. The backbone—a position not applied for nor wanted—she continues to create new glue to hold the dysfunctional group together. For Nia, family time feels more like herding cats than spending time with her brothers and feisty, aging parents.

Her heart has always been in her career with the Pueblo Police Department, especially since it will never be okay with her very Catholic mother to openly give her heart to any woman, until she meets a secretive waitress who has her at, Can I take your order?

And then it begins...

Three murders that are so gruesome, so horrible, they rock the small town to its core. Nia and her partner Oscar are left to piece together a deadly puzzle to find the key to unlock the monster they hunt.

Or, are they the hunted?

As they dissect the murder scenes where not one shred of evidence is left behind, more bodies begin to show up, each cleaner than the last, the shadowy specter that is the killer vanishing without a trace, making the woman Nia loves disappear right along with it.

When there is no evidence to follow, Nia must trust her instincts...or, is she being guided?

The Plan – ISBN – 978-1-948232-43-2

As the dark days of the Dust Bowl came to an end, the

midsection of the United States tried to rebuild and revitalize. In the small, dusty farming town of, Brooke View, Colorado, teenager, Eleanor Landry and her mother were dealing with her father, a self-appointment fire and brimstone preacher to his congregation of two. A plan to survive.

As the dark era of the robber baron comes to an end, giants of industry and innovation emerged with fabulous fortunes manifested in the mansions that dotted the landscape across the country. Lysette Landon, the teen daughter of the wealthiest family in Brooke View, was everything a good, proper girl of privilege should be. Only problem was, she wasn't dreaming of finding a young man to raise a family with. A plan to be free.

One look, one touch, all plans are off.

Secrets deeper and darker than the grave would bring Eleanor and Lysette together, their families connected by a web of lies and broken promises. A plan to escape.

Be careful because, life has other plans...

The Traveler Book One: The Hunted - ISBN - 978-1-948232-91-3

A story so epic one book can't contain it. BOOK ONE:

1977: In the era between flower power and the yuppie, Sonia Lucas is a young wife and mother, just starting out in life. Without warning, a strange presence and dark force enters her life, clouds building...

1917: ...and a storm brewing as the world reeled from the horrific events of World War I just before it was ravaged by a Spanish flu epidemic that would kill millions. Sephora Lloyd is a 16 year old girl lost in the responsibilities of an adult world helping to support herself and her mother. A beautiful young nun-in-training enters her life, bringing love and hope with her. That is, until a force bigger than either of them threatens everything Sephora holds dear.

Four women - three deaths - two words - one house
THE HUNTED

The Traveler Book Two: The Hunter - ISBN - 978-1-948232-93-7

A story so epic one book can't contain it. BOOK TWO:

1890: In the dying days of the Old West, Sally Little runs her booming brothel with the passion and tenacity the business of sex requires. Savvy and indulgent, there's one itch Sally can't let herself scratch. Afraid of hurting the woman she loves, she instead unleashes...

Present Day: ...her renovation crew and fixer upper TV show on a dilapidated mansion that has known nothing but death since a murder there in 1977. Samantha Leyton sees ratings gold in bringing the sagging old house to life, but instead she discovers only she has the power to unlock the mystery that hunted four women across time, leaving death and destruction in its wake. Can she release her sisters who came before her and finally be granted the gift of love that is stronger than any evil?

Four women - Three deaths - two words - one house
THE HUNTER

Finding Faith (Wynter Series Book 1) - ISBN - 978-1-952270-16-1

Faith Fitzgerald thought that if she got an education and became a high-powered attorney in Manhattan, maybe—just maybe—she'd gain the attention and respect of her absentee father. Considering he was the only parent she had left after her mother's suicide when Faith was just a child, she thought that's what it would take.

She was wrong.

What she dreamed would be glamorous and satisfying turned out to be grueling and thankless. Since she wasn't willing to play the game between the sheets, she was forced to stay in the cubicle jungle doing all the heavy lifting while the men got the credit and the rewards.

Deciding she is done, Faith packs up and, with the flip of the bird to the rearview mirror, leaves New York and heads home to Colorado. She has nothing there: no job, nowhere to live, no relationship with her father. Truth is, she barely has a relationship with herself.

On the drive home, she finds herself in Wynter, a tiny mountain town at the foot of the Rockies. Looking more like it belongs in a made-for-TV Christmas movie than on the map, Faith is utterly enchanted. When she tries her luck and buys a raffle ticket at Pop's, Wynter's charming café, her prize is far more than meets the eye—or the heart.

Enter Wyatt, a feisty, sexy southerner and waitress at Pop's, who just happens to be married to a local sheriff's deputy. All is not as it appears with the All-American boy and his Georgia peach.

A colorful cast of unforgettable and charming characters will teach the jaded attorney that sometimes to find yourself all you have to do is go back to the basics…and have a little Faith.

Taking Liberty (Wynter Series Book 2) - ISBN- 978-1-952270-24-6

A victim of a massive corporate downsize, Liberty Faulkner suddenly finds herself without a job, without a home, and without a plan. Though certainly not part of her vision, Libby decides that the familiar is the safest path back to her life goals. In this case, the devil she knows is home: the tiny mountain town of Wynter, Colorado, a close-knit place where everybody knows everybody and everybody's business. Seems like the perfect place for the twenty-five-year-old to start over and figure out who she is without being noticed…not.

Sergeant Grace Montez escaped her dead-end job and toxic relationship in New Mexico and moved to Wynter to help build their police department from scratch. Now an established figurehead in the community, she's got her professional life dialed in and even mentors new recruits on the force. After a challenging childhood and lifetime of abandonment and disappointment, Grace hasn't been interested in another relationship—especially because no one has caught her eye since a certain quirky college student who used to make her caramel macchiato at the local coffee shop moved away three years ago.

Now that quirky college student has returned as the beautiful, mature woman Libby has become. Can Grace keep her distance, or will she finally take liberties with what is being offered?

Justice Won (Wynter Series Book 3) - ISBN - 978-1-952270-36-9

In 1890, seventeen-year-old Justice Kilkoyne and her mother, Ninny, are one bad decision away from living on the streets of Azrael, Pennsylvania. Ninny's propensity for the bottle has left Justice to play the adult, her androgynous good looks helping her pass as a young man to gain employment and keep them—if just barely—above water.

Determined to find a better life for them, Justice saves every penny to get them on a train headed west to the sunshine of California. Before they can leave, the bigotry of one shopkeeper sends Justice on the run, chased by the police for a crime she didn't commit and straight into the unwitting arms of a stunning young prostitute, who, after an unexpected connection, becomes Justice's Angel.

The day arrives to leave Pennsylvania for good. As

Justice and Ninny get settled, they're surprised by the appearance of Angel, also wanting to start anew. When the trip is violently interrupted in Colorado, Angel just may be lost to Justice forever.

Can Justice find a new life when she makes her way to the fledgling mining town of Wynter, Colorado? Can her heart ever be whole again?

Curtain Call - ISBN - 978-1-952270-42-0

What do you do when you come from a long line of dancers that spans the globe and generations, yet you can't tell your right foot from your left? You fall in love with a dancer, of course!

Gray Rickman is an awkward seventeen-year-old when she first sets eyes on Christian Scott at the dance studio/theater Gray's parents own and run in Denver, Colorado.

Though only a handful of years older than Gray, Christian carries herself with poise and wisdom far beyond her years. A woman of few words, she speaks volumes with her body.

Before Gray even really knows what her type is, Christian stars in endless daydreams and even fulfills a couple of her fantasies before vanishing out of thin air, leaving Gray in an empty bed with nothing but bittersweet memories and broken dreams.

With no choice but to move on, Gray attempts love, even moving with her college girlfriend to New York

City to pursue a career in journalism. But her standard has been set, the bar way too high for any other woman to reach or clear. It's an unexpected encounter in an obvious place when Gray sets eyes on her dancer again. Will the bright lights of Broadway illuminate the way back to the woman of her dreams? Or will they blind her to any other possibility of happiness?

Break a leg, Gray. The Great White Way calls.

Encore Performance - ISBN - 978-1-952270-52-9

Grey Rickman, a journalist for The New York Times, is offered the opportunity of a lifetime and a huge boost to her career—ghostwriting a memoir for one of the world's most beloved actors. She is deeply in love with her girlfriend, dancer Christian Scott, and her world couldn't be better.

Christian, though proud of Grey and all that she's accomplished, is facing her own career dilemma. All she's ever wanted to do is perform and create, her body her kinetic canvas. But, in one of the few industries where youth matters above all else, her time is coming to make decisions that no woman in her mid-thirties should have to make: is it time to retire?

As the career of one begins to explode into the stratosphere and the other's implodes after a career-ending injury that makes any retirement discussion irrelevant, Grey and Christian begin to drift apart. Changing priorities and newly built walls lead to fears and accusations, further tearing at the fabric of the love they've worked years to create.

Will cooler heads prevail to warm up the hearts of the deeply passionate couple in time to create a new dream for their second act?

Swann Song - ISBN - 978-1-952270-63-5

Christine Swann is a world-famous singer/songwriter and lesbian icon, known for her edgy style and heart-pounding songs. Gorgeous, rich and miserable. Her music has always been her life, her escape from an unimaginable childhood, and choices no thirteen-year-old should have to make.

Now, pushing thirty, she wants out. From all of it.

Willow Bowman lives in the farmhouse her beloved grandmother left her, with her husband. A pediatric nurse and small-town girl, she relishes in the safety of her marriage that keeps difficult questions at bay and keeps her life quiet and peaceful, because that makes sense to her.

Until one night when Willow is driving home and is about to cross the old, rickety Dittman Bridge not far from the farmhouse, and she sees a figure jump off into the cold waters below.

The moment she jumps in and pulls the woman dressed in leather pants out, both their lives change forever.

Keeping Hope (Wynter Series Book 4) - ISBN - 978-1-952270-78-9

Twenty-four-year-old Hope DeSilva has been released from a three-year stint in a Georgia prison. After returning to her family property in a tiny Georgia town, she decides she's had enough of the poverty, violence, and progound family dysfunction. It's time to get out on her own. She buys a $400 car and heads to find work out west.

After the car breaks down in Colorado, she's given a ride into a mountain town called Wynter where she runs into brash, aggressive police officer Samantha Gains, who has not one ounce of patience or sympathy for a felon in her black-and-white world of right or wrong, good or bad.

But, running from her own family trauma and inexplicably bewitched by the young newcomer Hope, Samantha begins to realize that maybe her strict worldview isn't as simple as it seems. When a freak accident brings the two women together, it will take both of them letting go of their pasts to truly move on.

Take another trip to Wynter and revisit old friends as they work their magic to help Hope and Samantha find their footing—and ultimately bring them home.

She Who Would be King - ISBN - 978-1-952270-89-5

Cateline is the seventeen-year-old daughter of a nobleman in fourteenth-century France. It's a time when children aren't seen as those to be loved and cherished, but instead are used as pawns and bargaining chips on the chessboard of control and privilege.

She is married off to a prince in the country of Sursha, a Gaelic-speaking island nation near Ireland. Fergus, her betrothed, is next in line to take over once beloved King Carthac dies. Or is he?

Fallon, the youngest royal child and only girl, has been raised as one of the king's sons her entire life, for reasons she has never fully understood. A natural fighter, she was raised to be a warrior and head the Crown's Elite Guard assigned to protect her boorish brother Fergus.

Forced to fill in for her brother in an unexpected way, an instant attraction between Fallon and Cateline forms. In a game of thrones filled with deception and betrayal, even the most secret love can mean death.

Control - ISBN - 978-1-959929-01-7

Keller Mitchum has already lived a lifetime in eighteen years. Fully responsible for her five-year-old sister Parker, Keller has seen and experienced things in life that should exist in the most intense fictional plot. Wise beyond her years, she will do absolutely anything to keep Parker safe.

Garrison Davies is a twenty-three-year-old pilot in Massachusetts, working with her father in a small, family-owned cargo business. Independent, feisty, and brilliant at what she does, she makes little time for anything outside of her beloved planes and dogs. Her simple and structured world is turned on its head when a difficult situation lands two unexpected guests into her life and her house.

Garrison tries to make a safe space for Keller and Parker, only partially aware of the horrors they come from. As time passes, it becomes clear that it's not only the past that keeps the two sisters at arm's length. Can Garrison break through Keller's defenses and help her regain control?

www.ingramcontent.com/pod-product-compliance
Lightning Source LLC
Chambersburg PA
CBHW020240010826
48973CB00006B/1597